Jane-Emily

AND

Witches' Children

Jane-Emily
AND
Witches' Children

PATRICIA CLAPP

HARPER

NEW YORK · LONDON · TORONTO · SYDNEY

HARPER

"In Her Own Words" from Something About the Author: Autobiography Series by Sarkissian; Adele (Editor). 1987. Reprinted with permission of Gale, a division of Thomson Learning: www.thomsonrights.com. Fax 800-730-2215.

HarperCollins books may be purchased for educational, business, or sales promotional use. For information please write: Special Markets Department, HarperCollins Publishers, 10 East 53rd Street, New York, NY 10022.

First Harper paperback published 2007.

Designed by Jaime Putorti

Library of Congress Cataloging-in-Publication Data is available upon request.

ISBN: 978-0-06-124501-5
ISBN-10: 0-06-124501-1

07 08 09 10 11 ID/RRD 10 9 8 7 6 5 4 3 2 1

CONTENTS

Jane-Emily

*This book is dedicated
to the memories of those people
for whom it comes too late,
Elizabeth and Howard,
and Ethel and Grandmère*

ONE

There are times when the midsummer sun strikes cold, and when the leaping flames of a hearthfire give no heat. Times when the chill within us comes not from fears we know, but from fears unknown—and forever unknowable.

But on that sunny June afternoon when Jane and I first arrived at her grandmother's house in Lynn, my greatest fear was that I should be overcome by loneliness and boredom before the summer was done. The year was 1912, I was just eighteen, and the thought of leaving Martin Driscoll and being cooped up for the shining vacation months with elderly and quite awe-inspiring Mrs. Canfield, with the almost equally elderly, if more friendly, maid, Katie, and with my niece, nine-year-old Jane Canfield, was less than appealing.

Jane had been orphaned the year before when her mother, my elder sister Charlotte, and her father, Mrs. Canfield's son John, were killed. They had been driving their quiet old horse hitched to the buggy, for even though many people have automobiles now, Charlotte still liked the gentle pace of horse travel better than the dust and noise of motor cars. No one has ever been able to understand what the horse shied at, what frightened him so that he must have reared and turned, tipping the buggy and throwing Charlotte so hard against a great tree trunk that she died instantly. John, grasping the reins and striving to control the animal, was dragged quite horribly for some distance. No one saw it happen, and John never regained consciousness, so the cause of the accident has always been a mystery.

My mother and father, Martha and Charles Amory, took Jane, and gave her warmth and love and security, but Jane was still unnaturally withdrawn. She was bright and well-mannered and sweet, but she rarely laughed and I never saw her really *play*. She read, or sketched—she was quite gifted with her pencil—or just sat dreaming into space. I was very fond of Jane, and I tried to interest her in other things, such as the dolls Charlotte and I used to play with, or my bicycle, or any of the other oddments that remained around the house, but nothing roused more than a polite interest.

When Lydia Canfield wrote Mother, suggesting that Jane spend the summer with her, it was felt the change might do her good—take her out of herself a bit. I backed the idea enthusiastically until I learned that Mrs. Canfield seemed reluctant to assume the care of the child, even with Katie's help, and had suggested that I accompany her.

"But why me?" I wailed to Mother. "Jane's not a baby. She can look out for herself."

"Yes, I'm sure she can," Mother agreed. "But Lydia Canfield isn't used to young children and I certainly don't want her to spend the summer fretting. You could do a great many things for Jane that her grandmother might not know how to do."

"But *Mother!* Martin and I have a million plans for this summer! He's going to read Shakespeare out loud to me, and I'm going to teach him to play tennis. Besides, what could I do for Jane?"

"Braid her hair, and—"

"I don't see why I should give up a whole summer with Martin just to braid Jane's hair! He'll be going to college in September and I won't have seen him at *all!*"

"Louisa, you have seen enough of Martin Driscoll during the past six months to last for the next six years!"

"You don't like Martin. I know you don't."

"I don't dislike him. He's a perfectly nice boy. But it wouldn't do you any harm to meet some other young men."

"I'm not very likely to meet *anyone* locked up in that gloomy old cave in Lynn!"

But I knew it was a losing battle. Charlotte and I were raised in the school of strict obedience and when we were told, or even asked, to do something, we did it.

"It's going to be absolutely awful!" I muttered, "Martin will forget all about me and I won't meet another living soul and I'll probably end up an old maid!"

Mother laughed and hugged me. "That's extremely unlikely," she said. "And just remember, darling, if you and Jane are both miserable we can always cut the visit short."

How many times later I looked back, remembering those words. If I had forced myself to leave, if I had gone home and taken Jane with me, if we *had* "cut the visit short," would things have been different? Or would that last rainy night always have been waiting somewhere to happen? But at the time all I knew was that we were thirty miles from home, embarked on a summer which, while it might not be truly dismal, certainly promised no great diversion.

However, it always seems to me easier to be happy than unhappy, and since there I was, and there I was going to stay, it was only intelligent to find whatever pleasant aspects there might be in the months ahead. There would, for example, be letters from Martin, and these I looked forward to eagerly. The last evening, when he had come to say good-bye, we had sat in the porch hammock, his arm around my waist and my head on his shoulder, and he had promised to write every day.

"And you must only read the letters when you are alone, Louisa. When you can't be interrupted. Because I shall be writing my deepest thoughts, and you must read them just as you listen to me now. With your whole attention."

My eyes had misted as I promised. Martin's deepest thoughts were very beautiful.

"And you will write to *me* every day, Louisa?"

"Well, I'll try, Martin. But I may be busy sometimes—looking out for Jane, and everything. I may not be able to write *every* day." Somehow I could not bring myself to admit that I detested writing letters, and that they always came out sounding stiff and stupid.

Later, when we heard Father start to cough and clear his throat, the sound coming just as clearly as he intended it to through the open window, Martin kissed me good-bye quite passionately. When he left I stood at the top of the porch steps and waved as long as I could see him in the faint star-light, and then went into the house, my eyes filled with tears.

But the train trip, the first I had ever taken without my parents, was exciting, and somehow by the time Jane and I arrived in Lynn I was not as despondent as I had expected to be.

Jane and I had connecting rooms at the back of the big Canfield house, overlooking the garden. Large and square, each room had high, narrow windows framed in heavy drapes, looped back with thick silk cords. The June sun-shine came through my two windows now, falling in bright pools on the rose-patterned carpet. The windows were closed—in fact the whole house had an air of being closed—but I managed to raise both lower panes as far as they would go, delighting in the smell and freshness that drifted in.

"Jane," I called through the open doorway. "Are your windows open? Shall I raise them for you? They're quite stiff."

There was no answer, and I went to the door that led to Jane's room. She was standing by the closed window, her forehead against the glass, gazing out into the garden.

"Jane," I said again. "Don't you want the windows open? The air is wonderful!"

Jane turned slowly and looked at me. "What? I'm sorry. I wasn't listening. Isn't the garden beautiful?"

With affectionate exasperation I moved her so that I could lift the sash. "It's lovely. Here, smell! Isn't that better?"

"Thank you, Louisa."

"Get your bags unpacked and put some of your things away, then you can go out. I'll finish up for you."

With the first real enthusiasm I had seen Jane show in months she went quickly to the luggage rack at the foot of her bed where her valise lay open, and started taking her crisp summer dresses from it and hanging them in the tall wardrobe that filled one corner of the room. The rod was so high that she hopped up on a small two-step contrivance which stood in position by the wardrobe door.

"Your grandmother is well prepared for you, isn't she?" I said. "She must have known the rod would be too high for you to reach."

"This was made for Emily," Jane said. "This was her room."

"Emily?"

"My father's sister. She died, you know. Years ago, when she was just twelve."

"Oh. Yes, I think I do recall hearing your mother speak of her. I had forgotten. How very sad that she died when she was so young."

"I suppose it is," Jane said with that cool impersonality that children have for people they never knew. "Louisa, that's all my dresses. Can't I leave the rest until later? Nothing else will wrinkle."

"All right, go along. I'll be down soon."

"Thank you," said Jane, and was out the door into the hall in a flash. I heard her feet thudding down the carpeted stairs. A moment later a screen door slammed somewhere and then I saw her running across the yard, the sun shining on her long dark braids. She went straight as an arrow to a large bright reflecting ball which stood on its stone pedestal in the exact center of the garden, and I smiled as I remembered the amusingly distorted images that one could see in such silver globes.

Turning back to complete the unpacking, I thought that in spite of *my* feelings about it, this summer might truly be good for Jane. She already seemed happier and more at ease than I had seen her since her mother and father died.

It was close to an hour later before I had emptied the suitcases, put Jane's and my clothes neatly away, washed the train dust from my hands and face, changed out of my traveling suit, and straightened my hair. I inspected myself carefully in the tall mirror to be sure I looked neat enough to win Mrs. Canfield's approval; although I had seen her but rarely, I suspected she was not the sort of woman to tolerate laxity in dress or behavior.

My blond hair, too pale, and inclined to be overly curly, I had managed to brush successfully into a soft roll around my head, twisting the back into a thick knot. I moistened a finger with my tongue and smoothed my brows, accenting their brown arch, and brushing my lashes—which are very thick, as my hair is, but not as pale. My eyes are just plain blue, except that Martin once told me they turn green when I am angry.

The dress I had put on was a lilac voile, held snugly at the waist by a deeper violet sash, and it fell to my ankles. I felt that I looked quite presentable; and hoping fervently that I could live up to the outer image, I made my way through the long, carpeted corridor, down the wide angular staircase to the lower hall, across the dim parlor and out through one of the tall French doors that led to the garden.

Mrs. Canfield sat in one of several wicker chairs placed in the shade of a wide-branching tulip tree. She looked so straight and formal that I found myself walking decorously across the velvet grass to join her. As I approached she looked up and smiled.

"Ah, Louisa. How fresh you look, child! Sit here in the shade and tell me about your parents. They are well, I trust?"

"Quite well, thank you. They asked me to give you their very warmest greetings."

"How kind of them. And your trip was not too unpleasant?"

"Not at all. Both Jane and I enjoyed it."

"Perhaps a cup of tea would be refreshing. I have asked Katie to bring it out here."

"Thank you," I said. Mrs. Canfield made me feel ill at ease and unnaturally prim. Even my words sounded stiff. "How beautiful it is here! I don't wonder that Jane was so happy to come."

"Was she happy? How nice! Of course she was here often before—before the accident, but I did not know whether she would want to come back. It cannot be much entertainment for her, I'm afraid." She leaned forward slightly and laid her small hand on my arm. "I am most grateful to you, my dear, for consenting to spend the summer with her."

"I was glad to," I said, trusting that this was what might be called a "white fib."

I looked across the garden to where Jane was walking slowly up and down the bright rows of flowers, her hands clasped behind her back, seeming to examine each brilliant bloom.

"I love Jane so much, but I wish she was—well, not so *inside* herself. She doesn't laugh, or run, or play the way a little girl ought to. She's—she's too quiet!"

"I shall ask Katie to help me search out some of Emily's old toys," Mrs. Canfield said. "They are all packed away in the attic, and there might be something among them that would amuse Jane."

"I can help, if you like," I offered.

"That would be very kind of you, Louisa."

Involuntarily I glanced up at the house. It stood tall and dark gray, with gables and half-hidden dormers, its several brick chimneys soot-stained almost to black. In most of the rear windows the shades were drawn halfway down, rather like heavy-lidded eyes. Only the four windows on the second floor which were Jane's and mine stood wide open with the shades raised to the top, and two on the first floor in what I judged would be the kitchen. At least Katie believes in letting in a little air, I thought, but the attic probably hasn't seen a ray of sunshine in years. Strangely, I shivered a little and turned back to the lovely yard in which we sat.

As warm and lush and fragrant as it was, the garden had a certain strict control about it. The heavy-headed summer flowers grew neatly within their bounds, the tidy hedges of boxwood and privet were trimmed and even, the thick soft grass was perfectly cut and disciplined. But the rich scent of stock and viburnum drifted lazily on the air, birdcalls lilted from the top of the tulip tree, and bright rows of pansies marched along the sharply-edged borders, their gay faces lending a flippancy to the dignity of the place.

I felt the garden was much like Lydia Canfield herself. Restrained, calm, precise, yet with a natural force and energy which must require a constant effort to hold it always in control. She had been born and bred a Bostonian,

I knew, and had not moved to Lynn until the early years of her marriage. She was small, slim, determinedly erect, and I had never seen her dressed in anything other than black taffeta, her chin held high by a boned lace collar. Her hair, gleaming now blue-black in the sun, was just beginning to show bright silver threads in the intricate coronet of braids. She always wore the same four pieces of jewelry: her wide gold wedding band, two magnificent diamond rings, and a long jet chain from which hung an oval black locket, its smooth surface highlighted by another large diamond. She had what Jane called a "closed-up face," and although her voice was low and beautifully modulated, it lacked warmth. Somehow, through her cool reserve, she gave off an air of strength which was impressive. I was not exactly afraid of Lydia Canfield, but I was quite awed by her, and very much on my best behavior.

I heard the back screen door open and close, and turning, saw Katie coming across the yard with the tea tray. She set it on a low table by Mrs. Canfield's chair.

"I made sugar cookies for Jane," she said, "and there's milk for her in the little pitcher."

"You'll spoil her, Katie," I said lightly.

"Nonsense, Miss Louisa! She could use a mite of spoiling, seems to me. It doesn't set right to see a child so quiet." She turned to Mrs. Canfield. "Shall I fetch her, ma'am?"

"Please, Katie."

Her ample body in its neat gray uniform looked solid and dependable as she walked across the grass toward where Jane knelt by a pansy bed.

"Dear Katie," Mrs. Canfield murmured with a little smile. "Nothing could make her happier than having a child around to cater to. If we don't watch her she'll stuff Jane as full of goodies as a Christmas pudding."

"Has Katie been with you long?" I asked.

"Since I was married. She was only sixteen then, inexperienced, but quite desperately anxious to learn. Katie and I have been together for almost forty years. A very long time."

"She knew John, then."

"Oh, yes. From the time he was born. John was always so very fond of Katie!"

"And Emily, too?" I asked.

"Emily?" The barest suggestion of a frown touched her brow and was gone. "Emily was . . . rather different. She demanded a great deal, even from Katie."

"From the little I have seen of Katie I imagine she would enjoy putting herself out for any child."

"Katie is very fond of all children, fortunately. She has always had infinite patience with them. Even with Emily."

I could not help probing. "Even?" I repeated.

"Emily was . . . not particularly considerate of other people."

It seemed a surprising statement for a mother to make, and it embarrassed me a little.

"I suppose all children are a little selfish about their own interests," I said.

"No, not all," Mrs. Canfield replied. Then she lowered her eyes and leaning forward, lifted the silver teapot. "How do you like your tea, my dear?" she asked.

"Sugar, please. And lemon."

As the clear amber fluid flowed smoothly into the delicate cups I watched her face, puzzled by what she had said, and looking for some explanation. But the "closed-up" look was there and I felt unable to pursue the subject. Mrs. Canfield added sugar to my tea, and a thin slice of lemon studded with a clove, handing it to me just as Jane came across the grass toward us, and Katie went back into the house.

"Jane, dear," Mrs. Canfield said. "Did Katie tell you she made cookies for you? And here is your milk."

"Yes. She told me. May I have two?"

"If you like."

Jane chose one of the deeper chairs, pulling her legs under her and sitting comfortably curled while she nibbled round and round the edge of her cookie, her dark eyes full of quiet pleasure.

"Isn't it nice here, Louisa?" she said at last. "I told you it was. I said you would like it. Remember?"

"I do. And you were quite right."

"Even though I know you didn't want to leave Martin," she added.

"Oh—Martin," I said weakly, wishing Jane wouldn't be so outspoken.

Mrs. Canfield looked at me with polite interest. "Martin? He is your . . . beau?"

"Not exactly. At least, not yet."

"I think he is," Jane offered. "He's there at our house practically every minute. And he always wishes I wasn't around."

"Jane!" I had a strong desire to tell my niece to be quiet, but I didn't quite dare. "Martin is very fond of you."

"Oh, he likes me all right, but he still wishes I wasn't around." She turned to her grandmother. "He writes poetry about Louisa, and he can't read it to her when I'm there."

I could feel myself flushing with annoyance and embarrassment. To my relief Mrs. Canfield deftly turned the conversation.

"He must be very clever to write poetry," she said. "It is something I have never been able to do. Emily used to, however. Have you ever tried, Jane?"

"To write a poem? No, but I don't think it can be so very hard. Did Emily write good poetry? I mean, did it rhyme and everything?"

"Yes, it was quite good, as a matter of fact. I have a copybook somewhere in which she kept them. Perhaps I can find it for you. She wrote a very nice one about pansies once, I recall."

"I like the pansies," Jane said. "Will you come and look at them when you're done with your tea, Louisa? Some of them are enormous!"

"Perhaps."

"They look like tiny little people," Jane mused. "They all have faces, just like tiny people."

"That is what your Aunt Emily used to call them," Mrs. Canfield said. "Her pansy people. She would pick one and say that was the king, and another one would be the queen, and others were their subjects."

Jane looked up at her grandmother. "You mean she really picked them? Or she just *chose* them?"

"She picked them. She had a sandbox, I remember, and she used to stick the stems into the sand so the flowers would stand up."

There was deep concern in Jane's voice. "But didn't they die? With no water, didn't they die?"

"Why, yes," Mrs. Canfield said, "I fancy they did. But by then she was through playing with them."

"I wouldn't want them to die," Jane said positively. "I wouldn't pick them unless I was going to put them in water."

I set my empty cup on the tray and wiped my lips with my napkin. Jane looked so troubled that I could not remain put out by her remarks about Martin. Besides, he *did* write poetry, and he *didn't* like her around when he wanted to read it to me.

"Jane, everyone picks flowers," I said, "that's why people have gardens. And pansies grow better the more you pick them."

"It's all right if you're going to put them in water," Jane said. "But you should never make anything die!"

She swallowed the last bite of the second cookie, finished off her milk, and wiped her mouth on the back of her hand.

"Jane!" I started to remonstrate. "Use your napkin—"

"Let her be, Louisa," Mrs. Canfield said surprisingly. "Perhaps we fret too much about manners. There is plenty of time for those. For a little while let us both help her to enjoy herself." She gazed at Jane, and her eyes were brooding. "Time is so short—it goes so swiftly—"

I rose. "Jane, will you show me the pansies now?"

Jane bounced from her chair. "This way," she said, and pulled on my hand. "Come on, Louisa, *run!*"

Delighted at being freed from that formal tea table, I picked up my skirts and raced Jane across the grass. Beside me she laughed exultantly.

TWO

The soft summer days flowed by. Letters from Martin arrived regularly and they were the only thing that broke the unchanging rhythm of routine. I would take them to my room to read in private as I had promised to do, and open each one eagerly. Martin's handwriting was quite large and sprawly and what felt at first like a very thick and rewarding letter often turned out to be no more than a few lines scattered over several pages. But the lines were often poetry, which made me feel very special, and reading about the beauty of my hair or my eyes or my "rose-tipped" hands was flattering, to say the least. The letters made me miss him, and I longed to be home again where I could hear his light voice saying these sweet things to me, rather than having to decipher them from the written page.

Answering his letters was difficult, however, and mine were generally rambling accounts of uneventful days, spiced with a mention of my latest trip to the library or the progress of the campanula plants in the garden. I could have written a great deal about Jane, but I doubted that Martin would be interested in the fact that she was happier than in months.

She seemed to be lowering the wall she had built around herself, making herself more open to new experiences, more willing to be the warm, friendly child she had been before her parents died. In a sense I suppose she was making herself more vulnerable too, more easily hurt or frightened, but how could I know there could be anything in that quiet Lynn household to hurt or frighten her?

She spent almost all her waking hours in the garden and seemed content to play her own private games with the flowers, to follow Jacob, the weekly gardener, watching him weed and trim and rake. She tried her hand at pushing the lawn mower and was delighted when she could cut a clean straight path in the emerald grass.

Most of all she was fascinated by the reflecting ball.

"It used to be Emily's," she told me. "Emily wouldn't let anyone else look in it. *Ever!*"

"How do you know that?"

"Katie told me. Katie thinks it's marked with evil."

"Jane! What a thing to say!"

"I didn't say it, Katie did. Katie says no good ever came from anything that doesn't show the truth."

"And doesn't the reflecting ball show the truth?"

We were in the garden, and I was trying lackadaisically to write a letter to Martin. Jane went close to the silver ball, putting her face down near it.

"I guess not," she said, and giggled, a lovely sound. "I look like a frog, and I *know* I'm not a frog. But I have a flat nose, and bulgy eyes, and a big wide mouth!"

She stood staring into the silvery surface, making ridiculous faces and giggling at the reflection.

"I can look like a lot of different people," she said. She puffed out her rosy cheeks. "Now I look like Queen Victoria!"

I laughed at her. "How do you know what Queen Victoria looked like?"

"I've seen pictures, of course." She opened her eyes wide and tipped her head down slightly, looking upward into the ball through her dark lashes. "Now I look like Emily."

"Where did you see a picture of Emily?" I asked lazily. I could feel the sun warm on my head, and I felt pleasantly drowsy. After a moment I realized Jane had not answered. "Where did you see Emily's picture?" I repeated.

Jane stepped backward, away from the ball, her face very still. "I never did," she said softly.

"You must have, else how would you know you looked like her?"

"I never did," she said again, and suddenly her voice was angry. "I never saw a picture of Emily! But I looked like her! I know I did!" She came quickly to my chair, standing close beside it, her eyes stormy.

"Well, all right, dear," I said in surprise. "As you told me, you can look like all sorts of people in the ball. Queen Victoria, and a frog—why not Emily, too?" I put my unfinished letter and box of writing materials aside. "Let's see who I look like, shall we? Maybe I can be President Taft!"

"No! I don't want you to, Louisa. Anyway, you're just being silly about it! You couldn't look *anything* like President Taft, and I *did* look like Emily! So there!"

She stood a moment, her face flushed and her breath coming quickly. Then she buried her face in my shoulder, hugging me tight.

"I'm sorry, Louisa. I'm sorry! I don't know why I—I didn't mean to talk like that!"

She sounded deeply disturbed, and it puzzled me, but I thought it probably better to drop the whole subject.

I wondered once or twice about that odd little scene, and I hoped that being at the Canfield house would not create any morbid thoughts in Jane's mind. After all, it had been her father's home, and he was dead; her Aunt Emily had lived here and had died; Mr. Canfield, too, although I could not recall ever having heard much about him. I only knew that he had died before John and Charlotte were married, as had Emily, of course. But in the days that followed I put it out of my mind. There was no further reference to Emily, and I began to think I had imagined the whole incident.

It was at breakfast a week or so later that Mrs. Canfield looked up over a letter she was reading.

"Oh, how nice!" she said. "Adam is back! He asks to come and call."

I slipped my own letter from Martin into my lap to be savored later. Having no idea at all who Adam was, I tried to look interested. It was Jane who asked, "Adam who?"

"Forgive me," Mrs. Canfield said. "Of course you don't know him at all, do you? Adam Frost. He is Dr. Frost now, and he is back in town to work with his father. I suppose it will be Old Dr. Frost and Young Dr. Frost, won't it? How pleasant it will be to see him again!"

"Was he a friend of my father's?"

"Not a close friend. He and Emily were constant playmates from the time they were very small. Adam's mother was a dear friend of mine, and we often spent afternoons together with our children. After Mrs. Frost died Adam still came here frequently. I often thought it must have been simply from habit, because he and Emily had some memorable battles! They were the same age—that would make Adam twenty-four now. Quite young to have completed his medical training."

Jane swirled brown sugar artistically into her porridge. "I don't think twenty-four is so young," she said.

Lydia Canfield smiled at her. "No, I suppose not. But I assure you, it is." Turning to me, she went on, "Adam was always a brilliant boy. Not really a *genius,* I guess, but certainly very, very bright. He was a challenge to Emily. I remember she used to say she was going to marry him when she grew up."

Jane looked up from her cereal. "Did he want to marry Emily?"

"I don't expect she ever gave him a chance to say. It would not have been like her. She was used to announcing her wishes and having them obeyed."

"Did you do everything she wanted you to, Grandmother?" Jane asked with interest.

Mrs. Canfield looked at her thoughtfully. "Far more often than I should have, I fancy," she said. Then she reached over and patted Jane's hand. "But don't get your hopes up, child. I have learned a great deal since then."

"Well, *I* think it was silly of Emily to talk about getting married," Jane said, licking the last cream from her spoon. "*I* don't intend to think about getting married for years and years and years. Maybe never!" Folding her napkin, she slipped it into the heavy silver ring. "Excuse me, please, Grandmother."

Jane skipped out the swinging door, and we could hear her chattering to Katie in the kitchen. Mrs. Canfield looked down at Dr. Frost's letter again, as I clasped mine from Martin.

"I shall ask Adam to have supper with us on Sunday," she said. "I'm sure you will find him excellent company, Louisa."

"I am sure I shall," I agreed, but a doctor who was almost a genius sounded rather forbidding.

On Sunday when the noon meal was done Mrs. Canfield excused herself to lie down for a while, and Jane and I wandered into the garden.

"Oof, I'm full!" Jane remarked inelegantly, stretching out on her back on the grass.

"I'm not surprised. I counted the helpings of strawberry shortcake you had."

Jane grinned at me. "It was good." She patted her stomach. "I bet I'm getting fat. When we go home I'll probably be as fat as a pig. Granny Amory won't even know me."

"She will be pleased, though." I hesitated, and then added, "Will you hate to leave here when it is time to go?"

Jane pulled up a blade of grass and bit the tender end. "I don't know. I don't think so. I like it here, but it's really Emily's house. Not mine."

"Why, Jane," I said in surprise, "how silly! It's as much yours as hers. It was your father's house, too."

"I know. But it doesn't feel like his. It only feels like Emily's. And Grandmother's, of course."

"You think a lot about Emily, don't you?" I asked.

"Emily thinks a lot about me."

"Jane, don't be ridiculous! You're imagining things. Emily died years ago, long before you were even born."

"I know she did."

"Then don't you see—it's nonsense to say she thinks about you."

"She does, though. I feel her, a lot of times."

"Jane, don't talk like that! You can't 'feel' Emily. Emily isn't anything anymore—except a memory to the people who knew her. Just the memory of a poor little girl who died before she ever had a chance to grow up. And don't keep thinking so much about her! It isn't . . . well, it isn't *healthy*, Jane!"

"Don't worry, Louisa. I'm perfectly healthy. You just said I was getting fat."

I felt suddenly edgy and a little out of patience with her. "I don't mean that kind of healthy!"

Jane laid one little brown hand on my knee. "Don't worry, Louisa. Emily doesn't go skittering around the garden like a white cloud, and she doesn't make funny noises in the night, or anything scary like that. She's just *here*. And she knows I'm here, too. But she hasn't spoken to me yet."

"Well, you just tell me when she does," I said tartly, "because that's the day I'll give you a large dose of castor oil and put you to bed for a week! With *no* strawberry short-cake!"

Jane laughed. "You're funny, Louisa," she said. "I love you. I'm glad I have you."

"Well, if you really love me, stop talking nonsense," I said, but I couldn't help smiling at her.

Flopping over onto her stomach, her two feet waving in the air, she asked, "What are you going to wear tonight?"

"Tonight? Why, what I have on, I suppose. Should I be changing for some reason?"

She looked at me, amazed. "Dr. Frost is coming to supper! Didn't you remember? Wear your white dress, Louisa, with the blue sash. Please, will you? You haven't worn it since you've been here, and it's the prettiest of all your dresses."

"Why should I get all dressed up just because a friend of your grandmother's is coming to see her?"

"He's not too old for you. Maybe he'll fall in love with you."

"Why, naturally he will! How could he help it? He will walk into the parlor, take one look at me and throw himself flat on his face at my feet. Oh, Jane, you *are* a goose!"

"Is Martin in love with you?"

As a straight question I found it a little difficult to answer. "Why, I don't exactly know. I guess he is—sort of."

"Are you going to marry him?"

"Maybe. Someday. When he's through college."

"Dr. Frost is already through college. You wouldn't have to wait."

"Jane, would you mind very much letting me run my own life?"

"I only mentioned it. *I* think Martin's soppy!"

"Well, *I* like him very much! And I wish *he* was coming to supper instead of the brilliant Dr. Whatshisname!"

"Won't you even *talk* to him, Louisa?"

"To whom?"

"Brilliant Dr. Whatshisname."

I picked up my box of writing materials and laid it on my lap. "I'm sure I can find something to say to him," I replied. "Perhaps he'd like to hear about my tonsil operation. Now if you will very kindly be quiet, I am going to write to Martin!"

Jane got lazily to her feet and slipped her hand in mine, her mouth turning up in its own appealing way. "Wear the white dress anyhow, Louisa, will you? Please? Just for me."

It was a few minutes before six that evening, and I was just tying small pink bows on Jane's braids when we heard the sharp jangle of the doorbell.

"Oh, Louisa, he's here! Hurry!"

"Stand still! I can't tie bows when you wiggle! There. Now, let me look at you."

Her pink dotted swiss dress was fresh from Katie's skillful iron, her long white ribbed cotton stockings were smooth, and her black patent leather slippers gleamed from the trace of Vaseline I had rubbed into them.

"All right, go ahead. I'll be down in a minute or two." She bounced toward the door, her braids swinging. "And Jane! Walk! Like a lady! Don't go crashing down the stairs!"

She made me a mock curtsy. "Yes, ma'am," she said, and went mincing along the hall with exaggerated daintiness.

After a moment's hesitation I lifted the white dress from its hanger, and put it carefully over my head. The soft muslin felt light and cool as the skirt, with its dozens of tiny tucks, slipped easily over the starched petticoat. The neck was wide and square, edged with a lace ruffle, and wider ruffles fell from the short sleeves. The pale blue taffeta sash was crushed and fitted tight to my waist, making it look extremely small. I clipped flat blue bows onto my white slippers, tucked another into my hair, and took a careful look in the mirror. I couldn't help being satisfied with what I saw.

"Well, Dr. Whatshisname," I murmured, "here comes the irresistible Louisa Amory!"

There were voices from the parlor, and not wanting to interrupt a conversation, I paused by the open door. Mrs. Canfield sat in the small wing chair that she always preferred, and Jane was curled on a deep red velvet ottoman close beside her. Both their faces were smiling and lifted toward the man who stood talking, his back to the door. Beside the two small seated figures he seemed very tall. His head was narrow and well-shaped, his hair thick and dark and closely cropped, probably in an effort to discourage its definite tendency to curl. He stood easily, one hand in the pocket of his gray jacket, the other holding a pipe with which he gestured.

Lydia Canfield saw me in the doorway and held out her hand. "Come in, child. Adam, this is Louisa Amory, Jane's aunt."

He was quite nice-looking, with flat planes to his cheeks and jaw, and a sort of cleft in his chin. I remembered a silly rhyme Mother sometimes quoted. "Cleft in the chin, devil within," but this doctor looked anything but devilish.

"Miss Amory," he said. "I have wanted so much to meet you!"

Since he probably hadn't known I existed until five minutes before, I was inclined to doubt this remark.

"And I have been looking forward to meeting you, Dr. Frost. Mrs. Canfield speaks so highly of you."

I extended my hand and he took it. "Mrs. Canfield is prejudiced in my favor," he said rather pompously, "but I have no desire to change her opinion."

As I removed my hand from his and sat down, Jane said with suspicious innocence, "Dr. Frost, do you write poetry?"

The man looked at her in astonishment. "Poetry? Good heavens, no! Why?"

Jane smiled sweetly. "I just wondered. I think men who write poetry are kind of soppy, don't you?"

Before the surprised doctor could answer, Mrs. Canfield fixed her dark eyes on her granddaughter. "Jane, would you ring for Katie, please? We'll discuss poetry some other time. Right now I should prefer a glass of sherry."

THREE

As far as general table conversation went that Sunday night I would have done much better to have had my supper upstairs on a tray! I quickly discovered that the doctor and Mrs. Canfield had both traveled abroad, while I had never been out of Massachusetts. They began comparing impressions of places they had been and things they had seen, discussing some doors made by a man named Ghiberti, and something else called the Lion of Lucerne, about neither of which did I know anything. From time to time Dr. Frost would look at me with a politely expectant expression, but since there was no intelligent contribution that I could make, I could do no more than smile at him. As the meal went on, the smile became more fixed. Boredom crept over me, and I began to feel so countrified and lumpish that gradually I drifted into soothing thoughts of Martin. I was quite unprepared when Mrs. Canfield directed a remark to me.

"The Women's Social and Political Union, for example," she said. "What do you think, Louisa, of giving women the right to vote?"

I was too embarrassed to admit that I had not been listening to the talk, nor had I ever thought very much about women's rights. I could feel myself blushing as I tried desperately to reply.

"Why, I . . . I suppose women could vote as well as men," I stammered. "*I* wouldn't know much about voting, but some women are quite intelligent."

"I don't believe women would vote intelligently," Dr. Frost said. "I think they would vote emotionally."

That aroused me! He sounded so patronizing! "Perhaps that might not be altogether bad," I said. "I cannot see that the 'intelligent' voting of men has made the world such a perfect place."

"And you really believe that the unpredictable emotions of females would improve matters?" One of his dark eyebrows lifted maddeningly.

"'Females,' as you call them, are not always unpredictable, Doctor. For instance, when they are teased they are predictably annoyed!"

"I beg your pardon, Miss Amory! I had no intention of teasing you."

"Then you must consider women quite insensitive."

"In all honesty, Miss Amory, I must admit that I know very little about women except as patients. And as patients they are much easier to deal with than men."

"It's generous of you to say so. But I wasn't speaking of *sick* women. I was speaking of healthy, normal, everyday women!"

"I can see that I have a lot to learn about healthy, normal, everyday women. It will take some intensive study. I don't suppose you'd care to—"

"Offer myself as a textbook? No, thank you, Doctor. I would not make a patient teacher."

"A pity. You would certainly make an attractive one."

I took a deep breath. As Mrs. Canfield's guest I did not want to risk being rude, and yet Dr. Frost's air of amused superiority made me fume. With such dignity as I could muster I turned to Mrs. Canfield.

"It must be past Jane's bedtime," I said. "If you would excuse us—" I rose.

"If you think best, Louisa. But you will join us again, won't you?"

Immediately Dr. Frost was on his feet. "Please do," he urged. "Otherwise I shall feel that you are really annoyed with me."

I wanted to say, "I am!" but I wouldn't give him the satisfaction. "If it is not too late," I murmured. "Come, Jane."

Jane groaned softly, but she knew better than to argue. We left the dining room and went upstairs.

While I hung Jane's dress in her wardrobe she struggled with the buttons on her Ferris waist.

"I don't see why children always have to go to bed," she grumbled. "Just when things start to get interesting, it's always bedtime!"

"*You* may think all that talk about doors and lions and emotional women is interesting. *I* don't!"

"Anyway, Dr. Frost is handsome, isn't he? I think he's a lot handsomer than Martin."

I untied the bows from her hair and separated the braids with my fingers. "You are entitled to your opinion," I said coldly.

Apparently sensing my rough edges, she tried to soothe them. "You looked beautiful in your white dress, Louisa." Then she spoiled it by adding, "Dr. Frost thought so too."

Her hair snapped as I brushed it vigorously. "Don't be silly! He thinks I'm a complete dodo!"

"Maybe he does," she admitted with annoying candor, "but he still thinks you're pretty. He looked at you and I could see him getting all soft around the edges."

"Well, I hope he gets softer and softer until he melts!" I said inanely. "Go and brush your teeth."

A few minutes later I tucked her into the high brass bed and kissed her good night. As I pressed the light switch by the door she said. "Louisa, you know what?"

"What?"

"I bet Emily's plenty mad at Dr. Frost thinking you're pretty! She was going to marry him!"

"Well, it's too bad she didn't grow up and do just that! A bad-tempered, self-centered girl, and a know-it-all, show-offy man! A perfect combination!"

"Louisa?"

"Now what?"

"Please don't talk like that. Don't say things against Emily. It makes her mad. And when Emily was mad, she was *dreadful!*"

I paused for a second, and then went back to the bed and took her hand. "Jane," I said firmly, "stop thinking about Emily Canfield! She was a little girl who died a long time ago. She no longer knows anything, nor feels anything, nor gets 'mad' about anything! She just . . . rests quietly."

Her voice was surprisingly meek. "I hope you're right this time, Louisa. I really, truly do!"

As I came into the parlor Dr. Frost rose and Mrs. Canfield turned to me, smiling.

"I was just telling Adam how much I enjoy having Jane here this summer," she said. "I did not realize how greatly I missed a child around the place."

"Rather like having Emily back?" the doctor asked, re-seating himself near me.

"I suppose, in essence, that's what it is," Mrs. Canfield agreed. "Yet how different the two little girls are!"

"Do you think so? As I remember Emily, Jane looks a great deal like her."

"Yes, there is a strong family resemblance. But I was

thinking more of temperament. Jane is a quiet child, thoughtful and obedient. Her father was the same way. But not Emily."

Dr. Frost spoke feelingly. "Emily was a hellion!"

My eyebrows lifted in surprise. This was the first time I had heard Emily spoken of by anyone except her mother, and this new opinion startled me.

Mrs. Canfield sighed. "Well, she was certainly . . . diffi-cult," she said. Then she smiled. "Do you recall how Emily always said she was going to marry you, Adam?"

He laughed. "I do, indeed. I never had anything to say about it. Emily never *asked* me, she simply announced that was what she had planned."

"And you never demurred," Mrs. Canfield added.

"Not for long. It was much easier to go along with Emily than to have my face scratched when I disagreed."

"Yes, that is the way it was. Easier to go along with Emily than to disagree about anything." There was the briefest pause, then Mrs. Canfield smoothly changed the subject. "And now tell me, Adam. What are your plans? Are you home for good to work with your father?"

The talk continued for another half hour or so. When the little French clock on the mantelpiece chimed ten, Dr. Frost got to his feet.

"I hope we haven't bored you, Miss Amory. You have been very quiet all evening."

I tried to sound polite. "Oh, no," I said brightly. "It has been fascinating."

Looking very small beside the doctor, Mrs. Canfield laid her hand on his arm. "Adam, you must come here often this summer. Louisa needs young company."

I felt like a homely child being pushed forward by its mother! "Oh, I'm sure Dr. Frost is a very busy man—" I began, but he interrupted.

"Not nearly as busy as I hope to be. Thank you for a delicious supper, and for . . . " he paused and glanced at me, "for *stimulating* conversation! This has been a delightful evening."

And with that barbed remark, he left.

Usually when I went to bed I lay and thought about Martin. Remembering his soft voice, his soft blond hair, the strong sweet smell of the pomade he used to keep it smooth, all worked as a sort of lullaby to put me to sleep. But tonight I could not seem to concentrate on him. Instead I kept hearing Dr. Frost's deep voice saying, "Emily was a hellion!" and "It was much easier to go along with Emily than to have my face scratched." I recalled the odd note in Lydia Canfield's voice when she spoke of her daughter as being difficult. There had been no sadness, no regret, such as I felt whenever I thought of Charlotte. What kind of a child could Emily have been? What sort of little girl could die when still so young, and leave this kind of dark memory?

Sometime later I drifted off into a restless sleep, filled with confused dreams of a faceless Emily raising threatening, clawing hands, screaming, "Look out for me, Louisa, I'm a difficult hellion! Look out for me, Louisa—" And suddenly the sound of my name woke me, and it was Jane's voice calling.

"Louisa," I heard again.

I slipped out from under the sheet into the warm summer darkness of my room and went quietly to Jane's door. In a faint glow of light I could see her sitting up in bed.

"What is it, dear?"

"Louisa, what's that light?" she said, and her voice had a hushed sound, almost of fear.

"What light, Jane?"

"There—on my wall. A reflection or something. See it?"

On the wall opposite the garden windows, just above her bed, I could see a soft white blur of light. It was steady, and vaguely round, and very pale. It made Jane's eyes enormous dark pools in her small face.

"Why, it's moonlight, Jane. It must be."

She shook her head. "No, it isn't." Pushing back the cover, she slid out of the bed and went to the garden windows. "Louisa, come here."

I moved to stand beside her. Below us the garden lay in silent blackness, scenting the night. In the very center the reflecting ball stood, and its silver sphere glowed with a pure white light.

"How lovely!" I breathed. "The moonlight shining on that ball. That's what is reflected here in your room."

Jane slipped her hand into mine, and hers was shockingly cold. "Louisa," she whispered. "Look at the sky."

I raised my eyes to the pitch-dark tent overhead, even as I heard the first gentle pattering of rain.

"There isn't any moon, Louisa."

Suddenly I felt as chilled as though the night were mid-winter. Outside the window I could hear the sharp little sound of raindrops on the thick leaves of the tulip tree. As Jane and I stood there together we saw the white glow of the reflecting ball begin to lessen, and in a minute the garden lay unseen in utter darkness.

"Come to bed, Jane. It's gone now. It was nothing, dear — just some sort of reflection."

She allowed me to lead her toward the bed and pull the light cover over her.

"Reflection of what, Louisa?" she asked, and her voice was very small.

"Oh, darling, I don't know. The streetlamp, most likely."

"But there aren't any streetlamps in the back of the house."

I felt a strange reluctance to discuss it, that strange, white, sourceless light. "Jane, I don't know what it was. But it's gone now, and you must just go back to sleep. It's very late."

She turned away from me and burrowed into the pillow, as if for comfort. "All right, Louisa."

The soft obedience in her voice made me want to comfort her. "It's nothing to worry about, Jane. Just don't think about it anymore." She didn't answer, and after a moment I said, "Would you like me to stay with you until you go to sleep?"

She sounded very small, and somehow very alone. "No, thank you. I'm all right now."

"Well, good night then."

"Good night, Louisa."

I went back into my own room, and to bed, but it was not until the rain had stopped and the sky had started to lighten with early dawn that I slept.

FOUR

I woke the next morning with a heavy, oppressed feeling that I could not at first explain. Then, slowly, things came sifting back. The dinner conversation, Dr. Frost's exasperating superiority, the strange remarks about Emily—the reflecting ball! My eyes flew open. Jane! Was she all right?

Out of bed, I crossed past the windows on my way to her room, and glanced out. The morning was warm and damp after the rain, and Jane was already outdoors, walking delightedly barefoot in the wet grass. Since I had not been up to braid her hair it hung down her back, tied away from her face with a crisp bow. Katie must have done that, I thought. Jane had her jump rope looped over her shoulder, and when she reached the wide clear space, framed by flower beds, at the far end of the garden, she carefully arranged the ends of the rope just so in her hands and then began to jump. I could hear her chanting to herself, and I smiled as I saw her long hair flopping up and down, and the full skirt of her yellow dress bouncing. I could sense how cool and wet the grass must feel beneath her feet. As I watched, I heard Katie's voice calling from the kitchen door below me.

"Jane? Come along now, girl, and have your breakfast. The cinnamon buns are just hot from the oven."

"I'm coming, Katie."

With one last burst of skipping, just as fast as she could, she took the rope in one hand and started up the lawn toward the back door. Just as she came abreast of the reflecting ball she paused, staring at it. Then, chin high, she marched on by it and I heard the screen door slam lightly as she entered the house. I dressed quickly, a rose-colored cotton skirt and a pale-pink shirtwaist, and—perhaps inspired by Jane—I tied my own hair back with a rose ribbon. Running down the stairs and into the dining room, I found Mrs. Canfield and Jane already at the table. There was a letter from Martin beside my plate, and I slipped it into my lap as I sat down.

"I am so sorry," I said. "I never meant to sleep so late!"

Mrs. Canfield smiled. "My dear, I am delighted that you did. There is no necessity to live by the clock. I only trust it doesn't mean you had a sleepless night."

I glanced quickly at Jane. Her eyes were on her plate as she munched on a large cinnamon bun.

"No, no, not at all. I just . . . well, I just overslept!"

"And a very good morning for it, too. It's going to be dreadfully hot today, I'm afraid. The air seems quite heavy after last night's rain." Mrs. Canfield rang the little silver bell that stood by her place, and after a moment Katie came through the swinging door with a slice of cool, pale-green melon on a chilled plate.

"Morning, Miss Louisa. I'll have your eggs by the time you finish that."

"Good morning, Katie. And thank you for tying Jane's bow. If it *was* you . . . " I looked hesitantly at Mrs. Canfield.

"It's a fine thing to be fixing a little girl's hair again," Katie said. "I haven't your skill with braids, Miss Louisa, but there was many a time I used to tie Miss Emily's hair ribbons."

Placing the melon in front of me, she returned to the kitchen.

"What kind of hair did Emily have?" asked Jane.

"About the color of yours," Mrs. Canfield said. "Perhaps a little darker. It was very curly and I used to brush it around my finger to make ringlets. She wore two little bows to tie it back on each side of her face."

"Was she pretty?"

"I thought so."

"Do you think I'm pretty?"

"Jane! I exploded. "You know better than to ask a question like that!"

She looked at me, her large eyes calm. "I just wondered," she said. "It's hard to tell about yourself, you know."

Mrs. Canfield looked at Jane with fond amusement. "You need not fret, Jane," she said. "When the time comes that prettiness is most important to you, you will have no cause to worry. Now. Would you like another cinnamon bun?"

"No, thank you. I've had three. May I be excused?"

"Yes, dear. Of course."

Jane disappeared into the kitchen just as Katie set my breakfast plate in front of me. While I ate, Mrs. Canfield poured herself a second cup of coffee.

"Adam was interesting company last night, I thought," she said. "Did you like him, Louisa?"

My eyes were on my plate. "He seemed very nice."

"You were rather quiet all evening. I did hope you were not bored."

"Not at all," I lied smoothly.

She smiled. "Adam has always been quite a talker. Even when he was just a boy, he and Emily would chatter together for hours."

With sudden determination I said, "Mrs. Canfield, have you noticed that Jane seems ... well, overly preoccupied with ... with Emily?"

"With Emily?" The older woman looked at me with surprise. "I don't think I know just what you mean."

"I'm not sure I know just what I mean, either. It's only that Jane seems to take every opportunity to speak of Emily, to ask about her. Sometimes she even volunteers statements about her that she seems so . . . so *sure* of!"

"What, for example?"

"Well, she says she feels Emily is around here all the time."

"I think you make too much of such things, Louisa. The young have no conception of death, yet it has a mysterious appeal for them. I think Jane is simply rather intrigued by knowing that another little girl, one to whom she is related, lived here, played here, and—finally—died here."

"Perhaps," I said doubtfully, but after a second's thought I rushed on. "But Jane doesn't even seem to think of Emily as dead. It is more as though she were still here—Emily, I mean. I told you Jane said she could 'feel' her."

"Jane is imaginative, and sensitive, and probably lonely. Aren't imaginary playmates natural under such circumstances?"

"I suppose they are," I said. I was unsatisfied, and yet I could find no words to express the uneasiness I felt. Lydia Canfield was quite right. It was doubtless the result of a very active imagination feeding on a ready-made situation.

Just as we were about to leave the table the doorbell rang, and presently Katie entered the dining room, carrying a florist's box which she gave to Mrs. Canfield.

"A delivery boy just brought it," she said.

Mrs. Canfield lifted the pince-nez that were attached to a little gold clip on the bosom of her dress. Placing them on her nose, she looked at the box carefully.

"Dear me," she murmured. "Whoever do you suppose is sending flowers?"

She untied the single string and raised the lid. Turning

back green paper, she lifted a cluster of deep red roses from the box. "How lovely! But from whom? Ah, here is the card." She read it silently, her eyes bright behind the glasses. "Well, I am glad to see that young Adam still remembers his manners. Flowers for his hostess. He writes, 'Thank you so much for a delightful evening! Would you and Jane and Miss Amory be my guests at a Fourth of July band concert in the park tomorrow evening? I shall call for you at eight o'clock. Gratefully, Adam.' Now, isn't that thoughtful of him!"

"Very," I said, unenthusiastically.

"Gracious! I haven't been to a band concert in years! I think we are all going to enjoy ourselves tremendously!"

I wasn't as sure as she was, but I let it go.

Upstairs I made Jane's and my beds and tidied our rooms, deliberately putting off the pleasure of opening Martin's letter. Presently, however, I settled into the little armchair by the window and, slitting the envelope with my finger, drew out the folded pages. The large writing sprawled across them.

"Dear Louisa," I read. "I did not get any letter from you today. In fact I haven't had one for four days. I suppose you are very busy, going to one party after another." I snorted. The nearest thing to a party had been an evening of conversation I couldn't even understand! "I haven't called on any girls since you have been away, mostly because I haven't had much time, working in McHenry's Drug Store as I do. I did walk Susie Pepper home once or twice after she had come in just about closing time for a chocolate soda, but she doesn't really mean anything to me. I would never write poetry to Susie Pepper, even though she is a very nice girl and has invited me to take her to the Milford Fourth of July celebration."

I stopped for a moment and thought about Susie Pepper, a little brown button of a girl with teasing dark eyes that seemed to make boys feel eight feet tall. I had never thought Martin would be interested in anyone like her! So he was taking her to the Fourth of July celebration, was he? Well, I'd write him today and tell him I was going to the Lynn celebration! And I wouldn't set his mind at ease with details or explanations. It might do Martin good to worry a little!

"I think of you a lot, Louisa, and I miss you all the time. I have written a poem to show how well I remember you. Write me soon. Love, Martin."

A poem to show how well he remembered me? It sounded as though I had been gone for years! I didn't have any trouble remembering Martin! I thought about him for a minute, and realized with a shock that his face was very hazy in my mind! I knew that he had straight light hair, knew that his eyes were very large and pale blue and that he had to wear glasses when he studied. I knew that his kisses were very sweet—but I couldn't *see* him! Instead, a totally different face kept flashing through my mind. Deep, probing eyes under dark brows that matched the dark, crisp hair, a firm mouth above a lean, cleft chin—in exasperation I turned to the last page of Martin's letter to find the poem. It was titled "An Ode to Louisa's Lovely Face," and read:

> *Louisa has such yellow hair,*
> *Louisa's lips are red and fair.*
> *Louisa's eyes, now blue, now green—*
> *The loveliest face I've ever seen.*

With unaccountable vexation I decided the four lines made me sound like a piece of Scotch plaid! Had Martin's poetry always been as silly as that? I didn't think it could have been, else how had I always been so moved and touched by it? In quite a bad mood I stuffed the pages back into the envelope, added it to the pile in my dresser drawer, and picking up my writing box, I went downstairs and out the French doors to the garden.

Jane was sitting curled up in one of the deep, cushioned

wicker chairs under the tulip tree, and I settled comfortably in the chair next to hers, grateful for the shade. She had a tablet of paper on her lap, and she was chewing thoughtfully on the end of a pencil.

"Thinking great thoughts?" I asked.

"I'm writing a poem."

"I thought you didn't approve of poetry."

She looked at me reproachfully. "I like *good* poetry. I just don't like soppy poems like Martin writes."

"Louisa has such yellow hair, Louisa's lips are red and fair," I thought to myself. Yes, in all honesty it might be called soppy. "I didn't know you were a poet," I said to her.

"I never was before. I just thought I'd try."

"Well, if I can help you, let me know."

I was not too optimistic about the probable result of Jane's efforts. She was never overly inclined toward the written word. She loved to read, and read well, but writing was a chore for her, and her handwriting was still very youthful and unformed.

Feeling as uninspired as Jane looked, I tried to start a letter to Martin. I felt curiously unwilling to tell him how quiet and uneventful my life was in Lynn. If he chose to believe I spun on a carrousel of gaiety, let him! In this mood I wrote of "the fascinating, traveled young doctor" who had dined with us, and who was taking me (I somehow neglected to mention Jane and her grandmother) to the Fourth of July celebration. I wrote that I hoped he would have a pleasant evening with Susie Pepper and that her "constant chatter might not prove too bothersome." I thanked him for his poem and told him that Jane was "trying her hand at amusing little verses, too." And then I signed it "Your friend, Louisa," and shoved it into an envelope. Suddenly feeling quite cheerful, I looked at Jane who had been setting down a few words from time to time, then scratching them out and gazing off into space.

"You look as though it wasn't so easy to be a poet," I said.

"Things just don't come out right."

"I can sympathize. I have the same trouble writing letters. Why don't you leave it for a few minutes and do something else? It just might come easier when you try again."

She looked at me seriously. "Do you really think so?"

"It's possible."

"Well, it's not coming now, so I might as well." She slid out of the chair and, half skipping, went off down the garden. I watched her stop by one of the pansy beds and kneel on the grass, looking closely at the gay flowers.

She stayed quiet for a few minutes, and then she wandered aimlessly in the direction of the reflecting ball. When she was within a few feet of it she paused, and I thought at first she was going to avoid it. Then, as though on second thought, she walked very slowly close to it, placed her hands on either side of it, and—standing on tiptoe—peered in. I wondered with amusement whether she was making faces at herself again, but her back was toward me and I could not see her face.

Suddenly she turned and came running across the grass. Snatching up her pencil and tablet, she threw herself into the chair, pulled her feet under her, and scribbled furiously for a moment.

"There!" she said with triumph. "There's my poem. Do you want to read it?"

"Of course."

She handed me the tablet. In her loosely formed, downhill script I read:

> *Robed in velvet, jewel-toned,*
> *They stand in small majestic grace.*
> *Watching their garden kingdom grow*
> *With royal pleasure on each face.*

My delight was sincere, and quite apparent, I'm sure. "Why, Jane! That's charming! It's the pansies, isn't it?"

"Yes. Do you really like it?"

"I'm amazed! I think it's lovely!"

She preened herself with a little wiggle of her shoulders. "You don't need to sound so surprised. I *told* you I was going to be a poet."

A dark suspicion crossed my mind. "Jane. You didn't *read* this anywhere, did you?"

She looked at me indignantly. "No! I just wrote it! Just this minute, while I was sitting here. I walked around, like you said, and I looked at the pansies, and then I came back, but I still hadn't thought of anything to write, and then I looked in the reflecting ball because I didn't want to always be sort of . . . you know, scared of it—after last night—and while I was looking in it all of a sudden I just—" She stopped abruptly, her eyes moving from me to the silver globe.

"What, Jane?" I asked softly. "All of a sudden you just— what?"

Her voice was almost inaudible. "Just knew the whole poem. All of a sudden I just knew it."

A dozen half-formed thoughts flew through my mind, followed immediately by the knowledge that they could not be true.

"You see," I said gently. "I told you it would come if you just stopped trying for a minute."

She got out of the chair and stood close to me. "You really think that was it, Louisa?"

"Why, of course. It almost always works. And it's a very good thing to remember."

"I guess that's what it was, all right," she said doubtfully. Then, with more confidence, she repeated, "Yes, that's what it must have been. I just left it alone for a while and then it—just came to me!"

"Your grandmother will be very proud of you."

"Shall I take it in and show it to her?"

"Why don't you? But don't interrupt her if she's busy with something."

"I won't." Taking the tablet from me, she read again the four lines written there. "It really is very good, isn't it?" she said smugly.

Not a great deal later I was going through the upstairs hall on my way to my room to get a stamp for Martin's letter. As I passed the open door of Mrs. Canfield's room I heard her call me.

"Louisa. Would you come here a moment, please?"

I entered. The room was large and cool, the shades drawn halfway down to keep out most of the sunlight. The furniture was massive and dark, and it seemed an almost overpowering chamber for the very small woman who sat in a straight armchair by the window. Her hands were on the carved arms of the chair, but instead of resting easily as they generally did, the fingers were clenched tightly against the wood.

"Yes, Mrs. Canfield. Can I do something for you?"

"Louisa, sit down a moment." She indicated a small chair by the desk. Puzzled by something in her voice, I sat down quietly.

"Jane brought me a poem a little while ago. She said she had written it."

"Yes. I saw it. I thought it was quite good for a nine-year-old."

"Louisa, did Jane really tell you she had written it herself?"

"Why, I saw her, Mrs. Canfield! She tried for quite a long time, writing a line or two and then crossing it out, and she was becoming very impatient with herself. I suggested she leave it for a few minutes and perhaps it would come easier when she tried again, so she played around the garden for a little while, and then she came back and just sat down and wrote the four lines very quickly."

"I see." There was silence for a moment, then she said, "Open the second drawer of that desk, Louisa. It is not locked. I unlocked it myself just a few minutes ago."

I did as I was told, disclosing a tidy collection of letters, leather-covered books that looked like diaries, photograph albums—all the bits and pieces that strengthen memories.

"On the right there is a purple leather notebook. You see it?"

"Yes." I lifted it, smooth and cool, from the drawer.

"Open it from the back. You find where the writing ends? Several pages from the back?"

"Yes, ma'am."

"Turn back three pages—or is it four? You see a page with a verse on it? At the top is written the title, 'Pansy Song.'"

Even as I said the words, "Yes, I see it here," my eyes were racing down the page, through the four neat lines of exquisite penmanship. At the bottom was written, with something of a flourish, "By Emily Canfield." Slowly I lifted my eyes to the woman sitting quietly by the window. Leaning forward, she held out to me the sheet of paper with Jane's poem on it.

"Compare them," she said.

But I didn't need to. Line for line, word for word, the verse that Jane had written that morning and the verse that Emily had written more than a dozen years ago were absolutely identical.

FIVE

These "Emily-incidents" bothered me. The fact that Jane had seen herself in the reflecting ball as Emily was really no stranger than that she should have imagined herself to look like Queen Victoria, or a frog. But her distress when she disclaimed ever having seen a picture of Emily had been so real! Was it possible that in this house of well-preserved memories she had never glimpsed a photograph of her young aunt? Possible, I supposed, but unlikely. She must have seen one sometime, and simply forgotten.

But what about the light from the reflecting ball? *Emily's* reflecting ball? There had not been a moon. There were no streetlights in the rear of the house, as Jane had pointed out. Everyone had been in bed and there were no lights burning in any of the rooms. Yet how could I be sure of that? Mrs. Canfield—even Katie—might have left one on downstairs, either intentionally or inadvertently. If that were the case there was no mystery whatever.

As for Jane's poem, someone—sometime—might have read it to her. With her deep interest in the pansies it could well have recurred in her memory, even though she had no recollection of having heard it before. So all these things could be easily explained, if one thought about them logically.

And yet, for reasons I could not understand, these rational explanations did not satisfy me at all!

Fourth of July was hot and sunny, but there was a pleasant dry breeze. I washed Jane's hair and my own in the morning, and then we sat outdoors in the sun to dry it. I pulled a comb gently and easily through Jane's long straight silky mane. In my own hair the comb caught and pulled and knotted in the curls until I despaired of ever getting the snarls out.

"I don't see why I have to have a headful of lamb's wool," I said crossly. "Why couldn't I have nice smooth shining hair like yours, Jane?"

"If you did, you'd wish it was curly."

"Oh, no, I wouldn't!"

"Yes, you would. I wish *mine* was. Couldn't I put curling rags in mine, Louisa?"

"And have it come out looking like corkscrews? No! Just be grateful your hair is the way it is!"

"Emily had corkscrew curls. Grandmother said so."

I tugged viciously at the comb as it hit a particularly stubborn place. "Emily again! I don't care whether Emily's hair was bright green and grew in little bowknots all over her head! You are you and Emily was Emily and you are two different people and don't ever forget it! Besides, I'm tired of hearing about her!"

Jane grinned at me. "My, you are in a state today. Is it because we're going to see Dr. Frost tonight?"

"Certainly not!"

"I like him, Louisa. Do you?"

"I neither like him nor dislike him. I just don't think about him."

"Do you think about Martin?"

"Oh, Jane," I said in exasperation. "Can't you talk about anything except Martin or Dr. Frost? Martin's a very nice boy but I haven't seen him in weeks, and the doctor's a bore who talks about things I never heard of, and I don't care if I never see him again! There must be something else you can talk about!"

"I could talk about Emily," she offered.

"And Emily's *dead!* So just forget her, too! Now, turn around so I can braid your hair."

Jane gave me a long troubled look before she swiveled around on the grass. "I'd *like* to forget Emily, Louisa. I really would. She just won't let me."

I opened my mouth for a sharp retort, but something in her voice stopped me. Instead I leaned forward and kissed her sun-warmed hair before I started to plait it.

The prospect of seeing Dr. Frost again might not excite me, but the thought of a band concert and fireworks did. As I put on a blue skirt and my newest white shirtwaist, the one with the lace jabot, I thought hopefully that with music going on, there wouldn't be much opportunity for conversation, which would be all to the good. I clipped red bows to my white slippers, tied one in my hair, and was ready at eight o'clock when a great roaring and chuffing sounded outside the house.

Jane peered out of the parlor window to see Dr. Frost stepping down from a shining automobile. When the doorbell rang she could not wait for Katie, but went rushing to answer it herself.

"Is it yours? Are we going to ride in it? Will you blow the horn? A *lot?*"

"Yes, yes, yes, and yes." Dr. Frost came into the parlor, Jane's hand in his. "Good evening, Mrs. Canfield. Miss Amory. I suggest light scarves for your hair. It is apt to get a little windy."

"Good gracious," Lydia Canfield murmured, gazing out of

the window at the gleaming motor. "I have only ridden in an automobile two or three times before. I'm not at all sure—"

"I am," Dr. Frost said firmly. "You will enjoy it! It is quite safe, and very comfortable."

He helped us into the car, Jane and I in the back, and Mrs. Canfield sitting beside him.

"But you should be sitting with Louisa. I shall be quite all right in back with Jane."

The doctor patted her hand. "On the way home, perhaps. In case you get panicky and start to jump I want to be where I can grab you."

"Jump, Adam! Mercy! I won't dare to stir!"

He laughed, gave the crank a few strong turns, and we swung out of the drive and onto the street, becoming one of many automobiles all going in the direction of the park. Beside me Jane was in absolute bliss, holding her red-and-white-checked gingham dress down across her knees, feeling the wind in her face. In the front seat Mrs. Canfield sat erect, her feet planted firmly on the floor, her hands folded tightly in her lap. Dr. Frost drove easily and well, and it wasn't more than a few moments before Lydia Canfield began to relax a little. She turned her head from side to side, noticing the other motor cars, showing interest in the people strolling along the sidewalks. Presently she turned part way round in the seat.

"This is really very pleasant, isn't it, Louisa?" she shouted. I smiled and nodded, and she turned back, sitting more easily now, enjoying herself just as Dr. Frost had promised she would.

The park was beginning to fill as Dr. Frost helped us all from the car. From a trunk on the back of the automobile he took a red plaid wool rug and two small folding stools, then extended his other arm to Mrs. Canfield. Jane and I followed, and we walked across the grass to a spot where we could see the bandstand clearly.

Mrs. Canfield and I sat comfortably on the little canvas stools, while Jane and Dr. Frost settled on the rug at our feet. The band was just tuning up, and Jane giggled at the odd honks, snorts, and toots of the various instruments. Dr. Frost brought out his pipe and filled it, and then sat, knees drawn up and arms loosely around them, puffing contentedly. The Band Master tapped his baton against his music rack, there was a moment of silence, and then the marvelous, exciting blast of a Sousa march filled the park.

Jane said, "Ah!" in satisfaction, Mrs. Canfield's slippered toe tapped ever so slightly in time to the music, and Dr. Frost whistled the melody softly between his teeth. As for me, I shivered with delight as the waves of music washed around us.

There were the occasional pop-pop-pops of small firecrackers lighted by little boys on the fringes of the crowd. There was a smell of punk, its pungent scent helping to ward off mosquitoes. As the night grew darker there were the enchanted golden explosions of sparklers and, from somewhere a little distance away, the multicolored parabola of a skyrocket. The bandstand gleamed under the bright electric lights, the brass instruments looked bold and shining, the navy blue and red and gold uniforms of the musicians seemed splendid indeed. I was sorry when it was all over.

We walked slowly back to the automobile, but this time Mrs. Canfield took Jane's hand firmly in hers and they went on ahead. Dr. Frost offered me his arm, and I had no choice but to take it. People passed us on both sides of the hard dirt path, and he allowed them to come between us and the other two.

After a few idle comments on the concert he said, "Louisa Amory, will you have dinner with me sometime this week?"

Surprised by the sudden invitation, I didn't know what to say. "Well, I'm not sure . . . there's Jane, you see— "

"Jane is not included," he said flatly. "Do you like lobster?"

"Oh, I adore lobster! But—"

"Friday? I'll pick you up at six."

His confidence irked me. "I will speak to Mrs. Canfield. If
she doesn't mind—"

"She won't mind. Friday, then."

"I'll look forward to it," I said weakly. "Thank you."

When we reached home we all stood for a moment at the
door. The night stretched above us, dark and star-pinned, lit
from time to time with the beautiful flashes of fireworks.

"I cannot thank you enough, Adam," Mrs. Canfield said. "I
don't know when I have enjoyed an evening more!"

"On the strength of that, may I induce you to part with
Louisa on Friday? I should like to take her out to dinner."

There was no hesitation in her reply, and I suddenly wondered if the whole idea might have been hers. "Splendid! I
have felt quite guilty about her staying at home every night.
She should certainly get out more!"

Jane's dark eyes had been going from one to the other of
us, and now she started silently hopping up and down, singing to herself in an almost in-audible voice. "I bet it's going
to happen! I bet it's going to happen!"

I hoped Dr. Frost wouldn't hear her, but it was an idle
hope.

"And just exactly what is it that you bet is going to
happen, Jane?" he asked.

I pinioned Jane with the most threatening glare I could
manage, and her eyes dropped demurely.

"Oh, I don't think you'd be interested, Dr. Frost," she said.
"At least, not quite *yet!*"

SIX

The next morning I woke to a dark, humid, threatening day, and by the time we had finished breakfast thunder was rolling distantly and the first heavy sluggish raindrops were falling.

About midmorning Mrs. Canfield came into the laundry room in the basement where I was pressing out Jane's and my ribbons while Katie did the larger ironing. The little pot stove heated our irons, and the basement, smelling pleasantly of soap and starch and fresh clothes, was dry and warm.

"Jane is moping about, completely desolate," Mrs. Canfield said. "I thought perhaps this might be a good time to make a visit to the attic and see whether we can unearth any playthings for her."

"Of course! It's a wonderful idea! And just the day for it. I'll put these ribbons away and join you."

Jane was excited by the suggestion. "Oh, yes! What a good thing to do!" She was out of the bedroom door and into the hallway, calling, "Grandmother? Where are you? Louisa says we're going up to the attic!"

Lydia Canfield led the way along the carpeted corridor to the staircase that rose from the far end. "I don't recall what may be up there," she said. "It must be years since I've even been in the place."

At the top of the angular stairs there was a large hall. The first door stood open, and I could see Katie's immaculate room, looking lived in and comfortable.

Next came a bathroom, the tub setting high on white claw feet, and after that another small bedroom, apparently unused. Opposite these was a closed door. Mrs. Canfield turned the white china knob, but I had to help her push against the door to open it.

The moment it was opened we could hear the rain beating heavily on the raftered roof. The air in the room was unmoving, filled with the scent of mustiness, of old books and papers, of leather trunks and valises, of mothballs and camphor and dust. So little light came in through the two tiny windows tucked under the eaves that we could barely see. Mrs. Canfield pushed the electric switch by the door, and a small bulb cast a dim light through the center of the room. The shadows in the corners hung deep. Jane inhaled with pleasure.

"It's nice!" she said. "All cobwebby and moldy! Oh, *look* at all the things!"

Around three sides of the large room ranged trunks and barrels and boxes, and on a rod along the fourth side hung suits and dresses. An umbrella stand held canes, parasols, two or three ancient rifles and a rusting sword. A small sidesaddle rested on a wooden sawhorse, and I could see a doll carriage made of wicker with a sunshade dangling over it, a large and lavish dollhouse, boxes of games and piles of books.

Jane gave a little hop of excitement. "Oh, Grandmother! May I *poke*?"

Mrs. Canfield laughed. It was a particularly pretty laugh,

and I thought in amazement that it was the first time I had heard it.

"Yes, child. Go ahead and poke. I'm sure everything is covered with dust, but I don't suppose you care."

While Jane clambered around trunks and barrels, peering into boxes, I wandered along the rack of clothes. A number of dresses hung close together, looking like a rainbow. Shining satin, crisp taffeta, and soft velvet, sheer summer cottons, some very elegant and formal, others quite simple.

"These are beautiful, Mrs. Canfield," I said. "Whose were they?"

She came to stand beside me. "Those? They were mine."

"What lovely colors!" I found it difficult to imagine Lydia Canfield wearing anything but her constant black.

"Yes, they are, aren't they?" She smoothed the soft pile of a glowing garnet velvet gown. "Mr. Canfield and I went to New York one winter—just for a week. I wore this to a first night performance at Daly's Theatre."

"How long ago was that?" I asked.

"Oh, I can't think precisely. Emily was about four then— four or five—that must make it close to twenty years ago. We left Emily and John with Katie and the nursemaid, a nice young woman. Her name was Miss Simmons. Oh dear, what a fearsome time they had with Emily!"

"In what way?"

"She refused to eat, she simply stormed and cried and shrieked herself into a high fever." Mrs. Canfield gazed thoughtfully at the rich deep red. "I had forgotten that week."

"But why? What upset her so?"

"She did not want her father and me to leave her."

"But surely she was well cared for, and with her brother here—"

Mrs. Canfield turned her eyes to me, and they were quiet and brooding. "You did not know Emily, Louisa."

I could not imagine why the sturdy Katie had not administered a firm hand in punishment for such behavior. Surely, whatever Miss Simmons may have been, Katie was not one to tolerate temper tantrums. "I don't suppose Emily won out in this case, though, did she?" I asked.

"As a matter of fact, she did. Poor Miss Simmons was so distraught after a few days of this that she sent Mr. Canfield a telegram. He insisted we come home immediately. I remember how disappointed I was. We had planned to stay longer."

"It hardly seems possible," I began, and then stopped, realizing that any sort of judgment from me would be impertinent.

"It hardly seems possible that a child should not be better controlled. Is that what you were thinking? Or that she should have been so indulged? I can understand—but that is the way things were."

From a far corner of the attic came Jane's somewhat muffled voice. "I found a wonderful trunkful of things! Oh, I wish there was more light!"

I hardly heard Jane. My mind was still on Emily. It seemed incomprehensible to me that Mrs. Canfield should have permitted such behavior in her child.

Almost as though she read my thoughts Lydia Canfield said, "Looking back, I can see where I should have resisted more often, been firmer, for Emily's own sake. But it would have distressed her father, and . . . I loved him very much. It would have been most difficult to disregard his wishes."

"But could Mr. Canfield not see that such indulgence was harmful?"

"No, I think he could not. Emily was so charming—so irresistible—when things went as she wished. Often there were two or three weeks at a stretch when no one could have been more delightful than our daughter. Those were the times when my husband would point out to me that 'giving in to her,' as he said I called it, seemed not to be spoiling her at all. He wanted so much for her to be always happy! He . . . he *adored* her, Louisa. There is no other word for it."

I began to understand better, then. I could see that while Mrs. Canfield might well have had the strength of character to forbid or deny Emily certain requests, it would have been nearly impossible for her to override her husband, possibly even to anger him with her discipline. But surely John could not have been treated in the same permissive manner. I asked about him.

"No, John was raised quite differently, but then John was quite a different sort of child. I could reason with him, which I never could with Emily, and he would accept explanations. John and I were very close, always. Then, too, his father felt that a strict upbringing was quite proper for a boy. It was only Emily, you see. From the moment she was born she was the center of my husband's life. There was nothing he would not do for her."

I had almost forgotten Jane in thinking about that faraway child, Emily, when I heard the small voice again from the corner, annoyed.

"If somebody would just *help* me a little bit instead of standing and talking, I could get this trunk out where I could see it!"

I laughed and went to her, wending my way through the clutter in the dusky attic.

"I'm sorry, dear. What are you trying to do?"

"I *told* you! I'm trying to drag this trunk out where there's more light!"

I took hold of one leather strap on the side of the large old metal trunk and pulled it across the floor, Jane pushing sturdily from the back.

I opened the curved lid. In the top tray lay a number of dolls, their pretty faces smiling vacantly, except for one whose wax features were hideously misshapen.

"Oh, what a shame," I said. "Look. Her face has melted. I expect this attic gets very hot during the summer."

"No—no, it wasn't the attic heat. Emily—" Mrs. Canfield stopped.

Jane's eyes widened in horror. "You mean Emily did that? On *purpose*?"

There was no answer. The attic was very still for a moment. Then Jane shivered.

"I don't like to look at it," she said. "Cover it up, Louisa."

Silently Mrs. Canfield handed me a pale-pink shawl which she took from the clothes rack, and I gently wrapped the disfigured plaything in it and laid it to one side. Jane watched me, her eyes somber.

But there were other things in the lower part of the trunk that quickly took her mind away from the doll. Sets of blocks, a game of dominoes, delicate wooden jackstraws with their tiny hook. A wooden box with a sliding lid held a schoolroom with pupils and desks and the schoolmaster, each a flat wooden piece, brightly painted, and each with its small grooved base to hold it upright. As Jane discovered each new treasure I rose, dusted off my skirt, and wandered about the room. In one corner stood a chipped white-painted wooden pedestal, topped with a saucer-shaped piece.

"What stood on this?" I asked idly. "It seems to have been meant to hold something particular."

Mrs. Canfield joined me. "Oh, yes. Yes, that used to hold a reflecting ball in the garden. Like the one we have now."

"What happened to it?"

"It was broken."

There was an odd inflection in her voice that prevented me from asking any more. "Oh," was all I said. After a moment, gazing at the empty pedestal, Lydia Canfield went on, a strange smile on her face.

"Emily was always enraptured by the silver ball. She used

to stand gazing into it for quite long periods. One day—she was about ten, I believe—she had tried her hair a new way which I thought unbecoming, and I told her so. She was quite piqued with me, and ran out into the garden. I stood at the window watching her. I saw her go to the reflecting ball and stand there, staring into it. After a moment she stepped back, and, raising her hands, pushed the ball off the pedestal and onto the stone that surrounded it. It smashed, of course, into a thousand pieces. Emily came running into the house and up to her room, locking herself in. She would not open the door for me all day. When her father came home he went upstairs and she let him in at once. He asked her about the ball—I had told him of the incident—and she said that when she looked into it she saw a face that wasn't hers. It was an ugly face, she said, and she insisted that it must have been the face of someone else who had looked into the ball."

"Of someone else? But surely it was just the distortion such round objects give!"

"Of course it was. Her father tried to explain that to her, but Emily would have no part of it. Other people had been looking into her reflecting ball and she could see their ugly faces. She wanted a new ball, of course, one that only she would be permitted to look into."

"And her father got it for her."

"Naturally. And assured her that no one except Emily would ever look into it. That it was all hers. That is the one that stands out there now."

The rain drummed loud on the attic roof and I could barely hear Jane's voice above it. She sat cross-legged on the floor, cradling one of the dolls in her arms. She did not look up as she spoke.

"*I* looked into Emily's silver ball," she said. "I didn't know I wasn't supposed to."

"But of course you can, Jane," Mrs. Canfield answered. "It isn't Emily's any longer, you know."

Jane raised her eyes slowly to her grandmother's face. "Yes, it is," she said. "Emily's face still lives in it. I have seen it there."

"Nonsense, dear. You have seen the distortions, that's all. Just as Louisa said. Because the glass is curved—"

Jane interrupted. "No, Grandmother. It wasn't dis——, what you said. It was Emily in there. She looked out at me. I saw her."

Mrs. Canfield's eyes met mine for a long moment. Then she forced a smile. "I think we had better go downstairs now," she said. "This old attic is making us all quite fanciful!"

It was with relief that I closed the door behind us.

SEVEN

On Friday morning my daily letter from Martin arrived and I put it in my pocket to read later. I was busy with several small chores—some mending for Mrs. Canfield, helping Jane set up in her room the dollhouse which Jacob had brought down from the attic, pressing my yellow voile dress to wear that evening—so it wasn't until afternoon that I put my hand in my pocket for my handkerchief and felt the letter there. A little ashamed of my forgetfulness, I wandered out into the garden to read it.

The summer afternoon was hushed, with the shade stretching across the grass as the sun drooped lower. Fat bumblebees droned over the roses, a few butterflies made their staccato way from zinnia to balsam to phlox, resting still-winged for a second, and then zigzagging off again. I sat in my favorite chair under the tulip tree and pulled Martin's letter from its envelope.

"Dear Louisa," it said. "This will have to be a pretty short letter because I am going to Susie Pepper's house for supper. She's really a very nice girl and she thinks it's wonderful that I can write poetry. I showed her some I had written, but not any about you. She says she wishes I'd write some to her, but I haven't. I don't know why you thought Susie's talking might bother me. It doesn't at all. She asked me if I had heard from you and I told her about your letter—the one that said you were going to the Fourth of July celebration with that doctor. Susie says if he is a doctor he must be pretty old, and to tell you she's sorry you have to go out with old men. She sends you her love. So do I. Martin."

Impatiently I shoved the letter into the envelope, not even bothering to fold the pages neatly. Why, *Jane* could have written a more interesting letter than that! Feeling quite out of temper, I started back toward the house. As I crossed the soft lawn I came to the reflecting ball poised on its standard. Flagstones set around the base of the pedestal made a little island in the grass, and I walked close, stepping onto the stones. Slowly, very slowly, I leaned to peer into the ball. Its convex surface made my nose seem large, with the rest of my face fading back from it, but it was undeniably my face. That pile of ash-blond hair and those thick-lashed blue eyes were certainly Louisa Amory's. There was no trace of Emily in that reflected picture. It startled me suddenly to realize that I had not been sure I would see my own face. This odd business with a dead child is becoming real to you, I thought. Forget her!

But tell myself what I would, it was as if that man-made, silvered glass globe, resting on its painted wooden support, had some power—some fascination—some life of its own. It was all I could do to turn away from it and walk quickly into the house through the kitchen.

Katie was rinsing dishcloths at the sink. "I was watching you out the window," she said. "I was just coming to tell you it was time you started dressing for that dinner party."

"Not a party, Katie. Just dinner—with Dr. Frost."

She smiled at me. "And isn't that enough party for you?"

I must have looked embarrassed, because she went right on. "He's a fine man, that one. You could do a lot worse, Miss Louisa."

"I'm just having *dinner* with him, Katie. That's all."

"Well, everything has to start somewhere," she observed cheerfully. Then her tone changed. "I saw you out there by that reflecting ball. I keep away from that thing. I want no part of it."

"Oh, Katie, don't! You're beginning to sound as full of weird ideas as Jane!"

"Weird? Maybe so. But you didn't know Emily."

"That's what everyone keeps telling me," I said sharply, "and it's quite true. I didn't. But the child has been dead for a dozen years or more, and as sorry as I am that she died so young, nothing she used to do can make any difference to anyone or anything now!"

"It's making a difference to Jane. You know that yourself, Miss Louisa." She paused, and then went on. "That doll she found in the attic—the one with the melted face. She asked me how it happened."

"Did you tell her, Katie? Did you know?"

"Yes, I knew. But I didn't tell her. I think she knew most of it herself, somehow."

"What did happen to the doll?"

"Emily lost her temper with it one day because it wouldn't stand up. She held its face over my stove. Held it there until it melted. She said that would be a lesson to it."

I could feel my lips tighten with distaste. "How—how awful! But Katie, why do you think Jane knows?"

"When she asked me I told her I couldn't remember. But she stood there—looking at the stove. Then she said, 'That doll's face was made of wax. Wax melts easily, doesn't it, Katie?' I told her yes. And she kept staring at the stove, and all she said was, 'Oh, Emily! *Why?*'"

"I see," I said. Somehow the cheerful kitchen did not seem so cheerful. "Well, whatever she may have been, Emily is dead now. Let the poor girl rest in peace."

"I'd like nothing better, Miss Louisa! Nothing better in the whole world!"

There seemed nothing more to say. I went up the back stairs and as I entered my room Jane looked up from the dollhouse.

"Are you going to dress now, Louisa?"

"Yes," I said abstractedly.

"May I sit on your bed and watch?"

"I suppose so, if you really want to. It's hardly all that exciting, though."

"It is to me." She came bouncing through the doorway and threw herself down on my bed. "Are you going to wear the white dress again?"

"No. The yellow one."

"Oh. That's too bad. He would probably propose to you if you wore the white one."

"You know, Jane," I said rather huffily, "you really must learn not to meddle in grown-up affairs!"

Jane sighed. "In a minute you'll tell me to run along and play and let you dress in peace!"

Her tone mimicked mine so well I couldn't help but laugh. "All right," I said. "You win. I'll stop talking like an aunt, and you stop talking like Little Miss Know-it-all."

With good humor restored, Jane lay comfortably on the bed, her chin in her hands, her legs flopping up and down, making occasional comments as she watched me dress. I was just pinning my little cameo brooch into place when we heard the doorbell.

"There he is," Jane said quickly. "I'm going to answer."

Sliding off the bed, she went racing through the hall and down the stairs. Taking a thin scarf from my drawer, and tipping a drop of cologne on my handkerchief before plac-

ing it in my drawstring bag, I went along to Mrs. Canfield's
room to tell her I was leaving.

"I'm so glad Adam asked you," she said. "Enjoy yourself,
Louisa."

"Thank you. I'm sure I will."

Going down the sharply turning staircase, my first
glimpse of that dark head, those deep blue eyes looking up
at me, made me suddenly almost breathless. Whatever else
Dr. Frost might or might not be, he was certainly attractive!

"You know what your aunt looks like, Jane?" he asked.

"What?"

"Like summer. Just like summer coming down the stairs.
Good evening, Louisa."

"Good evening—Adam." If he could use first names, then
so could I.

"Shall we be on our way?" His eyes were smiling at me,
and I began to think the pompous doctor might just possibly be human.

"I'm quite ready." I turned to Jane. "Good night, dear. Go
to bed promptly."

Jane pulled me down for a kiss. "He's really very nice,
Louisa," she whispered. "Don't be mean to him."

"I'll try not to," I whispered back, and a minute later
Adam Frost was helping me into his automobile.

On the drive to the restaurant I found myself telling him
about my family, and the house in Milford, and he said he
had always liked the town, and perhaps I would allow him
to visit there sometime. I said I would, and asked him about
his medical career and how he had managed to complete his
training so quickly.

"It was quite simple. I managed two years in one."

"Mrs. Canfield told me you were extremely brilliant."

"Not really. It's just that I always knew I would be a
doctor. My mother died when I was small, and consequently
I spent most of my time with my father. From the time I was

eight or nine I used to go on some of his housecalls with him, and a couple of years later I used to help him prepare medications, and lend a hand in setting broken bones or applying dressings. During high school I transcribed some of his notes for him, and I think I read every medical book he owned. By the time I got to studying medicine formally I was pretty far ahead of the other men in the class."

"Are you a *good* doctor?" I asked, smiling at him.

He glanced at me, his eyes teasing. "*I* think so. Develop a slight sniffle or a minor cough and I'll come and tend you. Then you can see for yourself."

"Thank you," I laughed, "but I'll take your word for your medical talents." I settled back, feeling more comfortable with him than I ever expected to.

The restaurant was on the tip of the little peninsula just below Lynn, and from our table we could look through large open windows at the quiet water of the bay. We had lobster Thermidor, and a fresh, crisp bread, and a salad, with delicious hot coffee.

"Dining out is always exciting to me," I confessed. "It seems so—special!"

"This *is* special," he said. "Do you know this is the first time I've been out with a young lady in—well, months?"

Our eyes met and held. Then I looked away.

"Tell me about Emily," I said abruptly. "Tell me everything you remember about her."

He looked surprised. "How did we suddenly get to Emily?"

"It isn't sudden. Please. Tell me what you can."

He took a sip of coffee, set the cup down gently, and sat in silence for a minute. "Emily was the most strong-willed person I ever knew," he said presently. "I can't think of a time in her short life when she didn't get whatever she had set her heart on. It never mattered to her whether something was right or wrong, or whether it might hurt someone else. If it pleased Emily—that was all that mattered."

"Mrs. Canfield told me that Emily's father could deny her nothing. She said that he adored his daughter."

"I expect he did. The Canfield family hadn't produced many girls. I believe Mr. Canfield had brothers, and a number of uncles and male cousins, so when Emily was born he was ecstatic. Then, you see, as an infant she was rather sickly, and the poor man was probably terrified that he would lose her."

"When she did die, what was wrong with her?"

"She had pneumonia."

"Mrs. Canfield told me Emily had frequent colds, quite serious ones, she said."

"That's true. But you know, Louisa, there are people who can *make* themselves quite honestly sick. I've often thought that is just what Emily did."

"But why would she? No child enjoys being ill."

"Not even when it means you can demand that someone stay with you all the time? That is what Emily wanted, always. Someone with her. Her mother, or her father, her brother—even me. Oh, the hours I had to sit by her bed— waiting on her, hand and foot!"

"But why did you do it?"

"Habit, I suppose. I had always known Emily, you see. Besides, she could find ways to make life unbearable for anyone who crossed her!"

"Oh, Adam! How much could she do—a little girl!"

He finished his coffee and took his pipe from his pocket. "Do you mind if I smoke?"

I shook my head, and watched him tamp tobacco down into his pipe and then light it. I sniffed with pleasure as the first small puffs of smoke floated over the table. At last he spoke again.

"Do you know how Emily got the pneumonia that killed her?"

"No," I said. "I don't think I do."

"It was just after Christmas, I remember, and bitter cold. I had been with Emily one morning—one of the many times she was confined to bed with a very slight fever and a minor congestion—and she wanted me to have lunch with her and spend the afternoon. I told her I couldn't, that my father had promised to take me with him on some housecalls, and I had no intention of missing it. Emily was furious! She pounded on the bed, and said she didn't want to be all alone—she made quite an interesting scene."

"But she wouldn't have been alone, would she?" I asked. "Wasn't her mother in the house? And probably Katie?"

"Louisa, you don't understand. Emily wanted exactly what she wanted, and no half measures would do. In this case what she wanted was that I stay and play with her all afternoon."

"And did you?"

"No. And because of that I suppose I am partially responsible for Emily's death."

"What do you mean? How could you be?"

"After I had gone Emily apparently figured out in her devious little mind that if I was going to spend the afternoon with my *father*, who was her *doctor*, all she had to do was get the doctor to come and see *her*. I suppose it seemed like an easy solution, so she promptly told her mother that she felt much worse and Dr. Frost had better come and see her. But Mrs. Canfield didn't agree. She took Emily's temperature, found it improved, and—thinking she was being encouraging, I imagine—told Emily she was getting much better and could probably be up the next day. But that was not what Emily wanted."

"She wanted you," I said.

"She wanted her own way. She begged and cajoled her mother, and Mrs. Canfield pointed out to her that there were many people who were really very ill and needed the doctor, whereas Emily did not. That the doctor only had time to visit patients who were actually quite sick, and truly needed him. Then Emily asked her mother if Dr. Frost would come if she got very sick indeed, and Mrs. Canfield assured her that he would. Of course he would. And that was all it took."

"But I still don't understand."

"Mrs. Canfield offered to stay and read to Emily, but Emily said—ever so sweetly—that she thought she would have a little nap as soon as she finished her lunch, so her mother left her. At Emily's request Mrs. Canfield closed the door, telling her to call when she woke up. Emily never called. Mrs. Canfield, probably glad of the peace, didn't go back for two or three hours."

"And then?" I found I was sitting forward, my hands folded tight on the edge of the table.

"As she went along the upstairs corridor she could feel cold air from somewhere. When she opened Emily's door the room was freezing."

"And Emily?"

"Emily had apparently emptied the water from her bed-side carafe over her nightgown. She had pulled an armchair in front of the window, opened it wide, and was sitting there—drenched to the skin, and quite blue with cold. By that time her chest was so congested she could barely breathe. She was nearly unconscious."

I stared at him in amazement. "You mean she was delib-erately trying to make herself very ill?"

"I told you Emily had ways of getting what she wanted," Adam said quietly.

"And she died?"

"Very early the next morning. My father came, without me, ironically, but he could do nothing for her."

I shivered, and Adam reached out and laid one warm hand over mine. "Why do you want to know all this, Louisa? It was a long time ago. It's all over now."

"I'm not sure it is," I said very softly.

His hand tightened. "What do you mean?"

"Oh, Adam, I don't know!" I burst out. "But there have been things since Jane and I have been there—"

"What sort of things?"

"Oh, they sound ridiculous put into words—"

"Try."

"Well, one night—the same night you were there at the house for the first time—there was a strange light in Jane's room. She sleeps in Emily's old room, you know—it looks out over the garden."

"I know."

"It seemed as though that reflecting ball was shining into her room, somehow. And yet, how *could* it have been? There was no moon. But I saw it—I *did!*"

"Emily's reflecting ball," he said. "What else?"

"Oh, just little things. Jane says she sees Emily's face in the ball when she looks into it. And she wrote a poem—a little verse about the pansies—and she said that after she had been looking into the ball she 'just knew it,' and it was exactly—word for word—*exactly* like one Emily had written. Mrs. Canfield showed it to me in a notebook she kept."

"Jane had undoubtedly seen the notebook and something made her remember the poem."

"That's what I tell myself. But she *swears* she hadn't!"

"Louisa. Jane is an imaginative child, and right now she is living in a house where another little girl died. A little girl related to her. She is sleeping in that other child's room, playing with her toys, walking in the same garden, eating at the same table. Doesn't it seem rather natural that under these conditions a child like Jane might very well become overimaginative?"

"But *I* saw that light in her room, and the poem *was* the same! She didn't imagine those."

"When there is a logical explanation, Louisa, take it. The

light was some odd reflection, perhaps of a downstairs light shining out onto the ball in the garden. The poem—she *must* have seen that notebook! It could have been some time ago, even before her parents died. Things one reads or hears can lie forgotten in the brain for long periods, and then be suddenly brought to light."

"I know it must be that way," I said doubtfully.

"Of course it is!" He rose from his chair. "Come along. Let's go outside and look at the water for a while before it gets dark."

We went out onto the wide veranda that circled the restaurant, strolled down the steps and wandered along a narrow boardwalk across the sand. The sky was filled with the dusky brilliance of sunset, and the water gleamed in deep rose and gold. We stood at the end of the boardwalk, breathing in the salty smell, feeling the soft warm breeze against our faces. Our hands were loosely linked.

"Adam," I said, "you don't believe any of what I told you, do you?"

His voice was thoughtful. "I'm a doctor, Louisa, and medicine is a science. I suppose I think like a scientist—in fact, rather than in fancy. But as a doctor I know something else. I have seen men die when all my knowledge told me they would recover, and I have seen the reverse happen as well. I watched a man once—I expected each breath he drew would be his last. His wife was there, in the hospital, and she sat beside his bed, holding his two hands. She would not let them go. She kept talking to him—softly, just murmuring—and she held his hands so tightly that her own were white. She stayed there the whole night through. I told her to go and rest, that I would call her, but she refused to leave. 'He will die if I let go of him, Doctor,' she said, 'and I am not going to let him die.' The man's pulse was so faint I could barely find it. Respiration was almost nonexistent. I *knew* he could not live. And his wife leaned closer and she

called him—over and over she called his name—and she
never let go of his hands. Sometime—in the dark hours of
the morning—he opened his eyes, and he looked at her, and
he said, 'Don't let go.' 'I won't,' she said. By the time it was
light outdoors his pulse was firm, his breathing was normal,
and he was sleeping restfully."

"And he got well?"

"He got well."

"Oh, Adam, that's beautiful!"

"Yes, it is. But it's more than that. It is one of the strange
things that teach doctors how much they don't know." He
looked down at me, and the softness of night crept across
the water. "There is one thing this doctor does know, however," he said. "He is very glad you agreed to come tonight."

I looked up at him, determined to know. "Did Mrs. Canfield tell you to ask me?"

There was utter amazement on his face. "Did *what*?" He
took a deep breath. "Look here, Louisa Amory! I'm a big
boy now! I don't need anyone to make decisions for me."

"Then she didn't. I'm sorry. I mean—I'm sorry I thought
she might have. I'm *glad* she didn't!"

"For a very pretty girl you get some strange ideas," he
said. Then he pulled my hand through his arm. "Come on.
Let's walk down the beach a ways. And we are not going to
talk about anyone or anything but *you!* Understand?"

"Yes, Doctor," I said obediently.

"And one more thing! Tonight I am not a doctor. Tonight I
am Adam Frost, who is having a *dandy* time, thank you!"

It was really a very nice evening!

EIGHT

Although it was not very late when we came home the house was dark downstairs except for a soft light in the hall. Adam unlocked the door with my key, and as I stepped inside he caught my arm gently.

"Again soon, Louisa?" he asked softly. I nodded.

He put one hand under my chin and tipped my face up and for a minute I thought he was going to kiss me. Rather disappointingly he didn't. "Thank you for coming," he said. Then he laid his cheek against my hair. "You *smell* so good! All girl!"

He left and I closed the door after him. Feeling quietly happy, I slipped the bolt into place, turned out the light and went up the stairs, my way illuminated dimly by another light in the upstairs hall.

As I went down the corridor I saw that Mrs. Canfield's door was slightly ajar, and remembered that she had asked me to let her know when I came home. I knocked.

"Come in, Louisa," she said.

She was sitting up in bed, reading. As I entered she laid her book face down on her lap and took off her spectacles.

In the soft light from the bedside lamp her face looked gentle and serene.

"I just wanted to tell you I'm home, Mrs. Canfield," I said.

"Did you have a pleasant time, child? Adam is good company, isn't he?"

"Oh, yes! We had a lovely evening! Dinner, and a walk along the water—"

"Come and sit down for a moment and tell me about it. Unless you are very tired?"

"I'm not a bit tired!"

"Then stay a few minutes." She patted the edge of the bed, and I sat down, leaning back against one of the tall carved posts. We were both silent for a few seconds. Then, feeling that I had to know more, I said, "Mrs. Canfield, Adam talked about Emily tonight. I asked him to. He told me how she died."

"Oh?" Her tone made me wonder if I should have said it.

"The pneumonia," I persisted. "How she sat by the open window, wet to the skin—"

"Yes."

"It seems so incredible! Do you think she really knew what she was doing?"

"I'm sure she knew," Mrs. Canfield said quietly. "Whatever Emily happened to want she set herself to get, by one means or another. If I had been firm with her, if I had stood up against her whims, I could have disciplined her. And if I had, Louisa, I would have lost my husband's love completely. You may be too young to understand how much people will do—or leave undone—for love." She paused, then went on sadly, "I suppose the truth of it is that Emily and I both loved her father more than we did each other. Even for my daughter I could not displease my husband. And my daughter knew it."

"Adam says he feels it was his fault, in a way, that Emily died. If he had stayed with her—"

"Nonsense! I have always known that I . . . that if I had gone to Emily sooner it would not have happened. I knew the way her mind worked. I should never have supposed she would give in so gracefully. But it is easy to delude oneself, to believe what one wishes to believe." She sighed, and then added softly, "It is a terrible knowledge to live with, Louisa."

I leaned forward, laid my hand over hers. "Mrs. Canfield, I didn't mean to make you remember all these things. I'm so sorry!"

"It is not a case of remembering, child. One never forgets. One simply covers them up, hides them somewhere, builds a wall so they cannot be discovered. But since Jane has been here—well, I find that wall is not so strong. Jane has a way of getting through. I have become very fond of her, Louisa."

"It is because of Jane that I wanted to know about Emily. Jane seems . . . *obsessed* with her!"

Her dark eyes searched my face. *"Obsessed?"*

"She talks so much of her—she says she sees her face in the reflecting ball. And the other night . . . " I went on to tell her about the night that the ball sent the strange glow into Jane's room, and how I was at a loss to explain it.

There was a long moment's silence before Mrs. Canfield spoke again. When she did, it seemed to have no connection with what I had been saying.

"When Mr. Canfield died he was sitting in Emily's room, beside her empty bed. He often sat there. He . . . apparently had a heart attack. I heard him cry out his daughter's name. By the time I reached him he was lying across the bed. He must have died instantly."

"I don't understand," I said.

"And no one has ever been able to explain what could have made John's old horse bolt with the buggy that day. Never, *never* had it happened before. I think of these things, Louisa, and I remember how strong, how determined, how *ruthless* Emily was."

"Ruthless?"

"She wanted her own way. She did not like being alone. She wanted *her* people, *her* possessions, and *her* way. Always."

Suddenly I felt very cold and tired. My voice was hardly more than a whisper. "Mrs. Canfield. Are you saying that you think Emily is . . . is still getting her own way? You said she loved her father and her brother. That she liked to have them with her."

"So she did."

"Do you truly believe that she—"

"That in some way she 'took' John and her father to be with her? How can one ever know, Louisa? How can one ever know?"

I rose from the bed, feeling exhausted. "I'm sorry I mentioned these things, Mrs. Canfield. I should never have bothered you with Jane's . . . imaginings."

"Oh, yes, you should have. It is something I need to know about. Go to bed now, child. Go to bed and just remember the pleasant evening you have had. Good night, Louisa."

"Good night, Mrs. Canfield."

"And Louisa—don't fret."

I closed her door quietly and walked slowly down the hall to my room. For some reason I did not want the bright overhead light on. Rather than touch the wall switch I groped on the dresser for the candle and matches that were always there in case the electricity should fail. The candle flame reflected in the mirror that hung over the dresser, a small flickering light that showed me my own face, and— suddenly I gasped and pressed my hand hard upon my mouth to stifle a scream.

Behind me, looking over my shoulder, dim in the shadowy room, was another face—a face so contorted with hatred that I could feel the prickling of my hair against my scalp. Dark eyes glared into mine in the glass, lips were drawn back over teeth in a snarling grimace, black hair caught loosely from the face on either side, falling in long curls—Emily! I whirled, my back pressed hard against the edge of the dresser. There was no evil figure there, but the face remained. The face—a picture propped against my pillow—a picture Jane must have drawn, using charcoal for those dark, smoldering eyes, those clustered curls. It took all my strength to walk across the floor, to lift the hateful thing in my hand, to look at it closely. I switched on the light then—the more light the better!—and I could see it clearly. The childish way the corkscrew ringlets had been drawn, the clumsiness of the details, but the expression was there, the sheer hate, the venom—and something more too. Across one corner, exact and beautifully formed, was the signature "Emily Canfield." I knew beyond any possible doubt that if I were to compare it with something Emily had signed herself, there would not be a shred of difference.

My fright and shock were now changing to anger. I whipped into Jane's room, snapping on the light. She slept deeply, lying comfortably spread-eagled beneath the sheet, her hair spilling across her face in a dark cloud. Mercilessly I shook her.

"Jane! Jane, wake up this minute! Do you hear me? Wake up!"

She burrowed her head deeper into her arm. "Wake up, Jane! Now!"

Coming suddenly from sleep, she squinted her eyes against the brilliant light.

"Louisa! What is it? Is the house on fire?"

"You know what it is," I said, my voice low and filled with fury. "You drew that picture of Emily, didn't you? And left it on my bed to frighten me!"

"To *frighten* you? Oh, Louisa! Why would it frighten you? I never meant to do that! I just thought you'd like to see it."

"And the signature in the corner! The writing that says 'Emily Canfield.' Where did you copy that from?"

"I didn't copy anything from anything! I was just drawing a little before I went to sleep—Grandmother said it was all right—and I drew a picture of Emily, and it came out looking mad—because you were out with Dr. Frost, I guess—and I thought it was sort of funny. I thought you'd think it was funny, too. So I left it where you'd find it."

"What about the signature?" I repeated, stressing every word.

"The signature? I don't know. I just wrote down who it was, that's all."

"But that's not your writing, Jane. You copied it from somewhere, and I want to know where!"

Jane stared at me a moment, her lip quivering, and then she burst into tears. "Don't talk hard to me, Louisa! I never heard you talk like that before! You frighten me!" She reached out both arms to put them about my neck, but I caught her wrists and held her.

"Jane, where did you copy that signature from?"

"I didn't copy it, Louisa! I just . . ." She was sobbing so she could barely speak. I just held the pencil and it came out that way! *Please* don't be angry!"

I let go her wrists and held her close to me, smoothing her hair and murmuring to her. "I'm sorry, Jane. Oh, Jane, I'm *so* sorry! I shouldn't have spoken to you like that. It was just—oh, never mind! It's all right, darling, truly it is! Everything is all right!"

I held her until her sobbing stopped, and then I straightened her bed and made her comfortable again before I kissed her good night. Hating myself for what I had done to her, for the fear and anger and lack of control I had shown, I went slowly back into my room. As I passed her window I looked out on the sleeping garden.

Below me the reflecting ball glowed lucent.

NINE

I was pulled from a dark, fretful, heavy sleep the next morning by the feeling of a weight across my legs that kept me from moving. In quick panic I thrust one leg sideways as hard as I could. The weight was suddenly gone, there was a thud and someone said, "Ow!" I opened my eyes. Jane was sitting on the floor in her nightgown, looking at me reproachfully.

"You're still mad at me," she said, climbing back up on the bed.

"Mad at you? Why should I be mad at you?"

Then it all flooded back, the shock when I had seen the drawing of Emily, so alive and threatening in the shadowy room, the further shock and then the anger when I had seen that exquisite signature. I felt again the shame of losing my temper with Jane.

"Oh, Jane, darling! I'm not mad. I told you last night I was sorry. Don't you remember?"

"I wasn't sure. Well, that's all right, then! So now, tell me about last night. Was it nicer than you thought it would be?"

The pleasure of the evening before came back to me, and I smiled in spite of myself.

Jane crowed with delight. "It was! I can tell! Oh, I'm glad!"

"I'm glad you're glad."

"And you *like* him a lot better, too, don't you? Well, *that's* certainly a relief!"

I burrowed my face in the pillow to hide my silly grin. "Jane, you're impossible!"

"No, I'm not. You love me." She slithered off my bed and started into her room. As she passed my dresser she paused, and then picked up that horrible sketch. She stood studying it for a moment. "She's not very pretty in this picture. She was pretty in the picture Grandmother showed me, but not here."

"What picture did your grandmother show you?"

"It's in that black locket thing she wears. The one with the diamond or something stuck in the front of it. The back is a picture of Emily. Grandfather Canfield gave it to her when Emily died."

"I see."

"I thought I'd draw her the way she looked in the locket picture, but it didn't come out that way. It kept getting madder and madder while I drew." She laid the sketch carefully back on my dresser. "Emily doesn't let me draw her the way I want to. I don't think I'll try anymore."

"That's a very good idea," I said, slowly sitting up in bed. "In fact, I just wish you'd stop even *thinking* about her."

"I don't *mean* to think about her, she just comes popping into my head sometimes. And then I can't make her go away."

"When does she 'pop' into your head, Jane?" I sat on the edge of the bed. "Any special times?"

"Not really special. When everything is sort of quiet, I guess. When I'm a little sleepy, or when there isn't anybody to talk to, or when I'm in the garden—near that silvery ball thing. Mostly then. She kind of . . . lives in there."

"Oh, Jane, you know that's ridiculous!"

"Is it?" She looked up at me, her long hair loose around her face. "Well, she looks *out* of there quite a lot. Maybe she isn't *in* there, but she still looks out."

"Jane, I've tried to tell you! That's your own reflection—just distorted because the ball is round. You only *imagine* that it looks like Emily!" I could hear my voice rising. Jane looked at me thoughtfully and then turned and went into her room where she started to dress. Fuming, I began to put my own clothes on. A few moments later, half-dressed, I went to the connecting door. Jane sat on the floor, buckling her sandals.

"Jane," I said, trying desperately to sound calm. "Were you in the garden last night before you went to bed?"

She glanced up at me. "Yes. Grandmother and I went outside after supper."

"And did you look in the reflecting ball?"

"Yes. I always look in it when I'm outside, just to see if Emily's in there. She isn't always, you know. Sometimes it's only me." She looked down at the shoe as she slipped the strap through the buckle and added quickly, "And no matter *what* you say, Louisa, it isn't *always* me!"

I snatched a dress from my closet and put it on over my head, pulling it down into place with little angry tugs. I fastened the belt and went back into Jane's room.

"Come here and let me do your braids."

Silently she rose from the floor and stood with her back to me so that I could draw the brush through her hair. I could feel myself being a little rougher than necessary, but she said nothing. At last I burst out, "I'm going to ask your grandmother to have that silly ball put away!"

Jane's hair jerked from the brush as she turned and looked up at me. "Oh, no, Louisa! We mustn't do that! It's

Emily's special ball. She'd *never* forgive us if we took it away!"

I took her shoulders and held them tightly, leaning down to her. "Jane, I really couldn't care less about Emily! It's *you* I care about! She is dead! Do you understand? *Dead!* She was a spoiled, undisciplined, unkind little girl when she lived, and now she no longer lives. And whatever is done to that reflecting ball in the garden can make no difference to her now!"

Jane's eyes held mine. "That's not true, Louisa. And you know it isn't true. That ball belongs to Emily—it *still* does— and it would be dreadful to move it! Promise me you won't!"

"I will *not* promise! If you are going to upset yourself constantly with the thing, *I* am going to ask that it be moved!"

Great tears sprang to her eyes. "Please, Louisa, please don't! I'll stay away from it if you want. I won't go near the ball! But it's Emily's, and she has to have it there. Right there, where it is! It's the only way she can get through!"

"And that's precisely why I'm going to have it moved." I could feel my hands shaking as I gripped Jane's shoulders. "Because it's the only way she can get through!"

Jane stepped back, pulling herself gently from my grasp. Her eyes were dry now, but the tears had left streaks on her face. "You see, Louisa?" she said, and her voice was little more than a whisper. "You see? It isn't just me. *You* believe in Emily, too. And you *must not move that ball!*" Going to the door that led to the hall, she opened it and stood looking back at me. A wistful, almost sad, little smile touched her mouth. "Don't be frightened, Louisa. Leave the ball alone. I'll try not to go near it again."

She closed the door quietly behind her and went off down the hall. I recalled then that I had not braided her hair, but I felt too weak to call her back.

TEN

Something threatening seemed to hang over those hot, still July days. I was enjoying Adam's company, and should have been happy, but instead I was restless and uneasy, I found it difficult to settle down to needlework or reading, I preferred being with other people, rather than alone. I would often seek out Mrs. Canfield in her favorite spot under the tulip tree, and urge her to talk. One day I found the courage to ask her something that had puzzled me since that first evening when Adam came to supper.

"You talked about some lion, and some doors, I remember. I know I am ignorant, and I apologize, but it has bothered me ever since."

For a moment she looked baffled, then suddenly she smiled. "I remember now! The Lion of Lucerne. And it must have been Ghiberti's Doors, on the Basilica di San Giovanni in Florence. Poor Louisa! Why didn't you ask us then?"

"I felt so stupid!"

"It isn't stupidity, child. There is no real reason why you should know about them."

And she told me, about the beautiful golden doors, the

Gates of Paradise, on which Lorenzo Ghiberti spent fifty years of his life, depicting scenes from the Old and New Testaments with such skill and artistry that now, five hundred years later, they remained among the most exquisite portals in the world. About the tragic Lion, carved in the living rock, commemorating the seven hundred brave Swiss guards and their officers who were killed trying to defend Louis XVI and Marie Antoinette when the Paris mob stormed Versailles.

"Oh, I wish I could see these things," I said. "There is so *much* I haven't seen!"

"But there is time. You are very young, my dear."

On my next trip to the library I came home with an armful of travel books which made Jane break into an exasperating chant.

"I know why you're reading those, I know why you're reading those! You want to impress the Doctor, you want to impress the Doctor!"

"I want to improve my mind," I said loftily.

"Fiddlesticks!" was Jane's only comment.

Only one thing seemed to lift the nameless shadow hanging over those days. When Adam's office hours were over he often turned his automobile into the driveway and came strolling round the corner of the house, knowing just where to find us. Jane generally joined us when she saw him arrive, and I was both amused and embarrassed by the open delight she took in any small gestures he might make toward me. If he touched my arm or my hand, or let his eyes rest on me while we talked, Jane's lips would curve into her smug I-told-you-so smile. Mrs. Canfield noticed the child's behavior too, and once remarked, "Jane, I believe you are an inveterate matchmaker!"

Adam laughed, but with such affection Jane could not be offended. "You are one of my favorite people, Jane!"

"Even more than Em——" she began, and then broke off short.

There was a moment's silence, and then Adam said softly, "Than Emily? It's all right if you don't *want* to talk about her, Jane. But don't keep it buttoned up inside if you *do* want to. That can cause trouble." Their eyes met. "Will you remember that?" he added.

"Yes," Jane said. "I'll remember."

As the hot days continued Jane played for hours with the dollhouse, moving the dolls from place to place and carrying on their conversations. She called the father and mother simply Mr. and Mrs. Doll, but to my delight the children were named Sonny, Honey, Flotsam, and Jetsam. When she was outdoors I noticed that she never went near the reflecting ball. If it happened to be in her path she would make a quick wide circuit of it and continue on her way without even a sideways glance. Nor did she mention Emily.

Letters continued to arrive from Martin, although not with their former regularity, but there were times when I almost forgot to open them. My constantly deepening interest in Adam had pushed poor Martin way to the back of my mind.

We found so much that we both enjoyed: evening walks, tennis games, drifting in a canoe where willow trees dipped their long fingers in the water. Everything we did together was a delight! And always we talked, each of us eager to learn everything about the other. Adam was formally invited to dinner on occasion, and other times Katie would come from the kitchen to say diffidently that "there looked to be a lot of meat on that chicken that was for dinner—if Dr. Adam would like to stay, that is."

Generally "Dr. Adam" was very happy to stay, though there were times when he had professional calls to make, or when he had records to go over with his father. On one such evening he refused the casual invitation regretfully, and I walked through the house with him and out onto the veranda as he prepared to leave.

The long last rays of the summer sun fell across the porch, shining full on Adam's face. As he had once before, he put his hand under my chin and lifted it, but this time I saw the deep, deep blue eyes come closer until I closed my own.

"Louisa," he said softly, and I felt his lips warm and firm and demanding on mine. I had never known before what a kiss could be! Far too soon he lifted his head, and I leaned mine against his shoulder.

"You never kissed me before," I murmured, probably the most ridiculous remark I ever made!

"But I will again," he said, and did. "And again, and again, and again!"

Weak and breathless, I tried feebly to push him away. "Adam! The sun is shining!"

He held me close, laughing softly. "Sunlight—moonlight—who cares?"

"People might see us!"

"Do you mind?"

"Jane might!"

"Jane has. With great interest. Look." He turned me slightly so that I could see the drawing room window that overlooked the veranda. From behind the stiff lace curtain two shining dark eyes peered out with delighted fascination.

"Ooh, that little—" I gasped, but Adam stopped me with one firm kiss.

"I love you, Louisa," he said. "I don't care if the whole world knows!" And before I could say another word he was down the steps. "I'll see you tomorrow," he called, and with my feet barely touching the floor I floated into the house.

Jane was still standing by the front window, and she faced me as I came in.

"I saw you," she said, as though she made an admission.

"I know," I said dreamily.

"Aren't you cross with me?"

"No."

"*Really,* Louisa?" She sounded unbelieving.

"Really, Jane. I'm not cross with you or anybody in the whole wide world. I love you! I love everybody!" My voice seemed to be caroling in the silliest way! "I'm going upstairs and lie down on my bed until I wake up. Because this *has* to be a dream!"

Jane looked at me and shook her head. "Golly!" she said. "I never thought love made people like this! Don't go to sleep, Louisa. It's almost time for dinner."

It was later that evening and Jane and I were playing a game of croquet on which I could not seem to keep my mind, when Katie called me from the back door.

"Dr. Adam's on the telephone, Miss Louisa. He wants to talk to you. He says it's very important and to hurry!"

I dropped my mallet and ran into the house and through the hall to the little table where the telephone stood. My heart was thudding. What could be so important? And why the hurry? I picked up the receiver.

"Hello? Adam? What is it?"

"I love you."

"Oh, I'm glad! I'm glad! But what is it that's so important? Why did I have to come so fast?"

"So I could tell you again that I love you. I couldn't wait any longer."

I stopped dead and then started to giggle. "Oh, Adam, you idiot! And here I thought something terrible must have happened!"

"What a gloomy mind you have! But I do have something else to say. Dad wants you to come to dinner tomorrow night. Here."

"Oh, heavens! Your *father?* Oh, Adam, I'm scared!"

"Now don't get edgy. You'll like him. Everybody does. You'll come?"

"All right," I said weakly.

"And Louisa . . . wear that white dress. The one you had on the first time I saw you. Please?"

"All right," I said again.

"Till tomorrow then. I'll pick you up at six. Good night, Louisa."

"Good night," I said, and hung up.

I sat there on the little bench by the telephone table for a moment, and then a board creaked farther along the hall, and I looked up. Jane stood in the far shadows.

"I wasn't listening, Louisa," she said instantly. "Honest! I didn't listen until you stopped talking."

"His father wants to meet me," I said shakily. "I'm going there to dinner tomorrow night."

"Oh, Louisa!" she breathed, coming closer. "That is a good sign! What are you going to wear?"

"A blanket. And I'll pull it over my head and hide inside it!"

She giggled. "He'll think you're an Indian. You could wear your white dress."

"Thank you. As a matter of fact I'm going to. Adam asked me . . . I mean—well, I guess he liked it."

"I knew he would. Louisa, is it all right if I tell Grandmother you're going to dinner?"

"I guess so. It's not a secret. Nothing *could* be, with you around!"

She ran back to me and hugged me violently, "Oh, Louisa, I do love you!" she said, and skipped off down the hall.

I went upstairs and while I waited for Jane I sat in the little armchair gazing out at the soft summer night. The faint light that remained seemed to have gathered in the silver of the reflecting ball, but now it was not ominous, only beautiful. I don't mind about you anymore, Emily Canfield, I said to myself. You no longer live, but I do! I can see now why you always wanted Adam with you, why you wanted to marry him when you grew up. But you never grew up. It's my turn now, Emily, and there's nothing you can do!

I heard Jane enter her room from the hall, and then her light shone through our connecting door.

"Grandmother says how nice you're going to dinner," she reported. "She says—" Jane's voice stopped suddenly. "Louisa, come here a minute, please."

I don't know what there was in her voice that chilled me even before I went into the room. "What is it, Jane?"

"Look." She pointed to the floor by the dollhouse. One of the dolls, one of the girl children, lay on the carpet, little chips from her broken china head scattered around her.

"Your doll! She must have fallen out of the dollhouse and smashed." I bent to pick it up.

"Smashed on the *rug*, Louisa? On the soft *rug*?"

"The wind, perhaps. Or Katie, cleaning. She must have brushed by the doll somehow, or perhaps it was already on the floor and she stepped on it."

"It wasn't on the floor. I put the dolls to bed before dinner. And Katie hasn't been up here since."

I gathered the tiny chips in my hand. "Well, *something* broke it, Jane. Maybe it was cracked before. It's quite old, you know."

"It wasn't cracked, Louisa."

I looked up at her, slightly vexed. "All right, then, *you* tell *me* how it broke!"

Her voice was no more than a whisper. "I don't know how. But I know who. Emily broke it."

"Oh, Jane!"

"Emily did it, Louisa. She doesn't like us having her things."

"What things?"

"The reflecting ball, and the dollhouse—and maybe Dr. Adam, too."

I got to my feet, took her gently by the shoulders and

turned her toward me. "Jane, Emily could not have broken that doll. I don't know how it broke, but she couldn't have done it! She *couldn't* have! And you can't give her back the dollhouse, any more than I can give her back Adam. Emily's life is *over*, Jane! You *must* believe that!"

Jane took the doll and the tiny chips from my hand. "Poor Flotsam," she said. "I'll keep her somewhere safe. I don't want to throw her away."

I went back to my room while Jane undressed. When I looked out of the window again the garden slept in unbroken black. There was no light anywhere at all.

ELEVEN

Jane spent most of the next morning trying to glue Flot-sam's head together. She was not very successful.

"Why do you bother, dear?" I asked. "There are several other dolls."

She didn't look at me. "Somebody has to show her she can't always do just as she likes."

"Show who? *Flotsam?*"

"You know who."

Yes, I knew. And I didn't want to discuss it. Instead, I changed the subject.

"Oh, I wish dinner tonight were over with! Suppose Adam's father doesn't like me?"

"Grandmother says he's very nice! You mustn't be scared, Louisa."

"I'm not exactly *scared*—oh dear, yes I am too! I'm scared he'll think I'm just a frumpy country bumpkin! And I *am!*"

Jane was enchanted with the words. "Frumpy country bumpkin, frumpy country bumpkin," she kept repeating, until it finally came out "Frumpy cumpy crumpkin," which set her off into gales of laughter. It was the one bright spot in the day.

Adam had said he would call for me at six o'clock, but it couldn't have been more than four when I started to dress. I had spent the morning pressing every tiny ruffle on the white dress, so it looked as fresh as meadow daisies, but I agonized over whether to wear my tiny pearl earbobs, whether my white gloves would be too dressy, and what to do with my hair. It was not until I saw the approval in Adam's eyes that I was reassured.

The two Dr. Frosts lived in a rambling old house where they were tended with patient firmness by a tall, erect, soft-spoken Negro woman named Sarah. She greeted us in the hall when we arrived, and then Adam led me into a lovely large room, filled with beautiful old pieces of furniture, and lighted by the long shafts of early evening sunshine.

"Oh, Adam, it's charming!" I said. "Have you always lived here?"

"Always, and so did many Frosts before me." He stood tall and smiling, looking down at me. "I'm glad you like the house, Louisa. You look very right, standing in this room. As if you belonged here."

"Well, I'm glad I *look* right! I *feel* scared to death!"

"I know an excellent cure for that."

He kissed me slowly and deliberately, and my arms went tight around him and I wanted to be so close to him that nothing could ever, ever, ever come between us! I thought I heard footsteps, but I could not have moved if the roof had caved in on my head. Someone cleared his throat, Adam put me gently away from him, and I turned to see an older, burlier, grayer Adam standing in the doorway.

"Dad, this is Louisa Amory."

Dr. Frost came toward us, smiling. "Miss Amory," he said, taking my hand warmly in his.

"Do you know that ever since Adam told me you'd be dining with us tonight I have been in a state of panic?"

"*You?*" I said stupidly. "*I've* been in a dither all day, but why should you—"

"Being a father on display is unnerving. Sarah made me change when I came in; she all but inspected my fingernails and checked behind my ears before she would allow me to come downstairs."

I laughed, just as he had meant me to.

"I'm under an additional strain," Dr. Frost went on. "You see, you are the first girl my son has brought home since he was five. I knew this was something special."

I glanced at Adam, who was looking happily from one to the other of us like a little boy whose mother approves of his new playmate. He turned to his father.

"And now that you've seen her?" he asked.

"I don't know how you found her, Adam, but don't let her go!"

Dinner was delicious—Katie could have done no better—and Sarah, as she served it, beamed with pleasure. Later we returned to the drawing room where I managed to pour coffee without spilling a drop. As I passed Dr. Frost his cup he noticed me eyeing several bright little objects that hung from his watchchain.

"Those are my child-beguilers," he said, lifting the chain from the two pockets and handing it to me to look at. "It's almost as useful as my stethoscope."

There were some fraternal emblems and keys on the chain, and such other trinkets as a tiny gold whistle, a little doll with jointed limbs and jewelled eyes, a miniature harmonica, and a tiny enameled Easter egg with a scene inside.

"They distract the older children during my examination," Dr. Frost explained, "and the little ones find it excellent to cut teeth on."

"Completely unscientific," Adam said. "The American Medical Association would never approve!"

"More fools they." His father refastened the chain across his vest. "It was little Emily Canfield who first gave me the idea for that."

And suddenly I felt a chill in the room that had not been there before. I had forgotten Emily for hours, but now—as always—here she was again. My voice must have sounded strained, for Dr. Frost looked up at me quickly from under his shaggy brows when I spoke.

"Emily!" I said. "Always Emily!"

"You know about her, then."

"Oh, yes, I know about her. And I keep learning more all the time. How was she responsible for . . . what did you call them?"

"My child-beguilers. It was one of the many times Emily was ailing, or claimed to be. I put my stethoscope to her back and asked her to breathe deeply while I listened for congestion, but she flatly refused. This little gold whistle was on her bedtable, and I picked it up and admired it, and then asked her if she could blow it. When she blew, I listened. But I listened to her lungs, not to the whistle. It worked beautifully." He smiled, remembering.

"And didn't she realize what you were doing?"

"Not until it was too late. Then she was a blazing fury. She made me take the whistle away with me—said she was never going to blow it again. I must have used that trick on a thousand children since."

"I'm glad to know there was at least one person Emily couldn't get around," I said. "Everyone else seems to have been right under her thumb!"

"You *have* been hearing about her! Yes, if Jack Canfield hadn't been such a complete fool about that child—that's

Emily's father I'm talking about, Miss Amory, not her brother—if he'd taken the flat of his hand to her once or twice, if he had listened when I tried to talk to him . . ." I could hear real anger growing in the doctor's voice.

"Take it easy, Dad," Adam said. "It's all been over for a long time now."

"That's *right*," his father said vehemently, "and it didn't have to be! If that child had been raised properly then just as sure as God made little green apples she'd be alive now! But her father was her undoing. In his eyes she was the most wonderful creature ever born, and when she asked for the moon he gave it to her!"

"The moon," I repeated. "That silver ball in the garden. It's rather the same, isn't it?"

"It *was* the same. Jack took Emily outside one night to look at the moon. He told me she thought it was pretty, and she wanted it. Jack almost tore his hair out wondering what to do."

Adam grinned. "I can imagine you told him."

"I told him the smartest thing he could do would be to point out to his daughter that there would be many things in life she would want and not be able to have. But he said not if he had *his* way. As long as she wanted something he'd turn the world upside down to get it for her. That's when he bought her that first reflecting globe. Ridiculous foolishness, that's what it was!"

"And Mrs. Canfield couldn't do anything?"

Dr. Frost looked at me. "If you were a young woman passionately in love with your husband, could you continually and deliberately do what you knew would anger him most?"

"But if it were my child, and if I could see what was happening to her—"

"Emily was never really Lydia's child. From the moment she could speak, could differentiate between people, could make her simplest wants known, she belonged to her father."

Adam shifted in his chair. I was finding the conversation fascinating, and I hoped he wasn't getting restless. "Dad," he said, "you called Mrs. Canfield a woman 'passionately' in love with her husband. Isn't your imagination running away with you? I can't think of anyone less passionate than she is."

"You saw her only as Emily's mother, Adam. Believe me, she wasn't always the controlled, withdrawn woman she is now, not by a long shot! When I first knew her she was— oh, laugh if you want to, but she was like a little dark flame! She was bright and exciting, she could talk about almost anything, she stood out in every gathering. She used to have the most beautiful laugh . . ." He paused thoughtfully.

"She still does," I said. "Not often, but at least more than when Jane and I first arrived."

"That's the best news I've heard! Whatever you're doing, keep it up!"

"Were Emily and her mother alike? Would Emily have grown up to be like that? Lovely and fascinating?"

"On the surface, yes. She probably would have. But there was one tremendous difference between the two. Lydia liked nothing more than *giving* to those she loved, but Emily—Emily was a sultry person. Delightful when things were going her way, but when they didn't . . ." He shook his head. "Emily was not the real tragedy in that family, Miss Amory. The real tragedy was Lydia. A woman who loved her husband more than life itself, and a man—a man who came to love his child more than his wife."

"But *why*?" I asked. "It was Mrs. Canfield he loved and married—"

"But it was Emily he created. A being so perfect—in his

eyes—so enchanting, so . . . so everything her mother was, but one he had made himself. A daughter like that is a formidable rival for any woman."

"But after Emily died, when she was no longer there to divide them . . ."

The doctor's fingers drummed quietly on the arm of his chair, and he took a long time answering. "Jack never forgave Lydia for Emily's death."

All I could feel was shock. "And she loved him so much!"

"She loved him so much that she retreated into herself for protection. That is when she became the quiet, reserved woman she is today. It was the most heartbreaking thing I ever saw!" Dr. Frost slapped the chair arm in anger. "What fools people can be!" Then his deep eyes searched my face. "You know that black locket Lydia wears?"

"Yes, I know it. Jane said it held Emily's picture. She said that Mr. Canfield gave it to his wife after Emily died."

"He gave it to her the day Emily was buried. He told her to wear it always, so she would never forget the child."

"You mean . . . for *penance*?"

"That's as good a word as any."

I felt quick tears against my eyes. "Poor, poor Mrs. Canfield!"

Adam leaned forward and took my hand. "Louisa, don't let it upset you. It was all so long ago. And now there's Jane for her to love."

"Yes, there's Jane." And without really thinking. I added, "If Emily doesn't spoil it all."

Dr. Frost frowned. "Emily?"

"Louisa feels that Emily is still around, Dad," Adam said. "That she is still . . . evidencing herself from time to time."

"Oh dear," I interrupted, troubled, "it sounds so—"

"I think Dad ought to know, Louisa, that's all. But not to-night. I'll talk to him about it sometime. Right now I'm going to take you for a fast windy ride. It will blow some of those clouds out of your head."

Dr. Frost walked to the door with us. "I'm sorry I spouted on at such length," he said. "I hope you don't think me a complete bore."

"Never!" I assured him. "This has been one of the nicest evenings I've ever spent! Not even Emily could spoil it!"

TWELVE

Being in love that quiet New England summer made the days enchanted, and I was so filled with happiness I could barely contain it. I had written to my mother about Adam, and although the first letters mentioned him merely as a young friend of Mrs. Canfield's, his name had occurred more and more often. Knowing my mother well, I never doubted that she did a great deal of between-the-lines reading. As for poor Martin, my letters to him had dwindled to an occasional postcard, and then to nothing at all.

With my own heart filled with love, I watched with pleasure the closeness that grew between Jane and her grandmother. Mrs. Canfield taught Jane to knit, and they would sit together under the tulip tree, Mrs. Canfield's needles flying, while Jane laboriously picked up every stitch, the yarn pulling tight in her damp little hands. They took turns reading aloud to each other, and sometimes they went walking through the wide old streets of Lynn. I often gazed after them as they started out, Jane's head lifted as she chattered to her grandmother and the warm smile on Mrs. Canfield's face as she listened. And as I watched I found myself praying silently that nothing would shatter the new joy these two lonely people had found.

On an afternoon in mid-August I heard Adam's automobile turn into the driveway. I was in the parlor, one of Katie's broad aprons around my waist, emptying the whatnot closet of its collection of small china animals, delicate fans, and carved bits of jade and coral, getting ready to clean them. I left my task happily to open the front door for Adam.

"I'm in my working clothes," I said as he came into the hall. "You will just have to put up with me."

"Such a sloven!" he teased, his eyes filled with the admiration I always saw there. Then he looked inquiringly around. "Where is your shadow?"

"Jane? She and her grandmother have gone to the library," I said, leading him into the parlor.

"You mean we are *alone*?"

"What's the matter, Doctor? Are you afraid of me? Katie is in the kitchen. You can always scream for help."

"I won't make a sound," he whispered, and took me competently into his arms. It was a wonderful kiss, long and deep and satisfying. I laid my head against his shoulder and sighed with pleasure.

"I have been thinking of that all day," he said softly. "All the time Mrs. Edwards was telling me about the odd pain she has over her heart whenever she has a double helping of dessert, and all the time I was taking the cast off of little Tommy Gregory's arm, and all the time I was telling young Mrs. Chase that she had the loveliest baby I had ever seen, I was thinking 'I hope Louisa is all alone so I can give her the kind of kiss she really needs.'"

"What would they have said if they had known how divided your attentions were?"

"If they had ever met you they would say I had impeccable taste. Do you know I love you, Louisa?"

"I am beginning to gain that impression," I said.

"A remarkably astute young woman. Come over here and sit down. I have to talk to you."

With his arm around my shoulders we walked to the little carved cherrywood love seat.

"You sound very portentous," I said.

"I don't mean to. I have to leave you for a short time, and I don't want to at all. Yet, I'm excited about where I'm going."

"Where are you going?"

"Dr. Halleck is going to conduct a week's course in surgery at Harvard Medical. It is only for practicing physicians and he is one of the best men in the country. Dad says he feels I ought to go, and it would certainly be a magnificent opportunity."

"But of course you must go! A week, you said? Why, that's hardly any time at all!"

"What a cold, callous, uncaring creature! A week is nothing, she says!"

"I didn't say 'nothing,' I said '*hardly* anything.' There's a difference."

"What will you do all the time I'm away?"

"Oh, just the usual things, go dancing every night with mysterious men—spend the days opening their flowers and jewels and furs and other paltry gifts, nothing special."

Adam stopped me with another kiss. "You're a brat," he said, "but even so—when I come back I'll have something important to ask you."

"Oh," was all I could say. And if there had been any doubt in my mind as to what he meant it was removed by his next remark.

"I want to meet your parents, too, Louisa. The Sunday after I get home let's drive to Milford."

"All right." I burrowed my nose into his jacket. "When do you leave?"

"Tomorrow morning."

I jerked my head up to look at him. "*Tomorrow?* But . . . that . . . that's *tomorrow!*" I felt oddly empty. I told myself it was ridiculous, that a week was only seven days, but it seemed forever. I wondered how I had managed to be so casual when Adam had first mentioned it.

He rose, pulling me to my feet, and we walked slowly into the hall. Just inside the front door Adam turned me toward him and held me close. "Take care of yourself, darling," he said softly.

"I will."

He kissed me, so thoroughly that when he raised his head and took a step back I could feel myself trembling.

"That's so you won't forget me while you're dancing with all those strange men," he said, and ran down the steps. I stood waving after him.

Jane was desolate when I told her Adam had gone away for a week. "But he didn't say good-bye to me!" she mourned.

"Darling, you weren't here. And he couldn't wait."

"I suppose not," she said, sounding unconvinced. "But didn't he even ask you to marry him before he left?"

"Not . . . exactly."

Her eyes sparkled suddenly. "But he's going to?"

"Jane! It's none of—"

"I know, I know! It's none of my business! You needn't keep telling me. Well, I guess I don't need to worry. Maybe you managed all right, even without me around."

"Just barely, Jane," I said. "Just barely."

I asked Mrs. Canfield that evening if she would mind my leaving Jane all day on the Sunday that Adam and I went to Milford. I could feel myself blushing as I spoke.

"Certainly not, my dear." Her dark eyes twinkled, very much as Jane's had. "May I make the rather obvious assumption from this proposed visit home?"

I looked down, happy, but suddenly shy. "Yes, I think so."

"I am so glad for you, Louisa," she said warmly.

She rose from the small armchair and coming to me kissed my cheek gently. "I am very, very pleased, dear child! And your parents will be, too. God bless you, Louisa!"

I wrote to Mother to tell her of our impending visit, knowing she would undoubtedly interpret it correctly, and feeling I should give her a little time to get used to the idea. Then I settled down to wait out the week until Adam's return.

It was strange how much difference it made, not having him around. It was not simply that I missed him, which I did, very much. It was something more than that, something darker, almost . . . sinister. I felt unprotected. I found myself jumping at small night noises, avoiding the reflecting ball, searching Jane out frequently to be sure she was all right. There had been no further—what can I call them?—mysterious incidents since the girl doll was crushed, and yet I could never quite rid myself of the fear that there might be. Anywhere, at any time. At last, in a real effort to rid myself of these forebodings, I resorted to a surge of energetic domesticity. Poor Katie was nearly driven to distraction as I washed and ironed, swept and dusted, got under her feet and in her way.

On Thursday morning, half laughing at myself, I went to my closet and took out the white dress. Inspecting it critically, I found several tiny dust smudges on the full skirt. They rinsed out easily, and I took it outdoors to dry, placing the crooked end of the clothes hanger over a low branch of a tree near the reflecting ball. There was not even the breath of a breeze, but the sun was warm and would dry and freshen the frock nicely. From there I went into the kitchen and announced that I was going to give Jane's and my rooms a thorough cleaning. Katie looked at me, her lips pursed.

"Miss Louisa, those rooms were cleaned from top to

bottom just before you came. They don't need another going-over now."

"Oh, Katie, please let me! I know they're not dirty—you're a marvelous housekeeper! But I just want to *do* something! Would you rather I helped you here in the kitchen? I could bake something, if you like."

Faced with the two evils, Katie chose the one which would at least keep me out of her way.

"Oh, go along and clean then, Miss Louisa, if that's what you're of a mind to do. Here, get yourself one of my big aprons, and you'll find a bucket and scrub rags in the cellarway. But those rooms *don't* need it!"

As I tied one of her bibbed white aprons firmly around my waist, Katie looked at me shrewdly. "Doctor Adam coming back soon?" she asked.

"Yes. Tomorrow."

"Praise be," said Katie, and went back to her sink.

Jane was in the garden, tagging after Jacob as he staked up the tall dahlias. From the kitchen window I could see her lips go as she chattered to him constantly, and I could imagine his slow, patient, often humorous answers to her endless questions and comments. Picking up the bucket, the rags, the soap and the ammonia, I went marching up the stairs and along the corridor.

Just as I was going into Jane's room to strip and clean her bed, she appeared in the doorway, surveying the room in silence. She shook her head.

"I just don't understand you, Louisa," she said.

"What don't you understand?"

"Well, love is supposed to make people dreamy and sort of mushy. You've been charging aound all week as though you had to clean up the whole world—all by yourself."

"Never mind being clever. Just help me get this mattress off. You pull, I'll push."

Jane put all her wiry strength into a tremendous heave that jolted the heavy mattress off the bed and partially onto the floor. As I gave the corresponding push I heard something rip.

"Oh, dear," I said. "We've torn it somehow. Did it catch on a spring?" I went round to Jane's side of the bed, and together we tried to lift the mattress to see underneath. There was no visible tear. "It must be on the edge, Jane. Let's push it back on the bed and see."

"I don't see why *I* should have to push mattresses around just because *you* happen to feel like cleaning," Jane muttered, but she helped me wrestle the awkward weight back onto the high bed.

"There! See? There's a rip along this side. Thank goodness it's not very big." I knelt to see better. "It must have been torn before, though. There are old stitches in it."

Jane crouched beside me, her small fingers exploring the split in the fabric. "What a funny place to get a hole in a mattress," she said, and very suddenly there was an odd note in her voice. I looked at her quickly. She was frowning. "This was Emily's bed," she said softly.

"Oh, Jane, can't we forget Emily for once? I'll get some heavy thread. We can mend this again."

"Wait." She laid her hand acoss the tear and raised her eyes to mine. "Louisa, there's going to be something hidden in that hole."

"The family diamonds, no doubt. Oh, Jane, stop imagining!"

"I'm not imagining, Louisa." She put her fingers into the hole, probed for a moment, and then slowly withdrew them. Between her first and second fingers she held a small envelope. "Here."

I looked at her. "How did you know there was something in there?" I asked.

"I don't know how I knew," Jane said, "but I knew. Take it, Louisa."

Sitting back on my heels, I took the envelope from her hand. Jane got up and walked slowly to the window, looking down into the garden.

"Don't you want to see what it is?" I asked.

"No. I don't think so. You open it."

The outside of the envelope was blank. I brushed bits of mattress stuffing from it slowly, and noticed that it was sealed.

"You can't know that Emily hid this in there," I said. "It's probably cleaning instructions or something."

"No," Jane said, her back toward me. "It's something Emily put there. Why don't you read it?"

"I'm not sure that I should. I'm not sure either of us should. Maybe I ought to give it to Mrs. Canfield."

Jane whirled on me. "Read it, Louisa! Now! Tear it open and read it!"

"Really, Jane—"

Her eyes were wide and dark. "Louisa, read it!"

Reluctantly I slipped one finger under the flap of the envelope and ripped it open, drawing forth the single folded sheet of paper. Jane stood against the window, watching me. I smoothed the paper flat, revealing the lines of perfect script, exactly like the writing in the signature on the drawing Jane had made, just like the writing of the pansy poem in the purple leather notebook.

"What does it say, Louisa?" Jane's voice was little more than a breath.

I started to read and found that I had to clear my throat before I could make a sound. "'To Whom It May Concern,'" I read. "'I, Adam Frost, do solemnly swear . . . '" I stopped. "But this can't be right," I said. "It is Emily's handwriting, but it is in Adam's name!"

"Go on reading, Louisa."

"'. . . do solemnly swear that I will marry Emily Canfield when we are both old enough. If I should ever marry anyone except Emily, I will regret it to the last day of my life. This is Emily's solemn vow. Hereunto I do set my hand and seal.' That's what it says, Jane. It is signed—in a very different writing—Adam Frost."

Jane's voice cracked a little as she spoke. "That's all?"

"There's—there's a sort of brownish smear here. After the signature."

"That's blood. Emily made him sign it in blood."

I knelt there for a moment, holding the paper, and my hand trembled so that the paper shook. Then in a sudden fury I crumpled the crisp sheet and stood up.

"It's utter nonsense," I said angrily. "I just wish I had Emily Canfield here right this minute! I'd give that selfish, spoiled, nasty child a beating she wouldn't forget in a million years! The idea! Going around telling everyone else what they must and must not do! Who does she think she is?"

Jane hadn't moved from the window. "She's dead, Louisa. Remember? You told me yourself—she was a poor little girl who died before she ever had a chance to grow up. She has been dead for years. She is nothing at all now. You told me that, Louisa." Her voice was quiet and even.

"All right," I said, "I told you that. And it's true. She *is* dead! And she has been dead for years. And now she is nothing at all. And I don't want to hear anything more about Emily Canfield! Not *anything!*" I was facing Jane squarely, and my breath came so fast it almost choked me. "You are not to speak of her again—not *ever,* Jane! You are to leave her alone inside that infernal reflecting ball or wherever you think she is, and I don't want ever to hear you mention her name again. Not ever!"

Suddenly Jane's eyes filled with tears and she ran to me, her arms going tight around my waist. "I never thought she would hurt *you*, Louisa! I hate her for hurting *you*. It was all right when she wanted me to do things for her. I thought she just didn't want to be all alone. Dead like that, and all alone. But I won't let her hurt *you*, Louisa. I won't let her!"

Jane was sobbing now, almost hysterically, and I held her close against me. The paper was still clutched in my hand, and I threw it away from me. I smoothed Jane's hair, talking to her quietly.

"There, Jane. Don't cry. We're making much too much of this whole silly business! You and I both know it is nothing more than imagination and a lot of stories we have heard about a little girl named Emily Canfield."

Mrs. Canfield's voice came from the doorway. "Did I hear Jane *crying*? What is it, dear? Are you hurt, Jane?"

I looked at her over Jane's head. "It's nothing, Mrs. Canfield, really. She's all right."

Jane moved away from me, drawing her hand across her eyes. She turned to her grandmother. "It was Emily again," she said clearly. "She left a note hidden in her mattress and we found it. And it made Louisa mad, and scared too, I think. And *I'm* scared! And I don't like Emily anymore!"

Mrs. Canfield walked toward us. "A note? What do you mean? What sort of note?"

"Please, it's nothing," I said, but Jane snatched up the crushed ball of paper from the floor and thrust it into her grandmother's hand.

"There! She made Dr. Adam write it sometime—at least she wrote it, and made him sign it. In blood too! Just because *she* can't marry him, she isn't going to let anyone else marry him. Not even Louisa!"

Mrs. Canfield smoothed the paper out and read it slowly. She stood in silence, and neither Jane nor I said a word. She must have read it two or three times before she went through the door into my room and to the dresser where the candle and matches stood. Striking a match, she held it to one corner of the paper until it flared up, burning quickly. Then she dropped it into the empty metal wastebasket. Turning, she came back to the doorway, her voice as tight and cold as her face.

"Wash your face, Jane, and smooth your hair. Marshall's Dry Goods Store is having a sale of children's sandals. I think you better have a new pair. I'll be ready to go downtown with you in ten minutes."

She walked out into the corridor and down it to her room. Jane and I heard the door close behind her, and there seemed nothing for either of us to say.

I watched them leave the house a few minutes later, the two slim, straight figures, walking together. The large rooms seemed suddenly abnormally silent.

After I had forced myself to mend the mattress and make the bed I carried the cleaning things to the kitchen and put them away. Katie must have been upstairs in her room, for the kitchen, too, was quiet and empty. Pushing the screen door open, I stepped outside just as a slow dark cloud slipped across the sun, dimming the brilliant garden colors and making the air almost chill. I walked across the grass to the center of the lawn where I had hung my white dress, close beside the reflecting ball. As I lifted my hand to take it down I froze.

The soft folds of muslin were wrapped and twisted around the branch, delicate lace ruffles caught roughly to the sharp twigs. Before I even started to disentangle it I knew what I would find. The dress was ripped in a dozen places, long straight tears that might almost have been made by vicious wrenching hands. The lace hung loose from the fabric, there were great streaks of dirt, and greenish stains from the leaves. The lovely white dress in which I might have heard Adam propose to me was utter ruin, beyond any possible repair. A strong wind, almost a gale, might have blown a garment round and round a tree limb that way, might have rubbed it against smearing dirt. It might have, if there had been a strong wind. But the air was totally still, just as it had been all day. Ever since I had hung the dress outdoors.

THIRTEEN

The dark cloud that had hidden the sun seemed to grow, both actually and in my mind. There was an ominous foreboding over the house and all of us in it. Dinner that night was a quiet meal. I had no appetite, and I noticed that Mrs. Canfield ate only a few bites before placing her knife and fork together on her plate. Jane appeared to be coming down with a cold and complained that her throat hurt. The conversation lagged and it was with relief that we left the table.

When Jane was undressing for bed I sat in her room, gazing out of the window at the still night, drawing in a little earlier now. Rain was threatening, as it had been all afternoon. The garden lay in dark silence.

"Does Dr. Adam come back tomorrow?" Jane asked.

"He's expected to."

"I'll be glad. Things are better when he's here."

"We'll have him look at that sore throat of yours."

"I didn't mean that kind of thing."

"What kind, then?"

"Oh, just things. Everything." Our voices were soft and a

little slow, and our eyes did not meet. "How much longer will we be staying here, Louisa?"

Jane was buttoning the neck button of her long white nightdress, and above it her eyes were very dark.

"Why, I don't exactly know, Jane. Another two or three weeks, I suppose. Why?"

"I . . . just wondered."

"Do you want to go home to Milford?"

"Sort of, I do. Sometimes. Not always."

When I tucked the sheet over her a few moments later she put her arms around me and kissed my cheek. "I'm glad Dr. Adam will be back tomorrow," she said. "I'll feel better then."

When I had gone to bed myself I lay awake in the dark for hours. It was plain now that Emily could not be easily dismissed. Simple enough to call the various odd episodes imagination, or fancy, or coincidence, or whatever one liked—they happened, one after the other, each a little more intense than the last. Could they only happen here at Lynn, in Emily's old home? And could there be an Emily without Jane? It seemed always to be Jane who was—well—the catalyst. It was she who saw Emily in the reflecting ball, her wall on which the dim glow shone, her hand that drew the pictures and wrote the verse about the pansies. It was Jane who had attached importance to my white dress, ruined now and unwearable.

I told myself I was an adult, that I had outgrown childish superstition. There was no way a child long dead could really hurt Jane, no way that child could change what Adam and I felt for each other, or keep us from marrying. I told myself these things as I lay staring wide-eyed into the dark room, and I knew I did not believe them. Something of Emily still existed. Something spiteful, determined, selfish, and dangerous.

Friday morning rain fell from a lead-colored sky, quenching the beauty of the garden, muddying the pansies, darkening our small world. I prowled the house, wishing I could stop time, delay Adam's return until I knew what I was going to say to him. But the well-bred chiming of the formal little French clock in the parlor went on and on.

It was almost lunchtime when Jane came into my room. She leaned over the back of my chair, watching me buff my nails.

"That makes your hands look pretty," she said.

"Thank you."

"Is your white dress all clean and pressed? Shall I get it out of the closet?"

I didn't look at her. "I don't think I'll wear it tonight."

"But you *have* to! You really have to! It's the very most perfect time!" She ran to the closet. "Louisa, where is it? Your white dress isn't here."

"I know. I . . . put it somewhere else."

"Where? I'll get it."

I put the buffer back in my manicure case and closed it. "I'm not wearing the white dress tonight, Jane. Please don't discuss it anymore."

She came back to me slowly, and her eyes held what I had begun to think of as her "Emily-look." "Something has happened to it. What happened to your white dress, Louisa?"

I gazed back at her for a long minute and then I rose and went to my bureau. Opening the drawer, I pulled out the dress, rolled into a tight wad as I had stuffed it there. Without speaking I shook it out for her to see.

She didn't touch it. She put her hands behind her back, and stared at the long rents, the dirt and stains and trailing lace. When she spoke her voice was very small. "How did she do it?"

"I don't know that anyone did anything. I rinsed a few spots out and hung it from the tree to dry."

"What tree?"

"The tree nearest . . . the reflecting ball. When I went out to get it the . . . the wind, I guess, had wrapped it tight around the tree."

"When, Louisa?"

"Yesterday. When you and your grandmother had gone downtown to buy your new sandals."

Jane just looked at me for a long minute. Then she said, "There wasn't any wind yesterday, Louisa."

"No," I said slowly. "No, there wasn't any wind at all yesterday."

She walked to the window and looked down at the drenched garden. "She's getting very close, isn't she?" she whispered.

I rolled the dress into a ball and thrust it out of sight in the drawer. "You had better wash your hands," I said. "It must be time for lunch."

It was a little after four o'clock when I heard the newsboy's bicycle crunch on the gravel driveway, and then the soggy thump of the folded paper as it hit the porch. I opened the front door and went out to get it just as Adam's car turned in from the street. As much as I wanted to, I could not run and hide.

He was out of the car in a second, through the rain and up on the porch, and both his arms were around me tight. His voice was barely more than a breath when he said, "Oh, Louisa! How I missed you!"

His wool jacket was flecked with raindrops and I could feel their dampness against my cheek. I was grateful that I did not have to meet his eyes. His lips touched my hair, and then he held me away from him, looking at me as though he had never seen me before.

"I'm home, Louisa," he said. "Will you marry me?"

I pulled myself away and walked to the edge of the porch, my hands gripping the wet railing tightly.

"I don't know, Adam."

There was a flat silence for an instant and then he took two long steps after me, put his hands on my shoulders and turned me roughly toward him.

"What do you mean—you don't know?"

"I . . . I . . . oh, Adam, couldn't we go in the house? Or somewhere?"

I had never heard his voice so hard. "No," he said. "We could not go in the house or somewhere. What do you mean—you don't know?"

My voice shook, and I fought back tears that threatened to overflow. "Adam, I don't know what to say. And I . . . I can't talk to you here—like this. You don't seem like you!"

"I don't feel like me!" He took my hand and led me quickly and forcibly down the porch steps and into the car, opening the door for me. "Get in," he said.

"Adam, I can't just go riding off like this, without telling anyone—"

"Louisa, get in that car!"

A moment later we were splashing down the driveway and into the main road. The isinglass and canvas curtains that were snapped around the car made it shut in and private, and the rain drummed on the roof. Neither of us said a word. My eyes and throat stung with tears, and Adam's grim face beside me did nothing to ease my unhappiness. It must have been ten or fifteen minutes before we turned off the road and onto a muddy track that led partway into a broad wet field. He braked the car, cut off the engine, and turned to me.

"Now, Louisa, let's talk."

I blinked hard and nodded. "All right."

He didn't touch me. "Do you love me, Louisa?"

I looked up at him, my eyes brimming. "Oh, yes, Adam!"

"Will you marry me, Louisa?"

I shook my head helplessly. "I don't *know!*"

He put his hand tight on my shoulder. "Something has happened, hasn't it?" he said. "What?"

I tried to speak, but suddenly I was crying and couldn't stop. His arms went around me, my head was tight against his shoulder, and I could hear him murmuring to me.

"There, love. Don't cry! Don't cry. Whatever it is, it's all right. Wipe your eyes. There are things you have to tell me."

I felt him slip his clean cool handkerchief into my hand, and I mopped my face and tried to smooth my hair.

"It was Emily again," I said. And then somehow I was ridding myself of all of it. Things that had happened before he left which I had never told him about, like the picture Jane had drawn of an angry Emily, signed with that elegant script, and the girl doll, lying smashed on the bedroom carpet. The wind-blown dress, too, on a day when no wind blew, and the note hidden inside the mattress. Above all, I tried to tell him of the *feeling* that pervaded the house.

"She's *there*, Adam! We can no longer say she isn't. It's not just imagination. She is *there*, and she wants something, and she isn't going to leave without it. And I think what she wants—is you."

His voice was quiet and thoughtful. "Just how do you mean, that she wants me?"

"I think she doesn't intend to let us marry, Adam."

"Louisa—" He paused briefly as though gathering his thoughts. "Louisa, I can think of no way Emily—dead or alive—can stop that. If this . . . this *force* does exist, and I cannot say whether it really does, or whether each incident can be explained reasonably, but if it does, if Emily is indeed trying to get her own way again, then perhaps the sooner we are married, the better. Emily was never flatly denied anything. Maybe it's time she was."

"But I'm afraid," I whispered. "I am truly afraid! For Jane. It has always been Jane, you see, who has been *closest* to Emily. If Emily reached Jane—if she hurt her in any way, *any* way—I *couldn't* marry you! You know I couldn't. And Emily knows it too."

He held me very close for a moment and then gently let me go. Taking his pipe from his pocket, he filled and lit it, taking his time while we both sat in silence. The rain beat monotonously on the roof of the car and slid down the windshield so that we could see nothing except wet grayness outside. Puffing on the pipe, Adam took my hand in his.

"I remember the day Emily wrote the note you found," he said presently. "It was the same day she sat by the open window. I told you I had spent the morning there, playing in her room because she was not allowed out of bed. She had her dollhouse dolls and was making clothes for them. She said they were named Emily and Adam. I had little use for dolls and I told her so, but she insisted we have a wedding for them. She dressed the Emily doll in a lace handkerchief and said she was the bride, and then she proceeded to have a marriage ceremony. I had to speak for the Adam doll, while she talked for the bride. I thought it was dull and stupid, but I did it just the same. Finally I announced I was leaving because it was almost time to meet my father. She brought that note out from under her pillow—I don't know when she had written it—and told me I had to sign it before I could go."

He stopped speaking until I said softly, "And did you?"

"Not at first. I told her what I thought of the idea—that it was dumb, and who cared about getting married anyway."

"What did she do?" I asked. "What did Emily do?"

"She picked up a pair of scissors from her bedtable and aimed for my face. I was sitting on the edge of her bed. I twisted the scissors out of her hand, but not without jabbing myself with them, and then I slapped her. Hard. I remember how shocked at myself I was—little boys just didn't slap little girls, Louisa, it simply wasn't done. But at the same time I was so angry that I felt no remorse at all. She opened her mouth to yell—I think she was as amazed at my slapping her as I was—and I clamped my hand over her mouth and told her if she so much as made a sound I'd never play with her again. I can see her eyes now—huge and dark, like Jane's—looking at me over my hand across her mouth. They were filled with hate—her eyes—and then she closed them for a moment, and when she looked at me again she was crying. Very softly."

"She was clever, wasn't she?" I said quietly.

"Very. But I was too young to realize it. All I could think of was that if Mrs. Canfield walked in and found Emily crying she would want to know why, and Emily would say I had slapped her. And I would not have been able to deny it."

"So she asked you again to sign the paper."

"Yes. Very gently, and sweetly. She said she knew it was silly, and that it didn't really mean anything, but if I liked her I'd sign it. So I did. And then I left."

"And the little blood stain?"

"She took the finger I had cut and pressed it against the paper. At that point I didn't feel like making any more fuss. I let her."

"And after you left she must have used the scissors to cut the mattress and push the paper inside, and then sew it up."

"I suppose so. I never thought about it again. It was such a long time ago!" He opened the door of the automobile enough to knock his pipe out, and then put it in his pocket and turned to me. "Louisa, there is no possible way I can believe or disbelieve in these odd events that you feel Emily may be responsible for. I told you once before, I am a scientist and I believe in facts that can be proven. At the same time, I have seen things in medicine that cannot be explained. There is such an infinite amount that we do not know! But this I do know. I love you very much. I want to marry you. I cannot believe that anyone except ourselves can change this. Not Emily—not anyone."

I laid my head against his shoulder. It felt so strong. "I suppose not," I said.

"And nothing can happen to Jane through Emily, Louisa. Her 'power' can't reach that far."

"I know. It isn't possible really, is it?"

"No. It isn't possible." He put his hands on my arms and turned me to face him. "Louisa, will you marry me?" he said.

I looked at him for a long minute, seeing the crisp dark hair, the deep, deep blue eyes, the strong lines of temples and nose and jaw. Then I put both my arms around his neck and held him close.

"Oh, yes, Adam! Yes, and yes, and yes!"

FOURTEEN

*L*ate that night, long after Adam had left, I woke to a noise I could not at first identify. All I could hear was the rain, still coming down heavily, chilling the air with the promise of fall. Then suddenly it came again, frightening in the darkness. There was a pounding somewhere, and a voice—a voice calling my name.

"Louisa, Louisa, please wake up!"

I was out of bed and into Jane's room without even thinking.

"Jane? What is it, darling?"

There was no light to guide me, but I went straight to her bed. My hands felt across it. The covers were thrown back and the bed was empty. The pounding came again, as if from outdoors. I ran to the window, trying to look down into the heavy black wetness of the garden. I leaned my head out of the open window.

"Jane? Jane, where are you?"

Her voice, small and broken, came up to me. "Down here, Louisa. I'm locked out. Oh, *please* let me in!"

Barefooted and silent I opened the door of Jane's room

and fled along the corridor and down the staircase, through the hall and into the kitchen. It never occurred to me to wonder how my feet knew the way so unerringly without light. When there is something urgent to be done one does it, and wonders later how it was managed. I turned the knob on the back door that drew back the lock, and opened it. Jane crouched there, a small white figure in the dark. She was crying, and as I drew her in, my hands felt her cold, soaked, shivering little body in the dripping nightdress.

"Jane! What in the world—"

"Oh, Louisa, I'm so cold!"

I groped for the pull-chain that turned on the bright overhead light, and blinked in the sudden glare. Jane huddled against the closed door, her lips blue with cold, her teeth chattering, the water dripping from her hair and her body and nightgown into puddles on Katie's polished floor.

"Wait right there," I said. "Don't move!"

Running soundlessly, I turned on the downstairs hall light and raced up the stairs. From the bathroom I snatched a towel and from the foot of my bed I took the extra quilt that lay folded there. One more second to slip into my robe, and I was back down the stairs and into the kitchen. I stripped Jane's nightgown from her and toweled her as briskly as I could before I wrapped her in the quilt and sat her in Katie's rocking chair. Then I went to the stove and lit the flame under the teakettle. I measured tea into a strainer laid across the top of a cup, and while I waited for the water to boil I wrung the drenched nightdress into the sink. Jane huddled in the chair. She could not stop crying. The sobs continued, deep and slow, and the tears kept welling from her eyes. It seemed forever before I could pour the water through the strainer, stir in a large spoonful of sugar, and take the cup to Jane.

"Drink this," I said, "and don't try to talk until it's gone."

I had to hold the cup for her. She was still shaking so

with chills that her hands would not obey. When the last sip of tea was finished I set the cup on the table and knelt on the floor beside her.

"Now, Jane. Tell me now. What were you doing outdoors?"

"I dreamed, I think," she said. Her sore throat made her voice ragged. "It *must* have been a dream. I heard Emily calling me—it was a crying sort of voice. I know you don't like me to talk about Emily, Louisa, but I have to if I'm going to tell you—"

"Go on."

"Well, I thought I heard her calling me, and I got out of bed and looked out my window and I could see the reflecting ball all shiny and silvery in the rain, and she kept calling me—at least, I *thought* she was—and somehow I just went downstairs and out the back door. I left the door a little bit open so I could get in again—I never wanted to bother you, Louisa—but it must have shut all by itself. Then I couldn't open it. So I knocked, but you didn't wake up, and I was scared to ring the bell because I didn't want Grandmother and Katie to wake up, but you wouldn't, so I had to pound really hard. I'm sorry, Louisa."

"Jane, never mind about waking me up. What happened in the garden?"

"I don't exactly know. It wasn't anything *happening* really, it was just the way I felt out there.

"And how did you feel?"

"Sort of sorry for Emily at first. I truly thought I heard her and that she was crying, Louisa. I thought she was lonely, and wanted me to be with her. But then it got different—after I was outside, and after the kitchen door slammed shut—it was all different!"

I could hear Adam's voice saying "... and when she looked at me again she was crying. Very softly." And I could hear myself saying, "She was clever, wasn't she?"

"How was it different, Jane?" I asked. "Tell me all of it."

"It's so hard to explain how things make you *feel*—hearing the door blow shut frightened me. I felt as if I was all alone out there with Emily, and she wasn't lonely and crying anymore, she was *mad!*"

"How could you know she was mad?"

"I could feel her, Louisa! I could feel her all around me, and it wasn't a good feeling at all! And then that old ball stopped shining; it was shining when I woke up and looked out my window, and it was still shining after I got outside, but then when the door closed it stopped and I was out there and it was dark as anything, and Emily was everywhere and I was so cold and oh, Louisa, you sleep so *hard!*"

Jane was crying again, but quietly now. I gave her the corner of the blanket to dry her eyes and got to my feet. Even in the brightly lighted kitchen, huddled in my robe, I felt lost and chilled and frightened myself. I rinsed out the teacup, wiped up the puddles from the floor, and gathered up the wet bundle of Jane's nightdress.

"Come along now, darling. I'm going to get you into a tub of hot water."

"We'll wake Grandmother."

"Perhaps not. Be as quiet as you can."

I had to help her up the stairs, she was still trembling with violent chills. We closed the bathroom door and I ran the tub half full of hot water and eased her into it. While she hunched there, still shivering and coughing every few minutes, I hung her nightgown over a chair to dry, and found an extra comforter for her bed. I filled a hot-water bottle and slipped it between the sheets, and then tucked her into bed. I could think of nothing else to do for her, but I didn't like the pinched look on her face, nor the way her whole body shook. I wondered if I should call Mrs. Canfield, or Katie—or even Adam—but then Jane reached out her icy little hand and took mine.

"I'm sleepy, Louisa."

"And no wonder! Galloping around in the middle of the night! Go to sleep now, dear. I think you'll feel warmer soon."

I kissed her, and went back into my room. I turned on my light, closed the window, and drew the little armchair close beside it. And there, for the rest of the night, I sat and thought. I was no longer frightened. I was so filled with anger that there was no room for any other emotion. So dear little Emily was lonely, was she? Dear little Emily had her father with her, and her brother, and her brother's wife. I no longer doubted that in some way she had managed that. She had no reason to be lonely. No reason to keep torturing Jane.

But how does one deal with a little girl who no longer lives? They used to say that bell, book and candle could exorcise evil spirits, but I didn't believe Emily would respond to anything as classical as that. Emily was no ghost, wandering white-shrouded through the night, wailing through haunted hallways. But whoever she was, whatever she was—a memory, a feeling, the distillation of selfishness—there had to be an end to this!

When the sky began to lighten and the rain became visible instead of just an endless sound, I went quietly into Jane's room. She slept too deeply, and her breathing seemed too quick and shallow. Her face was no longer blue with cold; now it was flushed, and when I laid my hand gently on her forehead I could feel the heat of fever.

I dressed quickly, straightened my room, and when seven o'clock came I knocked softly on Mrs. Canfield's door.

She answered immediately, and I found her sitting up in bed, looking alert and calm, although I was sure I had awakened her.

"It's Jane, Mrs. Canfield. I think she is quite ill."

"Ill! But she seemed perfectly all right last night!"

"I know. I'll tell you all about it in just a moment, but I'm going to call Adam and I didn't want you to be alarmed when he arrived."

"Very well, child. Go and call him. I'll dress."

I had never telephoned Adam. I had to look his number up in the directory.

"Adam, it's Louisa," I said. "Jane is sick. She is feverish, and her breathing isn't right. She was outdoors last night, Adam, in the rain. I don't know how long. She didn't stop shivering for hours."

"Outside! What on earth for?"

"She thought she heard Emily—oh, Adam, that part doesn't matter right now! Please come. I'm worried about her."

"I'm on my way."

I went back to Mrs. Canfield's room. She was dressed, and as I sat there on the side of her bed she brushed out her long dark, silky hair, and I watched her rebraid it, her hands adept through long habit. I told her about the night before as simply as I could.

"I see," she said, tucking the last tortoise-shell hairpin into place. "I heard Katie go downstairs a few minutes ago. Have your breakfast, Louisa. I'll sit in Jane's room until Adam comes."

"I can eat later, Mrs. Canfield. In any case she is sound asleep."

"You've been up half the night, child. Go and have something to eat. It will do you good."

It seemed pointless to argue. As I started down the stairs I saw Mrs. Canfield go quietly into Jane's room. In the kitchen Katie eyed me curiously when I entered.

"Up early this morning, aren't you, Miss Louisa?"

"Jane's not well. I've called Dr. Adam."

"So it's Jane! I knew it was something. Poor lamb! She sick to her stomach?"

"No, she has a fever, I think."

"Kind of sudden-like, wasn't it?"

"Yes, I guess it was. Don't bother setting a place for me in the dining room, Katie. I'll just have some orange juice and coffee here."

"Strange she got sick so fast."

"Well, she . . . she seems to have gotten a chill last night. The weather was colder, you know, with the rain."

"Never knew a child yet who got a chill from being safe asleep in her bed all night." I didn't answer, and after a moment Katie went on. "Miss Louisa, when I came down this morning there was a cup and saucer rinsed out clean as you please setting beside my sink. It didn't get there by itself."

"No. I left it there."

"And the light was on in the downstairs hall."

"Oh. I guess I left it on. I'm sorry."

"And my sink cloth was damp and there were still a few wet smears on my kitchen floor. My sink cloth is always dry by morning. If it ain't used in the night, that is."

"I . . . I used that, too, Katie."

"Had a busy night, didn't you, Miss Louisa?" She set orange juice in front of me, broke an egg neatly into hot butter in a skillet, and poured steaming coffee into a cup. "If it's none of my business just say so, but it seems pretty plain something was going on here last night."

"Yes, something was, I guess. But I don't know exactly what."

She basted the golden egg yolk with the hot butter. "I could make a guess," she said. "'Twas Miss Emily again, wasn't it?"

I looked up at her quickly. "What makes you say that, Katie?"

She flipped the egg expertly onto a plate, added a slice of toast, and placed it on the table. "I told you once before,

Miss Louisa. There ain't much goes on in this house I don't know about, nor ever has been. I know it's wrong to speak ill of the dead, but there's trouble in this house—I can feel it. Don't ever forget I *knew* Miss Emily. I know what she could do, and what she *would* do. There was real evil in her sometimes. I don't know just what she's up to now, but there's something. If you want me, you call me. Good is still stronger than evil, and I'm a good woman, Miss Louisa, if I do say it as shouldn't. I have no fear of the likes of Emily— alive *or* dead."

"Thank you, Katie," I said. "I won't forget."

And then the doorbell rang, and Adam was there.

FIFTEEN

That Saturday seemed to go on forever. Adam stayed for perhaps an hour, his face grim, his mind entirely on Jane. We might have been nothing to each other for all the notice he took of me, and in a way I was glad.

He called for an extra pillow so that Jane could be raised slightly to ease the effort of breathing. He called for alcohol, with which we bathed her, for cool cloths for her burning forehead, and for cracked ice to moisten her mouth. He slipped spoonfuls of medicine between her lips, and wiped away the drops that spilled out. Katie and I ran his errands. Mrs. Canfield did not move from the side of the bed.

Once she looked up at Adam, her face very pale. "It is pneumonia, isn't it?" she asked.

"Yes."

"And there is not a great deal you can do, is there?"

"You mustn't worry, Mrs. Canfield."

"I asked you a question, Adam. There really is not very much you can do for her, is there?"

"No. Only care for her, make her comfortable as we can, and watch her."

The morning was still early, although it seemed as though it must be almost noontime, when Adam took my hand and led me into the hall.

"Louisa, I must get over to the hospital, but I'll be back by early afternoon. Nothing is going to happen for a while. Pneumonia follows a pattern up to a certain point. Jane won't reach that point for a while yet."

"When will she?"

"Not for four or five days, probably."

"But she's so sick! How can she go on—"

He put his arm around me, but said nothing. I walked down the stairs with him to the front door. He shouldered into his raincoat and picked up his hat as I opened the door. The rain fell heavily, cold and straight. I shivered just looking at it.

"Adam," I said, leaning my head against his arm, the rubbery smell of the raincoat in my nostrils. "Adam, Jane only had a little cold last night—how has this happened to her? Is it—can it be—Emily?"

He put his hands on my shoulders and moved me a little away from him so he could see my face. "Louisa, the child was outdoors for heaven knows how long in the pouring rain. She already had a cold, and then she got chilled through and soaked. This is precisely how pneumonia starts. Don't imagine anything else."

"But *why* did she go out?"

"She told you. She dreamed. Louisa, forget *why* she went. We have other things to think about now." He kissed me hard. "If you need me I'll be at the hospital."

I watched him go, getting into his car quickly after the crank spun the engine into life. The water splashed up around the wooden spokes of the wheels as he turned into the street.

Neither Mrs. Canfield nor I had any appetite for lunch when the time came, but Katie insisted that we eat, so first one of us and then the other left Jane's room and went downstairs. While I sat beside Jane, doing the small things Adam had showed us how to do to make her as comfortable as possible, she opened her eyes and looked straight at me. I leaned closer to her.

"Jane? How do you feel, darling?"

"It hurts to breathe."

"I know. Lie very still. It will be better soon."

"Louisa?"

"Yes, dear?"

"What's the matter with me?"

"You got a bad chill last night in the rain."

"Like Emily?"

"How do you know Emily got a chill?"

"I don't know. But when I was asleep just now—then I knew."

"You mean you dreamed again?"

"I guess so. Emily keeps talking to me. I wish she'd stop. Emily . . . didn't get well from her chill, did she, Louisa?"

"Jane, you mustn't talk so much. You must rest, darling, and be very quiet. You're going to be perfectly all right. Please, Jane, don't talk anymore."

Her eyes searched mine, and I forced myself to smile at her. I dared not let any trace of my own deep fear show lest she see it. After a moment she turned her head away slowly and her eyes closed and she slept again.

When Adam had said Jane's condition would not change very much for either better or worse for several days it seemed impossible. She was so very ill! But he was quite right. The dreadful fever continued, making the child's skin so hot that it seemed to burn my hand. She was restless and wakeful, exhausted by the dry, hacking cough and the fever. Breathing was painful, and the strange rhythm of it was terrible to hear. And there was so little any of us could do! The useless medicine, the cracked ice, the sponge baths,

Vaseline for her lips, the attempts to keep her quiet, to feed her unwanted spoonfuls of custard, or tiny sips of water or lemonade. We changed her sheets, we fanned her, we read to her. One of us, either Katie or Mrs. Canfield or I, was with her every minute, and Adam was there, and gone, and there again. I lost track of time and even of days.

The rain stopped after a nameless while, but the weather stayed cold and gray and raw. There was no wind, the air lay still and damp, and the sky lowered. The house felt cold, and everything was too quiet.

I watched Lydia Canfield with amazement through those days. Head high, always perfectly groomed, one might have thought her untouched by Jane's illness. But I knew now that her constant control was something into which she had been forced years ago, and that as long as she needed it, it would not desert her. I longed for her courage, but it was far, far beyond me. All too often, during the brief hours when I tried to sleep, I would press my face into the pillow so that Jane would not hear my weeping. Adam was my rock. Without him I could not have managed. But Lydia Canfield had no one.

Then one morning when I was sitting with Jane she woke from a brief nap and tried to speak. The words were almost unintelligible, and all I could understand was "Emily" repeated over and over.

"What is it, darling?" I leaned close to her. "Please, can't you tell me?"

But her eyes were glassy and staring and I knew suddenly that she was delirious. In her rough, gasping, croaking voice she kept muttering, and I could feel the chills start at the back of my neck. "Emily," she kept saying, and sometimes, "Please—no! Please, Emily—no!" And for the rest of that day she drifted in and out of the frightening delirium, and in and out of restless sleep, and when Adam came that evening he did not leave again.

"She'll reach a crisis tonight, I think," he said. "I want to be here."

"But you can't tell which way things will go?"

"She is very sick, Louisa."

And the dark came down, and the night began, and with it came the rain.

I tried to induce Mrs. Canfield to rest, but she refused. "We can't rest now, child. Not now."

And so we sat on either side of Jane's bed, Lydia Canfield and I. Adam came and went, doing what he could, sometimes going into the corridor and pacing up and down, his unlighted pipe clamped between his teeth. Katie carried her rocking chair up to my room and placed it just by the connecting door, and there she sat and rocked. Her hands were folded tight, and I knew she prayed.

The little parlor clock chimed the hours, and the night grew deeper, and then suddenly, from somewhere, vicious gusts of wind rose and the rain lashed in frenzy against the house. Katie jumped from her chair and I could hear windows slamming shut in my room before she came into Jane's.

It was almost as though that wind had been a signal. Jane's whole body stiffened and her thin hands caught firmly onto the light blanket. Her head turned violently back and forth against the pillow, her breathing was so rapid, so harsh, that it was agony to hear. Adam was beside the bed.

"Jane," he said. "Jane! Don't fight. Don't struggle, Jane. Try to breathe slower!"

But he might as well have spoken to the beating wind. Jane's eyes did not see him, she did not hear him. She clutched the edges of the bed, the sheet, the blanket, until the flesh across her straining knuckles was white. And then, almost as though her hands were being torn free, the fingers loosened bit by bit, until they slipped from their hold. I sighed with relief as I saw the child relax a little. Then she stiffened again, and again the weak hands fought for a firm grasp on the bed.

"She's trying not to let go," I breathed. "Oh, help her, Adam, help her!"

He took Jane's hands in his, almost prying the fingers away from their clutch at the bed. "I'm here, Jane. I'm here. Hold on tight. I won't let you go."

Lydia Canfield rose from her chair and stood straight and strong at the foot of the bed, gripping the brass rail. Her eyes seemed to bore into Jane as she watched the frail body shudder with each labored breath, watched those hands that tried to hold so tightly to Adam's, and yet—as if against their will—pulled slowly, slowly away.

And suddenly, across the sound of the rain, and the wind, and the terrible sound of Jane's breathing, Mrs. Canfield's voice cut through the room.

"No!" she said. "No!" And then with all the force she could summon, "No, Emily! *I will not allow it!*"

There was an instant in that room that I will never forget. An instant of such tension, such will, such unseen battle, that I was paralyzed by the pressure of it. I wanted to move, to scream, to do something that would break that silent struggle for dominance, but I couldn't.

Mrs. Canfield stood there, her gaze fastened on Jane's face. Suddenly great tears spilled from her eyes, and I could see her sag.

"Not Jane," she said, and her voice was a whispered plea. "Please, Emily, not Jane!" And immediately, as if regretting the moment's weakness, her back stiffened, and in spite of her tears the words came full and strong. "No, Emily! *You will not have Jane too!*"

With a clatter that brought a scream from my dry throat the shade on one of the windows snapped to the top. Katie, standing beside it, jumped back.

"Holy Mother of God!" she breathed.

Mrs. Canfield whirled around, and with a few quick steps she was across the room and staring from the window. Not knowing how I moved, I followed her. Below us, in the midnight of the garden, through the whipped black satin of the rain, the reflecting ball glowed with a white, triumphant brilliance.

When Mrs. Canfield ran from the room I was too stunned to follow her. Then I heard Katie calling as she ran down the corridor.

"Mrs. Canfield! Ma'am, don't go out there! Don't go! I'll do it—please let me do it! Please, ma'am, you mustn't! You don't know what she'll do!"

It made no sense. I wrapped my arms tight around myself to stop the shivering, my eyes fastened on that shining ball.

I heard the back door slam open, and then in the stream of light from the kitchen I saw Mrs. Canfield's slim black figure, buffeted by the wind, pushing across the drenched grass to that sourceless, evil light. For one split second she paused. Then she laid her hands on either side of the ball and I could see them silhouetted against the glow. Her body thrust forward, she strained to dislodge it. All time stopped. Then slowly, reluctantly, the ball rolled from its white pedestal and I could hear the crash as it shattered into a million colorless fragments on the flat stones. Behind me, from the bed, Jane screamed.

The child lay unmoving, but now her eyes were open. They stared toward the window, and yet they did not seem to see. Adam leaned over her, his fingers on her wrist.

In the garden Katie had her arms around Mrs. Canfield, and together, walking slowly in the rain, they moved toward the kitchen door. As though its purpose were ended, the wind fell to a whisper and ceased.

I went to the bed, and Jane's eyes looked straight at me.

Already the welcome gleam of sweat showed on her face, and her breathing came more easily.

"Hello, Louisa," she said.

The tears welled into my eyes so that I could barely see her as I knelt at the side of the bed. "Hello, darling."

"I'm tired, Louisa."

"I know, dear. Just rest. Just be very still and rest."

"Where is Grandmother?"

"She . . . she will be here in a minute, I think. Don't try to talk, Jane. Just rest."

"I want to see Grandmother."

And then Mrs. Canfield stood in the doorway, Katie's strong arms still around her, and the woman who had always looked so straight and sure rested against her maid like an exhausted child.

"Jane?" she said softly.

The little girl's head turned toward the voice. "Grandmother?" She looked at the woman with quiet interest. "You're all wet, Grandmother."

"I expect I am."

"Grandmother—"

"Yes, Jane?"

"It's all over now, isn't it?"

"Is it, dear? Oh, Jane, is it?"

"Yes. What did you do?"

"It doesn't matter. Sleep now."

"She wanted me."

"Yes. I know."

"I could feel her. I don't feel her anymore. How did you stop her?"

"I was her mother, Jane. I . . . I simply refused."

Adam put his hand on Jane's forehead, smoothing back the dampening hair. "Jane. I want you to rest now. You are not to talk anymore."

"There's just one thing, Dr. Adam. I have to know just one thing."

"What, Jane?"

She turned her eyes back to her grandmother. "It was the silvery ball, wasn't it?"

"Yes, dear."

"You broke it?"

"Yes."

"I thought so. I could feel it." Jane sighed deeply, a sigh of exhaustion, of relaxation, of relief. "I'm awfully sleepy," she said. She yawned mightily and her eyelids drooped as she looked at Lydia Canfield. "I'm sorry *you* had to do it, Grandmother. But I'm glad it's done."

Mrs. Canfield slipped free from Katie's arms and came to the bed. Holding her wet skirts back, she bent and kissed Jane on the forehead.

"Sleep now, Jane. Sleep well. God bless you."

Turning comfortably in the bed, the child curled into a ball, and as we watched she fell sound asleep.

SIXTEEN

After that dark, rain-drenched night I never heard Jane mention Emily again. If she thought of her, she gave no sign. She was well enough to be out of bed in a week, and by the time we were expected back in Milford, just before Labor Day, she was rosy and bright and healthy and ready for school.

The leave-taking from Mrs. Canfield and Katie was not as wistful as I had feared it might be. Plans were made for visiting back and forth at Thanksgiving and at Christmas, for now that Adam would be driving to Milford to see me he had offered to bring Mrs. Canfield with him on occasion. In addition it was agreed that I would come to Lynn from time to time in the fall, bringing Jane with me and staying at Mrs. Canfield's.

One morning shortly before Jane and I left Lynn I awoke to a busy thumping and bumping in the hall, and the brisk voices of Mrs. Canfield and Katie. When I went down to breakfast it was to find the front porch stacked with boxes, bags, and parcels.

"What in the world is going on?" I asked Mrs. Canfield.

"I decided it would be wise to clean out the attic. Good gracious, there are things up there, gathering dust, that I shall never want again. It seemed ridiculous to keep them when someone else might get some use from them. A charity truck is picking them up this morning."

"You mean you're throwing everything out? Those lovely dresses? And all the toys and books and things?"

"Those dresses are quite out of date, Louisa, and I really have no use for them. I had thought I might have the dressmaker in, however, for a few new ones. Something suitable, but perhaps not black."

"Good! It's high time you did! But the toys?"

"I shall keep some of them. Grandmothers' attics should always have a certain number of discarded playthings in them, but certainly not all the dull and dusty articles that were upstairs. Katie and I are trying to clear out the . . . cobwebs."

They did, too. Windows were opened wide to the last warm days of summer; the house seemed to lift its head, to come out of its dreams, to breathe deeply of fresh, clear air.

Just before we left I found a snapshot of Jane that Adam had taken earlier in the summer. It showed her in the garden, standing in front of the reflecting ball, her head tipped back and laughter on her face. Carefully, with my manicure scissors, I cut the face out in a little oval so that none of the reflecting ball showed. I took it to Mrs. Canfield.

"I thought you might like to have this," I said. "I'm sorry to have cut it, but—well, I didn't like the background."

She took it lovingly, her eyes caressing the pictured face. "Thank you, Louisa. I'm glad you cut it like this. It should fit almost exactly into my black locket."

Our eyes met, and she smiled. Quickly, feeling strangely close to tears, I put my arms around the awesome Mrs. Canfield and held her close. I didn't trust myself to speak at all.

*   *   *

As for Emily, that strange, dark spirit, perhaps she rests
now. I hope so. Perhaps she can be remembered as a troubled little girl who needed an authority and a discipline she
never got, a clever, intelligent little girl who died before she
had learned how to live. Again, I hope so. But I know there
will be sudden moments when any one of a hundred things
will make me remember that summer in Lynn. The sight of
a reflecting ball on someone's lawn; rows of bright-faced
pansies in a garden border; clothes hung out to dry and tor-
tured by the wind; a handwriting that is small and elegant
and spidery; heavy, driving summer rain, chilling the air
and enclosing fear and panic within four walls—so many
things!

Adam says in time we will all forget. But I do not think
he really believes that himself. We will wonder always. None
of it could have happened. And yet it did.

Or did it?

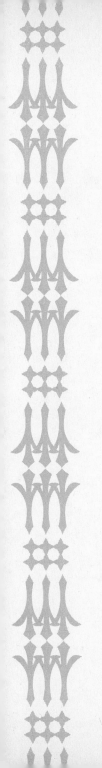

Witches' Children

For my husband, Edward,
and for our special ten—
Stacey, Julie, Andrew, Matt, and Amy,
Wendy, Jonathan, and Liza,
David and Jennifer—
with love.

ONE

1 was a little older than most of them, old enough, as John Proctor said, "to have a little sense in your head!" If I was not strong enough to resist the madness, how could children as young as Betty Parris and her cousin, Abigail Williams, withstand it? Surely they were helpless. Betty was but nine and Abigail eleven. Or were they helpless? Were any of us? Did we in fact make it happen?

It all began so quietly! I remember an ice-covered January afternoon when I opened the door to the kitchen of the Parris house to find Betty curled on one of the settles, moping with some minor ailment. Abigail sat erect, ankles properly crossed, on the facing settle, and Tituba was on a stool between them.

Tituba! A slender woman, soft-voiced, dark-eyed—eyes so dark in her pale brown face that they sometimes glowed like coals. The Reverend Samuel Parris had brought Tituba and her husband, John Indian, back with him from Barbados five or six years before. Tituba, always quiet and gentle, cherished and coddled Betty Parris far more than her parents ever did. The people of Massachusetts Bay Colony believed that life was a stern, demanding experience, and that children must be made strong enough to endure it. Coddling was not their way.

Tituba. What did she see in her cards? What did she see in the palms of our hands? Did she, in truth, know spells and magic learned in that mysterious distant island of Barbados? Looking back, it seems she was but the spark that lit the willing tinder of our stifled, repressed young minds. Who will ever be sure? It may be that if I put some of these thoughts on paper it will all come clearer to me. Perhaps I can find some sort of answer for myself, for God knows that if I cannot find such an answer I shall end my days in helpless agony!

Back to the beginning then, that January of 1692, when Salem Village lay quiet beneath banked snow. I have never lived anywhere but Salem, so I know little of how life may be in other New England towns. A man named Roger Conant first settled here many years ago in 1626, calling the place by an Indian name, Naumkeag, and planning to make a thriving fishing village of it. Some few years later it served as the start of the Massachusetts Bay Colony when one John Winthrop arrived from England with a charter for land and a little group of people in search of religious freedom. It became Salem then, and its new inhabitants turned to farming and the enjoyment of that freedom they had sought, though how they could speak of "freedom" or "enjoyment" it is hard for me to understand, since there seemed little of either in the strictures the elders believed in and enforced. Perhaps it was irksome only to the young, with their natural high spirits, which we were told to spend on productive tasks for the good of the community.

I always tried to be obedient, but that year it seemed that winter had lasted for an eternity. There was not even the excitement and sociability of such gatherings as husking bees or house raisings with the ground hard frozen, and in Salem there were no Christmas festivities such as there were in Plymouth and its neighboring settlements. Men found indoor chores to do, carpentering and repairing and the like, but for females the work continued on its unchanging, grinding daily round with only church services to break the pattern. 'Tis said the Devil finds work for idle hands, but I believe he finds it for idle minds as well, for though my hands were rarely idle, my mind was often dulled and empty of stimulation.

My name is Mary Warren, and I was a bound girl to John and Elizabeth Proctor, who had taken me in some years before when my parents died from the smallpox that had come again to scourge Salem Village. It was not easy to be bound out. Such a girl had little to call her own. Even a daughter living with her family had scant position unless she had been spoken for by some man, and marriage was considered a most solemn bond, not to be entered into until a lass reached twenty years or more. Then, too, a girl might think twice did she note the lives of married women who spent their days in household toil and their years in childbearing. Most likely, however, I would have settled for that had someone set his eyes favorably upon me, but there were at that time in Salem Village a great number of young girls and far too few young men to wed them. In any case, there I was with the Proctors, and I knew I should be grateful to them. I had a small room of my own, food to eat, sufficient modest clothing so I was always neat, and work enough to keep me busy from sunup to bedtime. But gratitude was not precisely what I felt.

John Proctor was a tall, strong, quiet man, for whom I had nothing but adoration. His wife, the gentle Elizabeth, was too sweet for my taste. I much preferred her husband's gruff commands to her soft requests. In my eyes John Proctor could do no wrong, and I worshiped him, blindly and secretly. The only other man I had known closely was my father, a stern, God-fearing soul who would have preferred several sturdy sons to one daughter. For Father the word *duty* replaced the word *love*. Now, in this somewhat warmer household, I found my healthy, eager, developing body responding to John Proctor's maleness. If he touched my shoulder in passing I thrilled. Whatever words he spoke to me I cherished, trying to believe they held more than the plain facts they stated. When he was within the house I pinched my cheeks often to bring color to my pale skin, and I brushed a damp finger upward on my lashes so they might better frame my eyes, always hoping he might notice the small green flecks deep in the brown. I would bite my lips to redden them and tighten the apron strings round my small waist until I nigh gasped. Ah, 'twas all vanity, and well I knew it even then, but young females are more given to feelings than to reason. In truth, I also knew that John Proctor saw naught that I wanted him to see. I was only Mary Warren, his bound girl.

It was Mistress Proctor, that bitter January afternoon, who asked me to carry a sack of potatoes to Reverend Parris's house, since it was custom for members of a congregation to augment a preacher's modest wage with foodstuffs and fuel for his fire. "And be sure to ask how Mistress Parris does, Mary, and say that I am deep concerned about her cough. And you may spend a short while with the girls, if you choose, but I shall need you home before sunset."

"Yes, ma'am," I said. Wrapped head to toe in every warm garment I possessed, I slipped and slid over the iced snow, teeth chattering, clutching the heavy sack of potatoes, to the neat small house where Samuel Parris lived with his wife, Elizabeth, his wife's niece, Abigail Williams, his daughter, Betty, and his slaves, Tituba and John Indian.

The door opened on warmth from the flames that frolicked in the great fireplace, silhouetting Tituba and the two girls. They turned to greet me as I entered.

"Potatoes," I said breathlessly, setting the heavy sack on the floor. I looked at the younger girl, huddled into a small quiet heap on the settle, her eyes wide as she gazed into the fire. "Is Betty ailing?" I asked.

"My Betty got herself a small 'gestion in her chest," Tituba said, smiling. "She be all right soon."

"Betty just likes to lie about and have Tituba fuss over her!" Abigail said in a high-pitched, fretful voice. "And surely there is naught else for any of us to do."

"There be aplenty to do," Tituba corrected. "That chicken to pluck so it can go in the pot with the carrots, and the potatoes Mary brought—"

"Oh, stuff!" Abigail thumped a small fist on the arm of the settle. "I have no love for plucking feathers off chickens! Come and sit down, Mary. Is it very cold outdoors?"

"'Tis frigid cold!" I unwound my several shawls and cloak and hung them on a wall peg, then sat down beside Abby, holding out my hands to the fire to warm them. "My fingers and toes seem made of ice!"

Tituba leaned down and slipped my shoes off, rubbing my woolen-stockinged feet in her slender hands.

"The fire soon warm you through," she said. "Betty, child, you want a drink of Tituba's herb tea? It help you feel better."

With a little sigh, Betty spoke. "No more tea, Tituba. I am full of tea!" Turning her dark eyes from the fire, she looked lovingly at Tituba. "But read my palm for me! Tell me what exciting things are going to happen to me!"

Tituba laughed softly. "Exciting things!" she echoed. "My Betty too young for excitements."

"She'll be an old, old woman before there is any excitement around here," Abigail said fretfully. "We all will! I don't think there has been a drop of excitement in Salem Village since it was settled!" She uncrossed her ankles and swung her legs vigorously. "There are times when I feel like that jug of cider Uncle Samuel had that blew the bung from its neck and splashed the rafters!"

I laughed at Abigail's scowling face. "And what sort of excitement would you have?" I asked.

"How can I know? I have never known any! Oh, Tituba, read Betty's hand! Mayhap you will see something to lighten this long horrid winter!"

"Yes, Tituba! Read my hand!" Betty coaxed. Sitting straighter on the settle, she thrust out her small palm toward Tituba. Resignedly, the woman took it gently in her own and began tracing its lines with her brown finger.

"Such a little hand," she said softly. "Too small to hold much things. I see one tall man, handsome in his face. He come a-riding up to this door and ask for little Betty Parris to be his wife."

Betty gazed down at her hand with interest. "Do you truly see that, Tituba? And is he very handsome?"

"Oh, very!" Tituba said solemnly.

"Oh, Betty," Abigail sighed. "You are such a baby! What do you care about handsome men? Tell *my* hand, Tituba, and tell me something *real*!" She held out her hand. "Tell me, Tituba!"

"You think Tituba have nothing more to do than play games with little girls," the woman murmured, taking Abby's hand. She stared at Abigail's palm, smoothing the fingers with her own, and I saw her dark eyes widen. Then she curled the fingers inward, forming a small closed fist. "Tituba see nothing," she said, and started to rise.

"If you can see things in Betty's hand, then you can see them in mine," Abby insisted. "Now, tell me! You *must* tell me!"

"Tituba don't *must* do anything, Abigail. You be but children. You best forget these nonsense things."

"There has to be something in my hand, and I want to

know what it is! Do please tell me, Tituba—here!" Again Abby held out her open hand.

Taking it reluctantly, Tituba rocked gently back and forth on her stool, her eyes intent. When she spoke her voice was low, and we had to strain to hear the words.

"I see trouble," she said. "I see big trouble, and there is you, Abigail, a-kicking up your heels, right in the middle of it."

Abigail wriggled forward on the settle, her narrow eyes shining. "What kind of trouble, Tituba?"

"I told you. Big trouble. Big black trouble."

"But what *kind*?"

"A bad kind."

"And why am I kicking up my heels?"

"Child, I only tells you what I see. I no can tell you *why*."

Removing her hand from Tituba's, Abby looked at it closely. "I don't see anything," she said. "I warrant you make it all up."

"Then don't ask me what I see," Tituba said calmly. Rising from the stool, she went to the wide, scrubbed wooden table in the center of the keeping room, picked up a knife, and started scraping carrots.

"Did you really see trouble in my hand?" Abby asked. Tituba did not answer, and the girl went on. "That would be exciting, and if you saw me kicking up my heels then I must like it—whatever it is, must I not?" Still Tituba said nothing. "Oh, Mary, would you not like Tituba to read your palm, too?"

I should very much have liked to hear what Tituba might see in my hand, but when I looked at the woman she seemed to have no interest in me. She cut the scraped carrot neatly into thirds and dropped it into an iron pot.

"Some other day, Abby, when Tituba is less busy, perhaps."

"Tituba can tell fortunes with cards, too, Mary. She can do all sorts of magic when she wants to, can't you, Tituba?"

The knife sliced into another carrot. "That for me to know," Tituba said. "Little girls like you have no need to know such things."

Abby's eyes were bright. "Tituba can put herself into a trance, Mary," she said. "Betty can do it, too, but I can't. But Tituba will teach me, won't you, Tituba?"

"No," said Tituba flatly.

"But if Betty can do it—"

"My baby be a peaceful child. If she trance herself it just be a deeper peace. But you—you is a different kind altogether!"

"What kind am I, Tituba? Tell me!"

"Don't bother me now. There be work to do. Can't trance myself out of work!"

Tituba seemed to have withdrawn from us. I hesitated, but then asked my question anyway. "Where did you learn to—to trance yourself, Tituba?"

Another carrot was sliced into the pot before she spoke. "In Barbados," she said then. "That where I learned many things."

"What sort of things?"

"Things white people don't know."

Betty leaned forward, her hands clasped together. "Tell us," she pleaded.

Tituba let the knife cease its work and stood straight, looking over our heads into some far distant place.

"I learn things that make life be better," she said softly. "Make you warm if you is cold. Make you feel you is somewhere else if you don't fancy the place you is in. Make you feel strong inside of you, even when you is weak. In Barbados all my people know such things. Some know more than others. My grandmam taught me much. . . ."

She stood quietly for a moment, and then with a quick

sigh sliced the last carrot into the heavy pot. Lifting it, she moved to the fireplace and hung it on one of the iron hooks. With her back to us she stood gazing into the flames before she spoke again. "But we not in Barbados now. Things here be very different. This Salem Village no understand how it is where John and I come from. Best you girls no think about such things. Nor you, my baby, Betty. Best you don't."

"But we *do* think about them," Abigail said with quiet satisfaction, "and you know we do, Tituba. Sometime you will teach us more of the—the 'things' you know! Sometime you will."

There came a tapping sound from the floor above and Tituba turned quickly away from the fire and started to the door that led to the hallway of the house and the steep stairs that went up from it.

"There be the mistress, a-tapping with her stick to call me," she said as she left us.

We could hear her quick steps as she mounted the stairs. I leaned toward the two younger girls.

"Can Tituba in truth do magic?" I asked.

"Of course," said Betty calmly.

"But how do you know? What have you seen her do?"

"I have seen her trance herself. And now I can do it, too."

"But I don't know what you mean," I said. "What is it, to trance yourself? What happens?"

"I don't know exactly, Mary," Betty said vaguely. "I just— oh, sometimes I sit and stare at the fire, or sometimes I stare into water—you know how quiet water is? In a bowl, or in some little pond? I look at it for a long time and then I—I go away, inside myself. It is beautiful, where I go, a place all filled with light. Heaven, it might be. It is—it is . . . well, then, it is *not* as it is here! Not cold! Just—beautiful!"

Abigail gave a little flounce of impatience. "Beautiful!" she repeated. "So it may be, but you do appear a ninny when you sit with your eyes fair pinned to the fire, taking no notice of anyone around you!"

"Then why do you want Tituba to teach you how to do it?" Betty asked.

"Oh, stuff!" Abigail got up quickly from the settle and moved restlessly about the keeping room, her long skirt over her woolen petticoats twitching as she walked. "Every day is like the day before! The same chores, the same food, the same people! If I could trance myself I would go to someplace exciting! Not just beautiful, like where Betty says she goes, but someplace where things would happen to me!"

Betty's brow wrinkled. "What sort of things, Abby? What do you wish would happen to you?"

Abby picked up a sliver of carrot from the table and crunched it between her white little teeth.

"Oh, who can say, Betty? But you know how sometimes in church meeting Uncle Samuel talks about the Devil and his works and how he lures people to do his bidding? And about the flames in Hell? And all the torments of the damned? That is what I like to listen to! *That* is exciting!"

Betty gasped. "Oh, Abby! Father just tells us such things to warn us. He does not want us to sin, for then we could not go to Heaven!"

Abigail lifted the paring knife from the table and flipped it so that it landed point down in the wood, the handle quivering.

"I think Heaven must be just like Salem Village," she said. "Everyone so good, and so pure. I become very weary of all the *Thou shalts* and *Thou shalt nots*! Someday I am going to do something shocking!"

I was amused. "What shocking thing will you do, Abby?"

"Oh, like—like—like screaming right out loud in Sabbath meeting! Just as loud as I can!"

I laughed, but poor little Betty looked distressed. "Abby! You wouldn't!"

Abigail's chin rose stubbornly. "Be not too sure, Betty Parris. For I feel at times that unless I do *something* shocking, I may blow like the cider jug and splash the whole village!"

Looking at her glittering eyes and her flushed face, I felt a certain sympathy for her. There were many times when I, too, secretly rebelled against the rigid behavior imposed on us.

I tried to sound more grown-up than I felt. "'Twill be better when you are older, Abby," I said. "I recall when I was your age, feeling that I would burst could I not shout, or run, or let my hair fly loose in the wind—but 'twill be easier soon. You will grow out of it."

Abigail eyed me closely, doubt written clear on her face. "Have *you*?" she asked.

I could not meet her gaze. I rose from my seat and moved to where my cloak and shawls hung. With my back to her I spoke calmly.

"Of course," I said. And knew I lied.

TWO

'Twas not easy to be bound out, to be little more than a servant to people who were not your own. John Proctor was tall and straight and ruggedly handsome. He owned a tavern on the Ipswich Road, hiring others to run it for him, since he preferred to spend as much time as possible at the farm called Groton, with its seven hundred demanding acres of fertile land. Elizabeth Proctor lived here with the five children (and now a new baby was on the way), and here I, too, spent most of my time, helping in the tavern only on rare occasions.

Writing now of what took place in that bewitched time, I must leave nothing out. I must confess what I would not have admitted then to a living soul. My love! My love for John. Always to myself I called him "John," though aloud I was ever careful to say "Master Proctor." It was a love made of dreams. Dreams of his touch, dreams of his knowing someday what I felt for him, dreams of speaking openly— but none of that was possible. Instead I did all that I could to please him. No stint at the spinning wheel was too long, no amount of scrubbing and cleaning was too tiring, no amount of hours spent by the hot fire, cooking dishes I thought he might savor, was regretted if he gave some small sign of satisfaction with my work. And sometimes he did, though he was never one to praise.

Elizabeth Proctor was a kind enough mistress, though her pregnancies were hard on her, causing her to be fussy and complaining till at times I wanted to slap her. And that, of course, was a childish desire that showed I was not as mature as I had wanted Abby to believe, or even to believe myself.

As I hurried home that January afternoon I thought of Tituba and the things she claimed she knew. I wished I had asked her to tell my fortune from my hand. Could it ever include John? The very possibility made me shiver and I swore I would have my palm read the next time I was with Tituba. John and me! Elizabeth gone somewhere, any-where—I truly did not anticipate *how* she would be gone. Just John and me together! To be close to him, to touch him—even the thought made me weak. I quickened my steps to reach home the sooner, and at a turn in the road nigh knocked over old Goody Good and little Dorcas, her daughter.

The old woman, who could not, I know, have been near as old as she seemed, peered at me through folds of filthy shawls and wisps of straggling hair, her reeking pipe clenched between her few remaining yellowed teeth.

"In a great hurry, ain't we, girl!" Her voice grated on me with its high pitch. "Cannot wait to get back to your hand-some master, eh?"

I tried to be calm. "'Tis frigid cold, Mistress Good. I have no desire to linger on the way."

"Very wise. John Proctor is not above taking the whip-ping stick to his jade, do he think it needed."

The idea made the blood rush to my face, and I knew the old crone saw it.

"Master Proctor does not believe in whipping," I said, trying to keep my voice steady.

"The more fool he, then. Dorcas and I will stop by later, I fancy. If *Master* Proctor is so kind he might find some scraps of food for us. The belly itself gets cold with nothing to warm it."

Though it would have been only Christian to feel sorry for her, I could not. I knew her husband was a lazy man who worked a bit from time to time if anyone would hire him, spending the few pence he made on drink, so that Goody Good was forced to beg for whatever she would have. Yet, even knowing this, I still wanted to back away from her, away from the stench of unwashed flesh and garments and hair, away from the horrible smell of her pipe. Heaven knew what she had been smoking in it! The child, Dorcas, no more than four years old, clutched her mother's skirt with a dirty, reddened hand, and stared at me with dark solemn eyes. Shifting as if to leave them, I pulled my cloak closer about me.

"I am sure Master Proctor will find something for you," I said, and hurried away.

Behind me I heard the old woman's cackling laugh. "Think you know him pretty well, don't 'e? He's a hard man, is John Proctor, but we'll see. We'll see."

"Old witch," I muttered to myself, and made my way back to Groton as swiftly as I could.

During the next day or so I thought often of the strange conversation that had taken place at the Parris house. Searching for an excuse to return, I bethought me of a piece of needlework I had started.

"'Tis a new stitch Abby Williams showed me," I told Mistress Proctor, "but I must not have watched her carefully. If I might ask her again—"

She gave permission, and I left the house as quickly as I

could, heading straight for the Parris keeping room. I can
still see that room so clearly. It was not unlike many others
in the houses of Salem Village. They were all warm, and
sometimes in the summer overly so, since the cooking fires
still needed to burn bright. They all had wood piled to feed
the hungry blaze; pails of water, carefully covered to keep
insects from falling into them; scoured tables and long comfortable settles and small stools. All had fragrant bunches
of herbs hanging from the raftered ceilings, drying, waiting
to be dropped by the sprig into a boiling soup kettle, or
pounded into powder and stored in heavy crocks to be used
later in food or as medications. Perhaps one difference lay
in the herbs themselves, for there were unfamiliar ones in
the Parris kitchen that Tituba claimed to have brought with
her from that far, mysterious Barbados. Though they looked
as dry and gray-brown as all the others, they seemed to
send a more exotic scent into the room, as strange and exciting as the island they came from.

I smelled them now as I opened the door, then instantly
forgot them in astonishment at the number of people in the
room. Betty Parris, Abby Williams, and Tituba, of course.
But there was Mary Walcott with her knitting, which she
scarce needed to watch, so skillful were her fingers. Mary
was seventeen, and lived with her aunt, Mistress Mary
Sibley. Elizabeth Booth and Susanna Sheldon sat near the
fire. Elizabeth was sixteen then, and Susanna two years
older, and both were bound girls as I was. I saw twelve-
year-old Anne Putnum, a thin, tense child with enormous
pale eyes, and Mercy Lewis, a rosy, happy girl who was
bound to the Putnums.

Tituba was the center of attention. She sat, back erect,
her white-turbaned head bent over cards she had laid out
upon the table. The room was deep in silence, as if every girl
were holding her breath, awaiting Tituba's words. When a
burning stick in the great fireplace snapped, I jumped.

Tituba looked intently at the cards spread before her, muttering something I could not catch. Then she gathered them together, working them in her hands, and laid them out again.

"What is it, Tituba?" Anne Putnum asked. "Tell us what the cards say."

"I have no liking for what the cards say," Tituba murmured, and again she gathered and reworked them.

Abby Williams sighed impatiently. "You sit there and stare at the cards, so they must say something. I want to know what it is!"

"You is a child wants to know too much. There be trouble in the cards, and Tituba goes better with no trouble."

"What kind of trouble?"

"Abigail, I told you—that day I looked at your hand—I told you there was big black trouble waiting! I try the cards, I think they may say different, but they tell the same thing. Now leave me be!"

"I don't like trouble," little Betty Parris whimpered, and her large eyes brimmed with tears. "Do not ask any more, Abby, please!"

Abigail folded her arms over her flat chest, sitting very straight. "Tituba told us she would read the cards for us," she said, "and she must! I want to know what they say! It may be that Tituba just says whatever she chooses, and there is naught in the silly cards at all!"

Tituba turned her dark, glowing eyes on Abby, and her face was stern. "You say that 'cause you affrighted to hear. If you did not believe in Tituba you would not pesk her to tell you things!"

"I am not afraid of anything, and you said you would tell us. *Saying* you see trouble doesn't mean 'tis *so*! Now, tell!"

Tituba gazed at Abigail for a long moment, her face unreadable. Then she lowered her eyes to the cards that lay spread on the table.

"Very well, then," she said. "I tell you. There is trouble such as you have never seen. Worse trouble than you little girls can think of."

"We have seen the smallpox," Anne Putnum said. "Surely no trouble can be worse than that."

"This be worse."

"As bad as the fire that destroyed two houses last month?" That was Mary Walcott, her fingers moving rapidly with needles and wool.

"This be far worse, for this be hellfire."

Huddled in a corner of the settle, Betty Parris covered her eyes with her hands and sobbed. Abigail glanced at her with impatience.

"Stop that, Betty," she said sharply. "'Tis all in sport! Be not so babyish!" Abigail turned back to Tituba. "How can the cards tell of something worse than the smallpox? Or fire?" she demanded.

"God send the sickness and the flames," Tituba replied. "But this—what I see in the cards—this come not from God."

"From where, then?"

"This trouble come from you, Abigail Williams! From you, from each one of you! You is all here, all you girls, and you hear me now! You is going to make people suffer worse than God do!"

Susanna Sheldon, blue eyes wide in her plain face, clasped her hands tight together in her lap. "But we—why should we make people suffer, Tituba? We are but ordinary girls. We do no harm."

"The harm be coming! And it come from all of you! There be blackness in some and it will pass to the others." She stabbed a forefinger at the cards. "It be all here. Trouble—blackness—the Devil himself—and death!"

It was then that Betty Parris shrieked and started to scream, so that we all but fell from our seats. She sat stiffly, as if frozen, her eyes tight shut, her face contorted, her fists clenched, scream after scream coming from her mouth. With a quick movement Tituba dashed the cards to the floor and went to Betty.

"Betty baby! Hush now! It be all nonsense, what the cards say. My baby must not fret herself!" Tituba tried to take Betty into her arms, but the child pulled away, her screams continuing as if she were powerless to stop them.

Mercy Lewis clapped her hands over her ears, her round face crumpling into tears. "Make her stop," she begged. "Make Betty stop that!"

Abigail's narrow eyes shone. "She's having a fit," she announced with relish. "That's what it is—a fit!"

At that moment Betty's father burst through the keeping-room door. He must have been in the small room he used as a study, working on one of his sermons, for his sandy hair was ruffled as if he had been running his fingers through it, and he grasped a Bible in one hand and a quill pen in the other.

"What is going on?" he demanded. "How can a man set down the words of the Gospel in such a furor? If you girls cannot be quiet—" His eyes went to Betty, as well they might, considering the screams that still rang through the room. "Betty! What childish nonsense is this? I am trying to listen to the voice of God and all I can hear is—"

As he father said "God," Betty's eyes flew open. She gave one last shriek, threw her arms about Tituba, and sobbed quietly. Reverend Parris drew a deep sigh of relief.

"There, that is better," he said, "though you know that I do not approve of babyish weeping, daughter. Dry your eyes now, and let me get on with my work." He moved to the door, saying, "Ah, it is not easy to be a man of God!" His last word seemed to echo as the door closed after him, and Betty shuddered violently, held close in Tituba's warm arms.

For a moment there was silence. Then Abigail grasped

Betty's shoulder and shook it, demanding her attention. "Betty! What took you? It was a fit, wasn't it?"

Betty lifted her head from Tituba's bosom and looked round the room at our stunned faces. Her expression was perfectly calm, her eyes wide and luminous. "Whatever are you all gaping at?" she asked. "Is something wrong with you?"

We looked at each other in wonder. "With *us*?" Anne Putnum asked. "'Twas you, Betty, screeching like the hounds of Hell were upon you!"

"Nonsense," Betty said primly. "You are imagining things." And sitting back on the settle, she straightened her cap, smoothed her dress, and smiled on us all. "Now," she said, "tell us what the cards truly say, Tituba."

With a long look at the little girl, Tituba rose, picked the strewn cards from the floor, and gathered them into a neat stack.

"No," she said. "Tituba has work to do."

THREE

More snow fell that night, and before John Proctor left in the morning for one of his rare visits to his tavern he paused beside me as I was sweeping the kitchen hearth.

"The new snow is not deep," he said. "I have left the shovel by the door. Clear the path, Mary, lest it freeze and become treacherous for your mistress. In her condition a fall could be dangerous."

"Yes, sir," I breathed, gazing up at his rough hair and deep-set blue eyes.

"You were very silent last night. Is aught wrong with you? You are in good health?"

"Oh, yes, sir! 'Twas just—oh, 'twas nothing."

"You had best tell me."

"Oh, little Betty Parris had a screaming fit yesterday. I cannot put it out of my mind."

He smiled, making pleasant crinkles beside his eyes. "Judging from my own, I would say children scream a great deal. That should not surprise you."

I looked down. There was no way I could explain to him how strangely frightening it had been. "No, sir," I said.

"You will not forget about the path."

"No, sir," I said again, and he left. The room seemed empty without him.

So it was that an hour or so later I was shoveling the path that led from the kitchen door when Abigail Williams came by, wrapped warm against the cold, her eyes sparkling in her thin face.

"How is Betty?" I asked. "Is she recovered today?"

"I suppose some might say so, but she is not! Oh, Mary, if you had but been with us last night when Uncle Samuel held our evening prayers!"

"'Tis bad enough here when Master Proctor holds ours," I said. "The heat from the fire makes me sleepy, and though the prayers are not of great length, still my knees do tire—"

"Oh, stuff!" Abby interrupted, twitching her red cloak tighter about her. "*We* must have prayers in Uncle's study where there is no fire, and the floor is so hard my bones creak, and he goes on and on and on—but last night, oh, Mary! You will never believe!" Those sly blue eyes were filled with excitement.

"How can I believe what I don't know?" I asked, and slid the shovel under the snow, filling it and throwing the snow aside. "You are telling me nothing!"

"Hush, and I will tell you! And stop shoveling! You must listen! So, last night at prayers, Uncle Samuel finished his reading from the Bible, and began the praying, which he seems dearly to love for he has much to say to God, and he asked God to give his daughter control over 'unseemly displays of emotion'—that is how he put it, Mary. And all of a sudden Betty fell flat forward on the floor and started screeching again until I thought my ears would burst, and she kicked her feet till she split the toe of her shoe, and she beat her hands on the floor, and shrieked and shrieked. And then I felt I was going to do the same thing—I could feel the screams coming up in my throat just from listening to her, and I wanted to leap around the room and make a great noise, and it was all so strange and exciting, and the next thing I knew I was running round and round and flapping my arms and shouting and it was the most wonderful feeling!" She paused, gasping for breath in the cold air.

All I could say was, "Abigail! You could not have!"

"But I did! And the oddest thing was that I hardly knew what I was doing! Tituba picked Betty up—Aunt Elizabeth had not come down to prayers because she felt the room was too cold and her coughing would start again—and John Indian just knelt there, staring, and then Uncle Samuel shouted at me, 'Abigail! Have you gone mad?' And I didn't really hear him, not really, and then he caught me and gave my face a slap, and I looked around and I didn't know quite what had been happening, and I felt so *wonderful*! It was almost as good as standing up in church and screaming, and I have always wanted to do that! You know I have!"

"But, Abigail!" I was nigh speechless. "How *could* you have behaved so?"

Her laugh was high-pitched and breathless. "I do not know. I saw Betty, and heard her, and then the strongest feeling came over me. I just had to—to—let go of myself! 'Twas very strange, indeed!"

"What did Reverend Parris do then?"

"He sent us to bed, Betty and me, and went up to talk to Aunt Elizabeth. And this morning at breakfast he looked as if we might fly up to the rafters right before his eyes!" She laughed again. "Poor Uncle Samuel! We did give him a fright!"

"I should think so, indeed!"

"Don't look so put out, Mary! I can't tell you how—how *exciting* it was! Like, oh, like being drenched with a cool rain after a stifling summer's day!"

I stared at her, and could feel the disapproval on my face. "I think I prefer a drink of cool water to being drenched by it," I said, and slid the shovel under the snow again.

She gave another quick little laugh. "Dear cautious Mary!" she said. "But come to our house this afternoon, for I mean to make Tituba tell us what the cards say. Nothing could be as terrible as she seems to believe, and I must know what she sees! Will you come?"

"I do not know," I said. "Perhaps."

"You will," Abby said confidently, and skipped back to the road.

And of course I did. Elizabeth Proctor was not mean about allowing a fair amount of freedom, and she did not object when I asked if I might go for a walk. Why did I not want to tell her where the walk would take me? Even then I must have sensed that it was wrong, but I felt pulled there by some force I could not resist.

The sky was a clear blue, the sun was shining, but with little warmth, and the snow was blindingly white and clean. I went quickly along the road to the crossing where I had met Goody Good, and then along the side road to the Parris house. I was almost there when I saw, coming from the opposite direction, Elizabeth Hubbard and Sarah Churchill. Sarah was bound out to George Jacobs, a sharp-tongued old man, toothless and lame, who could get about only with the aid of two canes. Elizabeth was an orphan (as the smallpox had made so many of us) and lived with her aunt, Mistress Griggs, wife of the doctor. As we met I greeted them and asked where they were going. They looked at each other almost guiltily before they replied, and then it was Sarah who spoke.

"We thought to visit the Parris house," she said. "We have heard of strange goings-on that take place there. Do you know aught of it?"

"Little," I told her, "though I have been there and seen Betty Parris in some sort of a taking, and Abigail Williams has told me the same happened again last night at prayers."

"But what of the slave, Tituba?" Elizabeth asked. "'Tis said she can read one's hand, or the cards, and see the future. That is what we want to hear!"

"She has said but little when I have been there, and all of it filled with mystery and doom."

"What doom can hang over us?" Elizabeth asked lightly. "And surely there is no mystery about us! In any case, are you going there, too?" Almost ashamed, I nodded. "Then come! We must not miss any of the circus!"

And so it was that we three arrived together to find the keeping room nigh filled with girls. All who had been there yesterday were there again, and now with Elizabeth Hubbard and Sarah and me there were ten of us, all clustered around Tituba, who sat like a queen at the table. On it were her cards, tarot cards she called them, and a shallow bowl of water.

That day she told our fortunes, though what she made up and what she may have "seen" I could not say, for her soft voice hesitated many times as if she chose not to speak of all that the cards showed her. She told Betty she would go on a long visit, but she could not, or would not, say where. She told Anne Putnum that her strength would become her undoing, which made little sense to any of us, and she told Mercy Lewis of a sickness that would all but kill her. She told Elizabeth Hubbard that she would look with her uncle, Dr. Griggs, upon such illness as had not been known before. I do not recall what other predictions Tituba made.

When at last it was my turn she stared at the cards for some moments before she spoke.

"A tall man," she said, "not young. He be close to you." I

felt a shiver of excitement. The tall man, not young, was surely John. "But there be something 'tween you," Tituba went on. "Something—"

"What?" I whispered. "What is between us?"

"A darkness. A great wall of darkness." Her eyes lifted from the cards and looked straight into mine. "Give me your hand," she said.

I held it out and could feel myself trembling as she delicately traced the lines in my palm.

"That man," Tituba said. "You hold his life in this hand, girl. That is all I have to tell you."

My mind whirled, thinking of ways in which I might rescue John from some danger, save him from some unknown fate. Tituba saw darkness between us, but I would cross that darkness to help him, for I held his life in my hands! I felt giddy with happiness at the thought.

Suddenly Anne Putnum spoke softly. "Look at Betty."

Betty sat stiffly, staring with unblinking eyes at the bowl of water on the table.

"She has tranced herself again," Abigail said, and the pleasure in her voice was evident. She leaned toward her cousin. "Betty," she whispered. "Betty Parris." The little girl did not move nor appear to hear. Abby clapped her hands sharply together, shouting Betty's name, and slowly Betty turned her head.

"You made me come back," she said reproachfully. "Why did you do that?"

"Oh, stuff! You were not anywhere but here. How could you come back?"

"I was not here. I was flying over a wide blue lake, and over trees, and into sunshine. I was not here."

Tense, pale-eyed little Anne Putnum began to shake. "That is what witches do," she said. "'Tis said that the body of a witch may be in one place while the witch herself is flying high above!"

"My baby's no witch," Tituba said firmly. "You is not to say such things."

"I did not say Betty was a witch," Anne said bravely. "I said that witches can do that. And we all know there *are* witches—the Bible tells us so. The Devil cannot do all his work alone, he must have others to aid him—and who better than a child who looks young and innocent, and can do her work unsuspected? Surely that might be the Devil's choice."

Mercy Lewis, the girl who lived and worked in Anne's house, spoke quickly. "Do not say such things, Anne Putnum! Betty is no more a witch than I am!"

"And who is to know that you are not?" Anne's thin voice was sharp. "And Tituba! Surely you are a witch, Tituba—tell us!"

Calmly the dark-skinned woman gazed at Anne. "There be many witches in Barbados," she said thoughtfully, "but they be not like witches here in this cold white place. In Barbados there be good witches who can cure bad sickness, and bring love to those who want it. They have potions and ways to do these things."

"And do you have these potions—and *ways*, Tituba?" Anne persisted.

Instead of answering directly, Tituba carefully moved the bowl of water closer to Anne. "Look into that bowl of water, Anne Putnum," she said, "and tell me what you see."

"I see nothing!"

"Because you no look. Look deep into it, now, keep your eyes wide, look, look deep. Say what you see."

With a strange reluctance Anne turned her eyes to the bowl of water, gazing into it while Tituba spoke softly. None of us dared breathe.

"Look deep, child, deep into the water. There are deep things in the water—things to see, things to know." Over and over Tituba repeated such words. At last she said, "Now. Tell me what you see."

Time seemed to stop before Anne spoke. When at last she did, her voice sounded as if it came from a long distance. It was faint, so faint we could barely hear her, and infinitely sad.

"I see the babies—my mother's babies—all those who were born before me and died so young. They lie there . . . white in their winding sheets . . . their hands are stretched out to me. They are crying. I cannot help them." Her voice rose. "I cannot *help* them!"

With a terrible cry Anne covered her face with her hands and wept, small screams coming with tears. A moment more and Betty joined her.

"I see them, too," she moaned. "They have no faces! They frighten me!" And throwing her head back so that it cracked against the settle, she shrieked.

In a trice the room was like Bedlam! One after another, the girls screamed and moaned and beat their heads with their hands. Only Mary Walcott and I sat silent, Mary going on with her knitting while her wide eyes went from face to face, I with a cold, sick fear flowing through me as I fought against joining my shrieks with the others.

FOUR

For three days I held myself away from the Parris house. It seemed to me three weeks. I scrubbed clothes, I washed and polished windows, I swept the floors, I cut kindling for the fires, I scoured pots and kettles, trying to exhaust the pounding energy I felt. My whole body longed for some sort of release. If I could have screamed as the girls screamed, or drummed my feet against the floor as Betty had, or beaten my head with my hands! My body seemed to hold a small fire that needed to burst into flame before it could burn itself out and give me peace. And each day was worse than the one before, so that on the fourth day I fled and joined the others in Reverend Parris's keeping room.

They were all there, and the very sight of the other girls eased me. Most of them were working dutifully on some piece of sewing or knitting, talking idly and calmly together. What had I been afraid of? We were young innocent girls. These were my friends. I could not think what had caused my deep unrest through the past three days!

"You are back with us, Mary," Elizabeth Hubbard said. "We have missed you."

"I was behind in my chores. I had much to do."

"It is best when we are all together," Abigail said. "We were just speaking of the strange goings-on when Tituba told Anne to gaze into the bowl of water. Do you recall?" I nodded. "I doubt that Anne truly saw anything in that bowl," Abby went on. "What could she have seen? 'Twas just water."

Anne Putnum looked up from the small stitches she was taking in the hem of an apron. Her thin face seemed even smaller, closely framed by her cap, and her lips were pressed tight together.

"I saw just what I told of. I thought, like you, that I should see naught, but they were there, in that water, all those dead babies my mother bore and buried. Plainly I saw them, their arms reached out . . ." Suddenly she shivered and dropped her eyes to her hemming.

"I do not believe you," Abigail said flatly.

"I care not what you believe, Abigail Williams. I know well what I saw!"

"Mistress Putnum speaks often of those infants," Mercy Lewis said in her slow, quiet voice. "I have heard her many times. Sometimes she weeps when she thinks of them."

"True," admitted Abigail. "I, too, have heard her. I expect that was in your mind, Anne, and you simply spoke of it."

"'Twas not in my mind! I did not believe Tituba had all the powers she said she had. I did not believe she could truly see our futures in the cards nor in our hands. And then she told me to look in the water—and I *saw*! I saw those babies! It was horrible!" Dropping her sewing, Anne put her hands over her eyes.

Abby gazed thoughtfully at her, the long narrow eyes secretive. "If Anne could see such clear pictures in a bowl of water, what might not the rest of us see if we tried?"

"I saw the babies, too," Betty Parris reminded them, her small voice high and clear. "'Twasn't just Anne."

"True, Betty. And surely, if two of us saw strange things in the water, others might do the same." Abby's voice was too quiet, too calm. It made me strangely uneasy.

"I think 'tis best forgotten," I said. "Neither Anne nor Betty liked what they saw."

"I was frightened!" Betty said. "So frightened I screamed!"

"So you must have believed in what you saw," Abby murmured. Then she looked up at us and smiled. "Tituba is not here to help us. Aunt Elizabeth has sent her on an errand. But perhaps we can see things by ourselves. How interesting that would be!" The blue eyes, beginning to sparkle now, slid from face to face. "I shall try first!"

Anne Putnum lifted her head. "And you will see nothing and will say I am a liar!"

"But Betty saw what you did, Anne. Surely I would not call my own cousin a liar. Oh, come! Let us have a little amusement!"

I did not know what was in Abby's mind, but I did not trust her. Those sly eyes ... "Do you think we should?" I asked.

"Oh, Mary, be not so prim! What harm can it do? And I am weary of sewing!"

She rose quickly, dropping her needlework on the settle behind her. Her face was suddenly flushed with excitement.

"Do you want the bowl of water, Abby?" Mary Walcott asked, her fingers knitting rapidly as if with a life of their own.

"No, I shall try without the water. I shall just close my eyes and think! But you must all help me!"

"But what are we to do?" Mercy asked. "We know nothing of these things."

Abigail gave a short gasp of laughter. "Then let us learn!" she said. She took a stand before the great fireplace, her back to the flames, her arms straight at her sides, her head lifted, her eyes tight closed.

For a moment she stood silent and unmoving. When she spoke her voice was hushed, barely a whisper.

"I am looking into darkness," she began. "I am looking into deep black darkness. My eyes are shut against the world. I am clearing my mind of all things. I am alone, standing in darkness. I feel the heat of the fire on my back."

Uncontrollably Sarah Churchill giggled. Betty Parris, leaning forward, her eyes intent on her cousin, muttered, "Hush!"

Abigail's high voice deepened. "In the darkness I can see whirls of color, brilliant, like the sun glittering on the sea. It blinds me!" She squeezed her eyes tighter. "Now the darkness rushes in again . . . there is no light. . . . I am all alone in the dark—wait! The dark becomes red, red mixed with blackness. A shape is forming . . . a figure. I cannot see it well. It is tall . . . it is taller than I. It stands above me—" Abby's head lifted, her eyes still clenched shut.

No one was laughing now. I felt a grip on my wrist, and, looking down, saw Anne Putnum's hand holding my arm in a grasp that whitened her knuckles.

"I cannot see the figure clearly," Abby's voice went on. "It is tall . . . and dark. It looms over me. It is black now, against the red. It is close to me—" The girl took a step back. "I see its long legs. It is coming closer . . . closer . . . closer . . ." She began moving slowly, edging round in a circle, her hands raised in front of her. Beside me Anne moaned softly. "I see no face . . . just great white teeth, like a dog's fangs. There are hands with long, hairy fingers. It comes closer . . . closer—" Suddenly her scream ripped through the room and my ears rang with it. "'Tis the Devil!" she shrieked. "'Tis Satan! His hands—his hands—his hands—"

Falling to the floor in a small heap, Abigail wrapped her arms about her head, swaying from side to side, still screaming. I could stand it no longer. In a flash I rose and bent over her, pulling her arms free and lifting her face. Her eyes were still tight shut, and I drew back my hand and slapped her blind face. The screaming stopped on a high note. Then Abigail's eyes opened slowly and she stared at me as if she had never seen me before. In all the room there was no sound. Abigail, eleven-year-old Abigail, gazed up at me.

"I saw the Devil," she said, and her words came slowly. "He is vastly tall, and black, and his hands reached out for me."

Without a sound Betty Parris slipped from the settle onto the floor in a dead faint. Abigail looked at her, and slowly a smile came over her face. She stood up, smoothing down her tumbled skirts.

"You see?" she said calmly. "We can do such things ourselves. Look at Betty. She knows. We have no need of Tituba, nor of bowls of water. We are enough. Now, which of you would choose to be next?"

But no one chose. We ministered to Betty, bathing her face, speaking softly to her, until she opened her eyes.

"I saw him, too," she whispered. "I saw the Devil, too."

Almost silently we gathered our shawls and our handwork together, and with not more than a word or two we left. The fresh cold air out of doors seemed like the very breath of life.

FIVE

Even then we could have stopped. Back in the busy, homely atmosphere of the Proctors' house I swore I would have no more to do with the girls when they indulged in their newfound sport. I told myself it was naught but nonsense and silly imaginings, and then I would think of Abby's face when I slapped her. She had said, "I saw the Devil." And I remembered the soft weight of little Betty's unconscious body, and I could hear her whisper, "I saw the Devil, too." And I knew that whatever it was, it was no longer nonsense, and that I had to know whatever more there was to know. There had been a nameless power in that room and I had seen it . . . felt it.

And the days went on and we met in the warm keeping room, and sometimes Tituba was there with her cards and her prophecies, and sometimes we, some of us, managed to put ourselves into that strange state where we knew naught of the room around us but filled our eyes with dark and unknown creatures, and sometimes we cried out in fear at what we saw. And yet we would not stop. The power was within ourselves, and stayed with us even when we were not together.

As hard as he might try, it was impossible for Reverend
Parris to stay in ignorance of what was happening in his
kitchen on those winter afternoons. Sanity seemed to have
deserted his household, and even though he was closed in
with his pen, his Bible, and his thoughts, he could not help
but hear the screams and wails and sobs that came from his
keeping room. As for Betty's mother, that poor woman, beset
by the noise, pulled herself from her bed, wrapped herself in
shawls, and came with cold bare feet to see what went on.
Mistress Parris staggered into the room, collapsing on a
settle in such a spasm of coughing that she could not speak.
Clutching her chest against the pain, she tried to gasp out
questions, but a hush settled over all of us and she learned
nothing.

That evening, however, she came downstairs again,
moving slowly, to join in the family prayers. Thus it was that
she was there to see Betty, head high when all others were
reverently bowed, staring straight ahead into space, fists
tight, lips drawn back from her teeth. Whenever Samuel
Parris mentioned the name of the Almighty, Betty made a
sound nigh to a beast's growl. When the Reverend began his
prayer, exhorting God to look upon these stricken children,
she screamed aloud, thudding the floor with her feet, pulling at her hair. Instantly Abby crouched on all fours and
went racing about the room, barking and snarling like a
dog. The prayer session came to an abrupt end, Mistress
Parris was taken in a swoon to her bed by an expressionless
John Indian, and Reverend Parris resorted again to prayer,
this time by himself.

In the Sibley house that same evening Mary Walcott sat
talking to Susanna Sheldon of what they had seen in the
Parris kitchen, when suddenly Susanna went into convulsions and within seconds Mary, too, was afflicted.

When news of this spread, as it inevitably and rapidly
did, the same misfortune descended on the house of Thomas

Putnum, where Anne Putnum and Mercy Lewis writhed on the floor, screaming as their muscles knotted painfully. Anne's limbs became so contorted her parents had to hold her firmly, lest she break the bones.

Now panic came to all of Salem Village. What caused these takings? Who would be next? For in a few days it developed that each of the ten girls who frequented the Parris home had been stricken with a seizure at one time or another. And I? Oh, yes, I, too.

It happened on a dark moonless night when I lay in my narrow bed at John Proctor's farm, tossing in my search for sleep. In the winter silence I kept hearing voices. Anne's, when she gazed into the bowl of clear water. Abby's, when she said she had seen the Devil. Tituba's, when she spoke of hellfire that was coming. I heard screeching, and the thud of small feet on wooden floors, and the crack of Betty's head against the settle, and screaming again, and moaning, and weeping. My heart seemed close to exploding through my chest. My nails dug into the flesh of my hands as I clenched them, and my skin was icy, and with no will of my own I opened my mouth and shrieked. And could not stop.

The door to my room flew open and John stood there, tall in his nightshirt, his nightcap askew upon his head, a lighted candle in his hand. Striding to the side of the bed, he looked down at me.

"What the devil ails you, girl?" he roared, trying to be heard above my screams. I could not answer.

Going to the washstand, he set the candle down, picked up the pitcher of icy water, and dashed a fair amount of it in my face. The screaming stopped as I glared up at him, and then I burst into tears. Curling into as tight a ball as I could, I hid my face and wept. John replaced the pitcher and thrust a towel at me.

"Dry yourself," he ordered, "and then tell me what insanity has taken you."

How could I explain? To one who had not heard nor seen what I had, the story would seem ridiculous. I tried, but even to my own ears it sounded like infantile maunderings. John stood beside my bed, shivering in the freezing night air. I repeated myself nigh a dozen times, saying again and again, "If you had heard them—or seen them—the screams . . ." At last he spoke.

"Hysterical females," he said coldly. "Aye, I have heard some talk of these seizures about the village, but I had not thought to have one in my own house. You will not visit the Parrises again unless I give permission, Mary. Is that clear?" I nodded, trying to still the foolish sobs. "The spinning is way behind," he added. "See that you get to it tomorrow."

"Yes, sir," I whispered.

With a rough pat on my shoulder, he left the room, taking the candle with him and leaving me in darkness. My skin felt warm where his hand had touched me. The rest of my body was icy cold.

In a village as small as Salem all that went on was common knowledge, and now the main concern of the people was our circle of young girls. Villagers recalled the family of God-fearing John Goodwin of Boston, whose children had fallen victims to just such seizures four years before, and had terrified everyone with their insane babblings and crazed antics. Ministers gathered and prayed over them, to no avail. At last the finger was pointed at a washerwoman, a Goody Glover, whom many had suspected of being a witch. Witch Glover was hanged, but it was not for some time after that the four Goodwin children were restored to their senses. Everyone in Salem Village had heard of Witch Glover, and a few of them had journeyed to Boston to watch the hanging, taking their children with them since, of course, such an exhibition would be an excellent object lesson to a child. So it was not surprising that now, in Salem Village, the word *witchcraft* began to be whispered about.

Reverend Parris was not a stupid man, nor an overly superstitious one, and he refused to heed the whispers. Instead he waited until an evening when Betty and Abigail began the twitching and moaning that betokened one of their attacks, and then he and John Indian carried them bodily to the home of Dr. Griggs. Elizabeth Hubbard, Mrs. Griggs's orphaned niece, opened the door, took one look at the two twisting, babbling figures, and started to twitch and grunt and moan herself. Into this walked Dr. Griggs.

Poor man! If we did not know what afflicted us, how could he? He consulted his books, he questioned and noted. Within a few days he saw each of us except me.

"Mary needs no doctor," said John Proctor flatly, when Reverend Parris asked him to allow me to be examined. And that was all he would say. But for the rest, good Dr. Griggs went from house to house visiting his troubled patients. He tried physics of various sorts, nostrums, concoctions, brews—none of them had any effect. The girls continued to jibber and jabber, to fling themselves from one end of the room to the other, to moan and groan and weep and scream. And in each case, Dr. Griggs observed, as soon as the wild antics ceased and sanity seemed restored, the girls looked as rested and happy as if naught but the sunniest good fortune had befallen them. On one occasion the doctor, thumbing through his medical books, came upon *Epilepsy,* and was sure he had found his diagnosis, but further reading removed even that possibility. Finally, his words to Reverend Parris were, "The evil hand is on them."

And now, indeed, Salem Village fell into a dither! The favored theory was that the girls were possessed, and that, of course, meant that the Devil was afoot in the little town, searching for young souls to make his own. And since the

Devil must needs have helpers to pursue his work, it followed that there must be witches. But who? And where?

Other villagers, of whom John Proctor was certainly one, disagreed. Did no one notice, they asked, how rosy and fresh and happy the girls appeared when they came out of their takings? Did no one notice that they were now the center of all attention, just the thing to please a young girl's vanity? Did no one notice that their fits took them only when there was an interested audience? John announced that I had been cured by sitting at the spinning wheel under the threat of a sound thrashing should I move without permission (though in fact he had never raised his hand against me), and advocated such treatment for all the afflicted.

The fact of the matter was that I had been forbidden to leave the Proctor farm, and knew only as much of what went on as I could glean from John's or Mistress Proctor's scant remarks. This enforced solitude had a divided effect— on the one hand making me much calmer in my mind, with no wild voices to excite me, on the other causing me to wish urgently that I could again join that circle and allow myself the release of the noise and movement and mystery.

There were several taverns in Salem Village besides John's, and one was a most respectable and homey place known as Ingersoll's ordinary. It stood close to the Parris house, and John Indian often worked there as helper to Deacon Nathaniel Ingersoll and his wife, Sarah, who ran the place. The ordinary was very much the center of Salem Village, with all manner of people stopping in for a drop of ale or cider, or a hot meat pasty, or simply to sit by the roaring fire and gossip. There came a morning when Mistress Proctor sent me there on an errand, carrying a large sack of goose down to Sarah Ingersoll for the making of quilts. Although the sack was large, it had little weight and I walked quickly, glad to be out of doors again, and away, for a time at least, from the accursed spinning wheel.

As I opened the door to the ordinary and stepped inside I suddenly dropped the sack, for there was Abigail Williams rolling on the wide plank floor in front of the fire, thrumming her heels on the floor and screaming.

I stood there, staring at her, and my blood began to pound. The rest of the room faded from my sight until there was only the blaze of the fire and Abby. My ears filled with her screams; my breathing grew so quick that it choked me. My hands were suddenly damp, I could feel beads of sweat on my brow, my knees weakened. Slowly I fell to the floor and my scream joined Abby's as I, too, rolled and thrummed my feet against the wooden boards. It was as if there had been a tightness in me that must have release, as if bonds that pinioned me were stricken off. I knew as from a great distance what I was doing, I could not stop myself, and I cared not. I relished it! I could barely see the white shocked faces that were turned upon us.

It was not until Abigail tried to throw herself into the fire and was held by a dozen sturdy customers who soothed and petted and comforted her—not until then did I, too, seem to come to my senses, sitting up with what must have been the look of a sheep upon my face, then hastening to smooth my apparel and regain what little dignity might be left me. All about the room there was the hum of voices.

"Possessed! They are possessed! The poor children . . . not strong enough to fight the black power that takes them . . . poor Abigail . . . poor Mary—possessed!"

That was the word that was repeated, that hissing, snake-like word, *possessed*. And in truth that is what I felt—that some unnameable thing was forcing me into these fits, something I was powerless to fight, did not want to fight. It was a terrifying thought!

Kind Sarah Ingersoll came to me, murmuring soft words, helping me tidy my clothing, accepting the sack of goose down and thanking me for its delivery, trying in every gentle way she knew to comfort me. I was grateful to her, but I could not wait to leave the tavern. When I did, it was to find Abigail by my side. She was cheerful, her bright face smiling composedly from out the red hood that framed it, and she hummed softly as we walked a little way together. After a few steps I could bear it no longer.

"Abby, what is happening to us?" I asked.

"Happening? Why, really, Mary, who can say?" She gave me one of her sly, sidelong glances, her eyes gleaming, and I could have sworn that she winked at me.

"Will you be at church meeting tomorrow?" she asked.

"Of course. Why would I not? We do always attend."

"'Twas an idle question. We have not seen you in the past few days. It will be pleasant if we are all together again. All us poor possessed little girls!"

With a merry laugh she turned and walked primly toward the Parris house.

SIX

During the few days that I had been kept at home by the Proctors, much had been taking place in Salem Village. Since Dr. Griggs had used the phrase "the evil hand is on them," no further thought was given to trying to cure us of our fits by medical means. Reverend Parris reasoned that if our bodies were not to blame, then it must be our souls, and this being within his province as minister, he set to work. He enlisted the aid of several ministers from the towns around Salem Village, such as Beverly and Ipswich and Salem Town, to add their prayers to his and to search with him for the cause of this most dreadful affliction.

When I followed Elizabeth and John Proctor into the church that Sabbath, it was to see two of these worthy men beside Reverend Parris. On his right was fierce Nicholas Noyes from Salem Town, and on his left mild John Hale from Beverly. The three solemn faces watched as the villagers entered and seated themselves. There seemed to be a current running through the meetinghouse—faint whispers, the craning of necks to see where the "poor possessed girls" were sitting, small restless movements. It was as though the congregation had gathered with the expectation of entertainment rather than of pious devotion. They had not long to wait.

Reverend Parris, his voice rising strong and clear in the crowded building, began his sermon. At the first sacred word he uttered, Abigail shrieked as if she had been bitten; at the second she was joined by two or three of the rest of us; at the third there was such commotion as could rarely have been heard in a house of worship; and at the fourth I heard my own voice join the rest. As from a distance I could hear the voices of the other two ministers, but what they said, or what took place for the scant rest of the service, I did not know. When I recovered my senses I was halfway home, being pulled along by a grim, striding John Proctor, with Elizabeth and the children hurrying close behind.

Bleak January moved into frigid February, and by an unspoken agreement Ingersoll's ordinary became our meeting place. Ever since that day when Abby had insisted we needed no help from Tituba, and had proved it by seeing Satan, Tituba had looked upon us with disapproval.

"You children be mixing with something too much for you," she told us. "You is playing with hellfire, and it going to burn you."

"But, Tituba," Abby reminded her, "'twas you who first taught us things. You read our palms, and told our fortunes with your cards."

"And I warned you! You 'member, Abigail? I warned you about big black trouble!"

"But we are not in any trouble, Tituba!"

"It be hanging right over your heads! I can see it!"

So it was Abby who first preferred Ingersoll's, where there were always people eager to watch and marvel at us, rather than the familiar keeping room at the Parris house, where Tituba's frown became deeper and deeper.

John might have forbidden me to join the others at Ingersoll's, but he did not. He seemed now to pay no attention to what we did nor what the villagers said of us.

"I have better things to do than bother with the ridiculous carryings-on of a handful of hysterical young females," he announced to Mistress Proctor. "Let them rid themselves of these antics and come back to their proper minds, and, please God, let it be soon!"

And stubbornly I told myself that if John had cared aught for me he would have kept me away from the others, kept me safe at home. Since he did not care, I would go as I chose! At Ingersoll's, surrounded by the other girls, I had a place of my own—a place of importance! People paid us attention!

There were days when we simply sat in the tavern, talking quietly together, nibbling on a piece of Sarah Ingersoll's spicy gingerbread, giggling a bit as young girls are wont to do. And then there were days when—oh, how can I tell it—when one of us began to feel that overpowering urge to move, to seek the release of small sounds, of moans, or small guttural barks. And the small sounds would grow, and other voices would join, and the movements became violent, and we would lose ourselves in our own actions, barely hearing the awed comments from those who watched us, barely hearing that whispered word, *possessed*.

And from these takings we emerged feeling refreshed, and ready to accept the cosseting and comfort that was lavished upon us. We were the center of interest in Salem Village, and even had we chosen to give up the mischief it was far too late. That became clear on the afternoon that Anne Putnum clapped her hands to her thin legs, hidden by her skirts.

"Oh," she screamed, and her voice was filled with pain. "Oh! I am being pinched! Don't! Don't! Stop! Oh, my legs!"

And then, at last and openly, the evil word *witch* joined the sibilant word *possessed*.

"Possessed by witches," the villagers murmured. "The poor children! But who? Who are the witches? Witches here in Salem Village?"

And there was no answer. Not then.

Mary Walcott's aunt, Mistress Mary Sibley, claimed she knew of a test that would identify a witch, and quietly sought out Tituba to discuss it. I do not know what was said, but they must have laid their plans secretly, since Goody Sibley admitted later it was a test that would not be sanctioned by any church or minister, and it was arranged for a day when Samuel Parris would be away from home.

We were bidden to gather once again in the Parris keeping room, and as some of us passed by Ingersoll's on our way, I saw old Goody Good standing by the tavern door, her reeking pipe in her mouth, watching us closely. Beside her, ancient and ailing Goody Osburne stood, leaning heavily on her stick, and the two old crones mumbled together as they saw us go past. Both women were looked down upon by the villagers, Goody Good because of her begging and her filthy appearance, Goody Osburne because she was said to have taken William Osburne to her bed long before she wed him. So they stood alone, those two, and watched us enter the Parris house, and we closed the heavy door on their curious faces.

Mistress Sibley was there with Tituba and John Indian, who was holding a hungry-looking small dog by a rope. Wide-eyed and uneasy, we seated ourselves on the stools and settles as Goody Sibley rolled up her sleeves in the heat of the blazing fire and spoke briskly.

"If so be in truth you poor children are possessed by witches," she said, "then 'twere well to find these creatures and have an end to the trouble!" She nodded at Mary Walcott, who sat, eyes downcast, working on her knitting. "My poor niece is so often taken with great spasms of her body and wild imaginings of her mind that I tremble for her health, and so it must be with all of you. So let us try to spy out those who harm you with their black powers, so we may all return to peace."

She picked up a small blue bowl and, without changing her crisp tone, went on. "Now, here in this bowl I have rye meal, and I am going to mix it with urine from all of you children."

Our eyes flew to Goody Sibley's face. "What?" gasped Anne Putnum.

The woman nodded calmly. "Betake yourselves to the small shed behind this room and make use of the chamber pot you will find there. I will wait."

By twos and threes, red-faced, we left the keeping room for the frigid cold of the shed, following instructions, hurrying back to the warmth as soon as we could. As I resumed my seat on one of the long settles I glanced at Abigail, who was opposite me on the other side of the hearth. She sat demurely, ankles crossed, hands folded in her lap, her head lowered, but I could see her expression, and with shock I realized she was doing all she could to keep from laughing aloud. For myself, I was terrified. There seemed an unholy air about what we were doing, smacking of what little I had heard of conjuring and black magic.

When the last girl returned from the shed, Mistress Sibley handed John Indian a wooden dipper and bade him fill it from the chamber pot. He looked uneasily at Tituba, who nodded to him slightly. John handed her the end of the little dog's rope and left the room.

In the few seconds that he was gone none of us spoke. My eyes wandered to a window, and I could see Goody Good and Goody Osburne outside, craning as if trying to observe what we were up to. If they but knew!

John returned, holding the filled dipper well away from himself, and handed it to Goody Sibley, who poured a small amount into the bowl of rye meal. Using a spoon, she mixed

it well, and then shaped it into a small cake and laid it in
the hot ashes on the edge of the fire. As though we were ex-
pecting some toothsome treat she said smoothly, "It should
not take long to bake."

As we sat there, silent, there came a small tapping on
the outer door, and I knew it must be the two old women,
Good and Osburne, hoping to come in and see for themselves what was taking place. Throwing a shawl about her
shoulders, Tituba opened the door, said a few quiet words to
the women outside, and then went out, closing the door
behind her.

We tried to make conversation, but the room seemed
wrapped in stillness. Presently Goody Sibley poked at the
cake with a long fork and declared it done. Spearing it with
the fork, she waved it from side to side, letting it cool
slightly.

"Now," she said to John Indian, "free the dog."

John untied the rope from about the dog's scrawny neck,
and Mistress Sibley held the cake out to it. The poor beast
must have been half-starved, for after one inquisitive sniff
it gulped the cake down with apparent pleasure. My stomach heaved at the thought!

We sat staring at the dog, at Mistress Sibley, at John
Indian, waiting for something to happen. Goody Sibley
smiled at us.

"The little dog will tell us who the witches are," she said.
"You will see!"

A moment later the door opened and Tituba entered, followed by Goody Good, mouthing her noisome pipe, and
Goody Osburne, leaning heavily upon her stick. The dog
turned toward the sound of the opening door, ears pricked
forward. In a moment of impatience Tituba made a shooing
motion with her hand and bade the animal to "get you
gone!" Goody Good snickered around her pipe, and Mistress
Osburne lifted her stick to lay it aside. Perhaps believing it

was about to be thrashed, the dog lifted its lip in a snarl, crouched back, and began to growl. The short hairs on its back bristled; its teeth were bared. John Indian moved to the door and opened it again. Sidling around the three women, the beast tucked its tail between its legs and bolted.

"So!" said Mistress Sibley. "So! 'Tis you! You three are the witches!"

We stared at each other, bewildered. Betty Parris lifted her arms toward Tituba, that warm loving slave who had so often held and petted her.

"Tituba!" she cried. "Not my Tituba!"

Then she fell to the floor in a deep swoon, whilst the rest of us sat white-faced and shaken.

SEVEN

The word spread like fire in a thatched roof, and the names of Tituba, Goody Good, and Goody Osburne were flung from end to end of Salem Village. They could not have been better chosen. Tituba was of a different color, came from a distant and unknown land, and even spoke in a manner unlike the villagers, her voice being softer and more musical to the ear. 'Twas well known, too, that she could read palms and tell the tarot cards, and had, in fact, done so for many of the women. Certainly these things should be considered.

As for Goody Good, everything about her fitted the concept of a witch—her begging, her curt, rough speech, her slovenly, unkempt appearance, her pipe. The naming of Goody Good roused little surprise.

And Goody Osburne's unseemly behavior with her hired man had put her into disfavor with most of the village. Nor had she been to Sabbath meeting in many weeks, though I think she could not be blamed, since once there she was ignored by everyone.

In any case, these three were accepted by Salem Village as

the cause of our fits and pains and babblings, and Reverend Parris, overlooking the manner in which the naming had been done, now joined with John Hale and Nicholas Noyes in questioning us. Since we had not made the accusations it seemed easier now to accept them. Anne admitted that she had known 'twas Goody Good who pinched her, but had been "afeared to say the name." Abigail confessed that she, too, had been pinched by Goody Good.

"And Goody Osburne was with her and scratched me, but I dared not tell," she added.

And those respected men of the cloth hung upon our every word, so that we tried to satisfy them. But little was said of Tituba. In truth, we did not dare. She may have been the one to set our minds on this strange road, but only because of our coaxing. She had disapproved of us, she had warned us, and we had not listened. And by her own word Tituba knew more of witchcraft than she had ever revealed to us.

But though we might hold our tongues regarding her, others did not. To the people of Salem Village, Tituba was their choice for a witch, and they made it known on the twenty-ninth day of February, that day which, with its own magic, comes only once every four years. Formal complaints were sworn out and warrants were issued for Mistress Good, Mistress Osburne, and Tituba. All three were taken to Ipswich Prison to await an examination of the evidence against them.

With Tituba gone from the Parris house Betty appeared to draw into herself until she could scarce be reached by word nor touch. It no longer took the flickering flames nor the stillness of water to send her wide eyes staring into space; she spent most of her time that way. She slept poorly, had no appetite, lost her soft rosiness. She was listless and spoke rarely, and often would sit sobbing quietly with no seeming cause. Her mother, more free of her racking cough now that the early days of spring brought a mildness in the weather, tried to tempt her with food, tried to rouse her interest in daily living, tried to soothe her into sleep. But it had been a long time since Mistress Parris had devoted attention to her daughter. Her place had been filled by Tituba, and with Tituba absent, no one and nothing could reach the child.

As for the rest of us, we could go to any extremes of behavior, secure in the knowledge that we were "possessed." We could name our tormentors as we cowered in corners or under the furniture—"I see the shape of Goody Good! She tries to burn me with her pipe!" As we writhed on the floor of Ingersoll's ordinary it was because "Goody Osburne is sticking needles into me!" As we screamed and shrieked and ran about the room, always filled with onlookers, we cried that one witch or another was "trying to get her hands on my throat!"

And if it was often Abigail, though sometimes Anne Putnum, who began these fits, they were swiftly joined by the rest of us. It was nigh to impossible to witness these explosions of released emotion without feeling oneself slide into them. When one girl screeched, in a moment we all screeched. When one girl threw herself to the floor and rolled in apparent agony, so did we all. When one saw the "shape" of witches, they were visible to each of us. We were caught. Frightened, bewildered, confused, but caught, in a coil of our own making.

If, sometimes, I was able to withhold myself from their takings, able to sit with my hands clenched tight together and my teeth clamped against the jerking and the screaming that invaded me, it was only with the most supreme, exhausting force of will. To be there, wherever we poor "possessed" girls were, was to share in the hysteria.

Then why did I go to Ingersoll's almost daily?

How could I not?

*   *   *

I suppose it is natural for young girls to rebel against the strictures of older women, who seem never to recall when they, too, felt the rioting juices of youth. Some mothers may look upon their daughters and think, "Ah, yes. I remember how it was to be that young." But the mistress of a bound girl does not, nor do other unrelated persons. And this may be part of the reason why those we named as witches—and God help us, how many there were!—were never the parents of those of us fortunate enough to have such. But with the others we were ruthless. It is but rarely that youth has power over its elders, and power is a heady brew.

It was on a Tuesday, the first day of March, when the sky was spring blue and the air had a softness in it, that hearings were held for Goody Good, Goody Osburne, and Tituba. I think there was not a soul in Salem Village who was not there, and many had come from the small towns around us, Beverly and Ipswich, Lynn and Topsfield. At first it was thought to have the hearings in Ingersoll's ordinary, but the size of the gathering made that impossible. Instead the excited audience, wet-lipped with anticipation, was herded into the church, where the ten of us "poor possessed children" were seated together in a place of honor. Reverend Parris's tall chair was turned about for the accused to stand upon and be well viewed, and a long table was set before it. Here sat one Ezekial Cheever as secretary, and the two magistrates, John Hathorne and Jonathan Corwin.

Sarah Good was led into the room.

Ragged, underfed, and scorned as she might be, that day she seemed uncaring of Salem Village's opinion of her. With a firm step she walked to the chair, clambered up on it, and stood, chin high, pipe in her mouth, surveying the assembly with a sparkle in her eye. It was but rarely, if ever, that Goody Good could have stood above the crowd with every eye upon her, every ear pricked to hear what she might say.

It was John Hathorne who spoke first, and his deep voice seemed to savor the words.

"Sarah Good, what evil spirit have you familiarity with?"

Goody Good looked down at him. "None!" she said shortly.

"Have you made no contract with the Devil?"

"No."

"Why do you hurt these children?"

Goody Good stared at each of us, taking her time. At last she said, "I do not hurt them. I scorn it!"

Magistrate Hathorne rose from his chair and walked deliberately to Mistress Good. Standing beside her, he put his hands behind his back beneath his coattails, gazing at the ten of us, sitting demurely in a row, our eyes on our folded hands.

"Children," he said, "I ask you now to look upon Sarah Good. Look well, and tell us if this is the person who has hurt and tormented you!"

With the others I raised my eyes and stared at that dirty, wrinkled face, the same face I had seen so many times in the village. Shrewish, stench-ridden, a nuisance to the town—but, witch?

Beside me Anne Putnum lifted her voice in a shriek, Abigail Williams fell to the floor and lay there writhing, little Betty Parris stiffened in her chair and beat her head against its high back, Mary Walcott threw herself down beside Abigail—and I? And I? My heart breaks to tell it, but my voice joined the rest. And throughout the crowded room there ran a sound like the escape of a long-held breath. This was what the audience had come to see.

Hathorne's strong voice rang out above the clamor.

"Sarah Good, do you not see now what you have done? Why do you not tell us the truth? Why do you torment these poor children?"

The old woman's voice was shrill. "I do not torment them! You bring others here, and now you charge me with it!"

Question and answer, the voices rose hotly against each other.

"We brought you here—"

"But you brought in two more—"

"Who was it then that tormented the children?"

"It was Osburne!"

We had quieted, and now as the magistrate faced us and we looked back at him, breathing quickly after our exertions, I felt—and I believe the others did, too—exhilarated and cleansed.

"Tell us, children, and be not afraid to speak the truth— is it Sarah Good who torments you?"

Mercy Lewis's slow voice came first. "'Tis both, sir. Goody Good and Goody Osburne both."

"They afflict us sorely," Elizabeth Booth cried out. "They hurt and torment us!"

"'Tis their shapes that come," Abigail said. "'Tis no matter where their bodies are, be they in Ipswich jail or in their own homes! 'Tis their shapes that fly at us through doors and windows!"

"Their shapes, aye, their shapes! If we touch them there is nothing there!" That was Susanna Sheldon, covering her eyes as if to keep out a fearsome sight.

"But they touch us." Anne Putnum's voice was calm. "They pinch us, and pull our hair. They stick us with needles and reach for our throats to strangle us."

"Hah!" said Sarah Good, and she spat on the floor, barely missing the sleeve of John Hathorne's coat. Quickly, and with scant ceremony, Goody Good was led from the room. In a few moments Goody Osburne took her place.

Elderly and unwell, she was a pitiable creature, but there was little pity in the faces of those who stared up at her. Leaning heavily upon the high back of Reverend Parris's chair, her voice a-quaver, she answered much the same questions as had been put to Goody Good.

No, she was not familiar with any evil spirit. No, she made no contract with the Devil. No, she had never hurt these children, nor any others, in her life.

"What familiarity have you with Sarah Good?" asked Hathorne.

"None."

"Where did you last see her?"

"One day, a-going to town."

"Sarah Good saith that it was you that hurt the children."

The woman's voice trembled even more. "I do not know that the Devil goes about in my likeness to do any hurt."

And then again we were asked to stand and look upon Goody Osburne, and say if we did know her, and then again came our voices, telling of the mischief she had done us. And when we were finished John Hathorne smiled at his success, and Goody Osburne was led away.

We knew, all of us, who was to come next. If there was one who might, in truth, be a witch, it was surely Tituba. What powers had she? What might she do to us? How could we protect ourselves? And so it was that the moment Tituba came through the door we immediately fell into such a taking that nothing could be heard above the noise we made.

But Tituba was wise. If telling the truth, as Goody Good and Goody Osburne had done, was to be disbelieved, then she would spin the tales this roomful of listeners wanted to hear. In spite of ourselves we hushed lest we miss some part of what she said.

"Who is it hurts these children?"

Tituba's voice, soft, low, musical, made everyone strain to hear her. "The Devil, for aught I know."

"Did you never see the Devil?"

"The Devil came to me, and bid me serve him."

A sigh drifted over the room, and we, in our seats below Tituba, leaned back easily in our chairs, our eyes fastened on her calm face, a sense of peace flowing through us as she told her story—the story that Salem Village wanted to accept.

Four women sometimes hurt the children, Tituba told them—Goody Osburne and Goody Good, and two others whom she did not know. They had wanted her to hurt the children also, but she would not until they promised to hurt her much more badly if she refused.

And then she spoke of a little black man—"Hairy like a beast, he is, but goes upright like a man"—and a tall man from Boston, who came to her demanding that she harm us. "He came with Goody Osburne," Tituba said calmly.

"This tall man from Boston. What clothes doth he go in?"

"He goes in black clothes. A tall man, with white hair, I think. He brought with him a book."

"What sort of book?"

"The Devil's book. He wanted me to sign."

"Were there other names in the book?"

"Aye. Goody Good. Her name was there. And Osburne, too."

"How many names were there?"

"There were nine names."

A gasp went up from those assembled. Nine names! Then—why, then the end had not come with the arrest of the three women! There were others, other witches, and the tall man himself. And the little black man! The hunt must go on!

With determination Magistrate Hathorne resumed his questioning, and Tituba continued her story. She told of a great black dog that appeared to her, saying, "Serve me," and that when she replied that she was afraid, the dog threatened hideous punishments did she not obey. She spoke of a red cat and a black cat, of a hog, and of a yellow bird that was always with the "tall man from Boston." She spoke of riding upon sticks through the air.

"Do you go over the trees or through them?"

"We see nothing, but are there presently," said Tituba.

"Did you not pinch Elizabeth Hubbard this morning?" demanded Hathorne.

"The tall man brought her to me and made me pinch her."

"Why did you go to Thomas Putnum's last night and hurt his child?"

"They pull and haul me and make me go."

"And what would they have you do?"

"Kill her with a knife."

"Why did you not tell your master?"

"I was afraid. They said they would cut off my head if I told."

"What attendants hath Sarah Good?"

"A yellow bird, and she would have given me one."

"What food did she give it?"

"It did suck between her fingers."

At that there was a sudden gasp from the listeners, who had hung upon each quiet word. 'Twas well known that a yellow bird was one of the Devil's recognized associates, and common knowledge that one way to prove a witch was by any small growth upon her body, for it was by means of these unholy teats that witches suckled their familiars, those creatures—whatever they might be, cats, rats, dogs, or birds—that did the bidding of their masters. Even John Hathorne's eyes narrowed as if he were searching Tituba's body for a similar excrescence, but he continued quickly in his questioning lest this fountain of information run dry.

"A yellow bird," he repeated. "And what hath Sarah Osburne?"

"Yesterday she had a thing with a head like a woman, with two legs and wings."

Instantly Abigail's voice rose clearly in the whispering room. "Aye," she said. "I have seen that creature, and it turned into the shape of Goody Osburne."

Anne Putnum nodded solemnly, her eyes wide, and without thinking the rest of us nodded with her. I could see Ezekial Cheever, the secretary, his nose close to the paper, his eyes darting about the room to note all our actions, writing as rapidly as he could with his long quill pen, the tip of his tongue showing between his lips.

The questioning went on and on, and shocked satisfaction was on every face. A confessed witch, one who had shared words with Satan, one who had flown upon her stick above the trees, one who was telling them all the secrets of that frightening, hideous, black nether world—this was what they wanted.

Tituba's melodic voice seemed almost to chant her responses. I felt lulled and calm, and I began to see clearly the things of which she spoke. That tall man dressed in black with his Devil's book was real to me. The yellow bird, suckling obscenely between Sarah Good's fingers. The red cats, the black ones, the hog, the dog. The woman's shape with wings that Abby said had turned into Goody Osburne's shape. I, too, could see it. If Tituba spoke of these things then they must be so, for her voice wrapped me round as a blanket might swaddle an infant, her words drifted into my mind and settled there. Something far stronger than I had moved into me until I felt at peace, with no will of my own. And if such a feeling had come real to me, then surely that band of girls surrounding me must feel the same. If Tituba had been labeled witch, then we had become the witch's children.

It seemed as if from a distance that I heard John Hathorne's final words. "Who is it hurts these children now?"

But Tituba, now that she had told of her alliance with the Devil, thus betraying him, could see no more of his fiendish works. Her voice seemed weary when she answered. "I am blind now. I cannot see."

She was led from the room, and only then did I realize that Betty Parris had sat silent through Tituba's hearing, her eyes fixed emptily on space.

Within a short time the three women were removed to the prison in Boston, there to await a formal trial.

EIGHT

If Tituba had not said there were nine names written in the Devil's book, would it all have been over then? Would the people of Salem Village have gone into their fields to prepare them for the spring planting, as John Proctor, removing himself as far as possible from the unease that was everywhere, proceeded to do? Could we have put an end then to our exhibitions? Or were we truly possessed by black power? Today, so much later, I still do not know.

In the early March days that followed the imprisonment of Tituba, Goody Good, and Goody Osburne, we were frequently called together by whatever men of the law or the church chose to question us. John Hathorne and Jonathan Corwin, Reverend Parris and Reverend Hale and Reverend Noyes, all of them spent time with us, asking, demanding, pleading.

"Who afflicts thee?" we were asked time and again. "Who is the cause of your pain and distress? What tall man from Boston hath appeared to thee? Hast there been a hairy little black man?" But none of these questions could we answer.

"'Tis your duty to aid us in searching out this evil," we were told. "Look deep into yourselves, use this power that God hath seen fit to give you, and tell us the names of those you see."

And we lowered our eyes in modest fashion and said little.

Betty Parris said least of all. She became increasingly pale and nervous, and wept when the ministers and magistrates spoke to her, no matter how gently. At home she barely touched her food and tossed restlessly at night, arising with dark hollow eyes and shaking hands. That first week in March Mistress Parris sent Betty off to stay with family friends, the Stephen Sewalls, in Salem Town, a few miles from the village. If Reverend Parris preferred to keep his small daughter at home where he could watch and pray over her, dislodging the evil spirits from her frail body, he was unable to convince his wife. So Betty was taken from the group, and would to God the same had been done for all of us!

As for the nine of us left, Abigail Williams became our leader. When Abby chose to spend a few hours at Ingersoll's, most of us joined her. If she was stricken of a sudden and moaned in pain, we felt the same agony. We saw dim shapes around us, but could see no faces and so, for a while, we could name no names.

"'Tis a pity you cannot put as much energy into your work about my house as you put into your antics at Ingersoll's," John Proctor said to me one evening as we sat at supper. "I hear you and your friends become more violent each day."

His words hurt. I faced him angrily. "But can you not see that we suffer?" I snapped.

"If you suffer it is by your own doing. To have named as witch two helpless women, and a third most likely because her skin is black, to have done that is evil mischief. May it all fall upon your own heads!"

I was unable to keep the tears from my eyes. Mistress Proctor laid her hand gently over mine.

"Thee must not speak so of our Mary, John. What she does is by no will of her own."

"Then 'tis time she had a will of her own rather than aping the madness of those she calls friends!" He raised the knife he held and pointed it at me. "Left to themselves," he said, his deep eyes boring into mine, "these girls will make devils of us all!" And he threw down the knife, rose from the table, and left.

Elizabeth Proctor tried to soothe me. "John speaks only from concern for you," she said. "He feels you do harm to yourself, and it distresses him. Try to understand, child."

But I could not. I wanted strength and comfort from him, not blame and doubt.

Friday, the eleventh of March, was declared by the various ministers as a day of fasting and prayer in Salem Village, a day of bringing God's attention to the little town and the misery that had befallen it. The local folk gathered in the meetinghouse, where first one man of God and then another beseeched the Almighty to look upon us, his poor possessed children, and give us the strength to name our tormentors. The voices went on and on, the pleading rose, there was the constant small rustle of assenting words from the townspeople. Suddenly Anne Putnum lifted her thin hand and pointed upward to the strong beams that held the roof.

"There!" she screamed. "There—on that beam—there she sits! Do you see her? A witch! A witch! Martha Cory is a witch!"

The villagers sat stunned. Martha Cory? That respectable

woman? A woman who, like John Proctor, had expressed great skepticism about our fits? A constant attender of church services? Not Martha Cory! Her absence that day was her undoing.

On the following morning Anne's uncle, Edward Putnum, and Ezekial Cheever paid a visit to Martha Cory. Before they left they talked with Anne.

"Can you see Goody Cory's shape, Anne? Is it clear to you?"

Anne, eyes tightly closed, shook her head. "No," she said, "I see nothing."

"Cannot you see what her shape is wearing? How is she clothed? We want no errors here."

The words of Tituba were graven in Anne's mind. "I am blind now," she told them. "I cannot see."

Her Uncle Edward's voice was gentle. "Why can you not see, Anne? Why are you blind?"

"Martha Cory hath blinded me. She knows that you come to her to accuse her. She knows that I named her. She hath blinded me."

Reluctantly the two men paid their call on Goody Cory, prepared perhaps at first to keep their minds open. They were met by an amused woman who laughed at their questions, and then turned serious.

"'Twould serve your purpose better," she snapped at them, "were you to stop the mouths of the scandalmongers. Talk is loose in Salem Village, and well ye know it! Stop the talk and you will stop this nonsense!"

Ezekial Cheever was shocked. "You call it nonsense, ma'am, when already three witches have been named?"

"'Tis a long mile between the naming and the truth," Martha Cory said. "For me, I do not believe in witches!"

In Salem Village such words were the greatest blasphemy. If there was God and His angels—and who would deny that?—then it followed that there was the Devil and his witches. To believe or disbelieve in one was to believe or disbelieve in both. And if one did not believe in God, it must be because one had sided with Satan.

On Saturday, March 19, a warrant was sworn out for Martha Cory's arrest, but since the next day was the Sabbath, delivery of the warrant was put off until the Monday.

In the meantime a former resident of Salem Village returned to town.

NINE

Before Samuel Parris had been appointed minister to Salem Village, the post had been held by one Deodat Lawson, who had later been called to a more important church in Boston. In recent weeks Lawson had received confusing and confused letters from such fellow clergymen as Reverend Parris, Reverend Hale, and Reverend Noyes, begging him to return and aid them in hunting down unnamed witches. Witches in quiet little Salem Village? Lawson must have felt an amused incredulity on that Saturday, March 19, as his horse clopped down the familiar dusty road. Dismounting at Ingersoll's ordinary to refresh himself, he pushed open the heavy door and may well have thought he was entering into Hell.

A few candles, added to the reddish glow of the low fire on the hearth, laid flickering shadows across white faces that lined the room, all watching a figure that twisted and screamed upon the floor. Deodat Lawson stopped short.

"What ails the female?" he demanded of the nearest face. "Who is she? Why does no one help her?"

"'Tis Mary Walcott, Reverend, Mistress Sibley's niece. She says a witch has bitten her."

"A witch? Here? And did no one see it happen?"

"Oh, we never see them, Reverend. Only the possessed girls see them. And then they claim to see only the shapes of the witches. Thank God you have come, sir! 'Tis a fearsome thing, not knowing which of our neighbors is a witch!"

Taking a candle from its socket on the tavern wall, Lawson strode to the girl and knelt beside her, his cloak swirling out about him.

"Mary," he said firmly. "Mary Walcott!"

At the unfamiliar voice Mary stopped her screams and opened her eyes, staring up at him. "I do not know you," she murmured.

"That matters not. Show me where a witch hath bitten thee."

Her eyes fastened on his face, Mary slowly pushed back one sleeve of her gown, holding her arm out to him. "There," she said. "She bit me there."

"Hmm," said Deodat Lawson.

From the circle of dim faces came questions. "Are there marks on her arm, Reverend? Can you see the marks of witch's teeth?"

The minister spoke cautiously. "There is a red mark of some sort," he admitted. "What may have caused it I could not say."

And who could blame Reverend Lawson if the thought ran through his mind that Mary might well have inflicted the slight wound with her own teeth? In any case he helped her to her feet, noting, as others had done, that she seemed none the worse for her experience, and then retired thoughtfully to the taproom.

It was evening when he arrived at Samuel Parris's home, and he was surprised at the number of villagers who had gathered there. Anne Putnum sat close to Abigail, both of them deep in a whispered conversation.

After quick introductions Reverend Parris led Lawson into the small, chilly room that served as his study, closing the door firmly behind them. In the keeping room the talk moved to whether Reverend Lawson would be able to identify the children's tormentors.

"He saw where Mary Walcott were bitten at Ingersoll's," someone said. "That should be proof enough."

"Aye, for some of us 'tis more proof, did we need it, but Reverend Lawson comes late to our trouble. He knows naught of what Salem Village has seen. Even for us 'twere hard to believe in the beginning."

"Do the Reverend bide here a bit, he will believe!"

"Mayhap, but recall the Reverend were ever a cautious man."

Slowly Abigail laid down her sewing, and rose to her feet. Then, as if blown by some gigantic wind, she whirled once around the keeping room, dashed out, and ran along the corridor to the study, flinging open the door. Arms flapping wildly, narrow eyes glassy bright, she darted into the room, bringing both men to their feet.

"Whish!" she shouted. "Whish! Whish! I am going to fly!" Circling the small room, she rushed out again and her racing steps could be heard running up the stairs and down, through the keeping room, back into the study and out again.

The two men followed her to the study door, gazing after her.

"You see?" Parris said helplessly. "This is the way things are. I know not where to turn."

In the keeping room those who heard him nodded their heads in sympathy, and then listened as Deodat Lawson's voice came clearly.

"But surely, Samuel, it could be mischief. Play-acting. A

mere child trying to draw attention to herself. Flying, indeed!"

From the keeping room Abigail's voice rose in a ringing scream. "I won't! I won't! Oh, help me! Help me!"

The two reverends reached the keeping-room door to see Abby thrusting her arms out before her as if trying to hold off some pressing force. Around her hovered the villagers, eagerly watching Lawson to see how he would respond to this behavior that had become so familiar to them.

Anne Putnum stood in shadow, her back against the wall, hands clasped tightly. Her eyes were fastened on Abby, and her lips seemed to be framing two words, repeating them silently over and over.

As if wrestling with Satan himself, Abby fought wildly, beating with clenched fists against the empty air, as Anne cowered, watching. Mistress Elizabeth Parris moved toward her niece.

"Abby! Abby, child! What is it? What frightens you?"

"Do you not see her?" Abby shrieked. "Why, there she stands! Oh no, I won't! I won't!" Her cap loosened and fell, her hair tangled as she shook her head violently from side to side. "I won't! I am sure it is none of God's book! It is the Devil's book for all I know!"

Suddenly she dashed to the fireplace and snatched a burning brand from the low flames, waving it before her. "Go! Go! I will not sign the book!" Hurling the brand into a corner of the room, she ran back and grasped more, throwing them helter-skelter. There was sudden movement as people twitched their garments from the small fires, stamped to put them out, or managed to toss them back into the great fireplace. Like a terrified animal Abigail panted and fought until with one last wail she sank to the floor, barely conscious. Deodat Lawson bent down to her.

"Who was it, Abigail? Tell us whom you saw."

But it was Anne Putnum's voice that answered from the

shadows by the wall. "And did you not see her then? 'Twas a shape. The shape of Rebecca Nurse."

Closeted again with Samuel Parris, Reverend Lawson made his disbelief plain.

"It's impossible, Sam! I knew Mistress Nurse well when I served here, and there could be no one more Christian and devout than she! An old, old woman, deaf and filled with the aches of age, loved by every member of that large family she has raised. No, Sam, I can't believe it!"

"And yet you saw Abigail fighting as if for her very life! Could you doubt that?"

"Aye, I watched her, Sam, and I confess I know not what to make of it. The child seemed terrified—seemed, in truth, to be battling some evil force. But that the force was Goody Nurse—that, my friend, I cannot credit!"

Reverend Lawson was not the only one. Certainly the name flew about the village, but in every case it aroused doubt.

On the next day, however, the Sunday, there was fresh food for consideration for all those who appeared at the church meeting, and who, in all of Salem Village, did not? Even Martha Cory was there! Since the warrant had not yet been served for her arrest she was free to come and go as she chose, and, intrepid woman that she was, she chose to attend church. To all appearances she sat stolid and quiet, paying no attention to the whispered remarks, the staring and pointing of those around her. But as the services began it became apparent that, though Martha Cory might be there in the flesh, causing no trouble, behaving as any churchgoer should, the shape of Martha Cory was at work amongst us.

At first our twitchings and cowerings were slight, but presently Abigail, then Anne, then the rest of us cried out as we had done so often before.

With an effort the Reverend Lawson, asked to conduct the service, did his best to lift his voice above our shriller ones, and words of his prayer rang through our clamor. Then Abigail jumped to her feet.

"Look!" she cried. "There sits Goody Cory on the beam, suckling a yellow bird between her fingers!"

Even as I knew the words to be those that Tituba had used against Sarah Good, so, as truly, did it seem that I could see the shape of Martha Cory upon the beam. With the others I pointed. Anne Putnum rose quickly and stepped forward.

"There is the bird," she said clearly. "It flies from the beam now, now it perches on Reverend Lawson's hat—there, where it hangs on the peg."

It was her father's strong hand that pulled Anne back into her seat, and we said no more. But we had said enough.

On Monday morning Martha Cory took her place, as had others before her, on the minister's chair in the meeting-house. Her hands tied loosely together, she stood straight, looking down at us with scornful eyes.

Magistrate Hathorne opened the questioning. "You are now in the hands of authority," he said. "Tell me now why you hurt these persons."

Mistress Cory's words were strong and clear. "I do not!"

"Who doth?"

And just as strongly, "Pray, give me leave to go to prayer."

"We do not send for you to go to prayer," said Hathorne sternly. "Tell me why you hurt these." A broad gesture of his arm indicated the row where we all sat silently.

"I am an innocent person," Goody Cory announced. "I never had to do with witchcraft since I was born. I am a gospel woman."

"She's a gospel *witch!*" one of us cried out, and in an instant the rest took up the chant. "Gospel witch! Gospel witch!"

No one could speak through the noise we made, until suddenly Anne Putnum jumped up. "Goody Cory prays to the Devil," she said. "When in my father's house I saw her shape, hers and another's. They were praying to the Devil. That is where Goody Cory's prayers go!"

Abigail's voice came next. "Look!" she commanded. "Look now! The tall man from Boston whispers in her ear! Do you not see?"

Immediately Hathorne spoke. "What did he say to you?" he demanded of Goody Cory.

Her head held high, the woman answered. "We must not believe all that these distracted children say."

But Hathorne was insistent. "Cannot you tell what that man whispered?"

"I saw nobody," Mistress Cory answered, and bit her lip.

Immediately all of us bit ours, Mercy Lewis until the blood came.

"See you now," said Hathorne, "as you bite your lip, so do they theirs."

"What harm is there in it?" asked Mistress Cory calmly.

Unexpectedly John Hathorne ordered that her hands be untied. As the knot was loosened the woman flexed her fingers.

Abigail sprang from her seat, rubbing her arm. "Goody Cory hath pinched me," she cried out.

Immediately we were all a-twitch and a-scream until the magistrates retied Martha Cory's hands. Instantly we were quiet.

"Do you not see these children are rational and sober as their neighbors when your hands are fastened?" he said to her.

The woman simply stared at him coldly and shifted her feet a bit on the chair. At once all our feet were shifting and stamping on the board floor.

Facing the woman squarely, his voice lifted above the

thunder of our moving feet, John Hathorne spoke. "What do you say to all these things that are apparent?"

And angrily, Mistress Cory answered him. "If you will all go hang me, how can I help it?"

Presently Goody Cory was released from the chair and led from the room. Her husband, Giles, an old and slow-witted man who knew little beyond the demands of a farmer's life, was brought in. He seemed anxious to do correctly whatever was expected of him.

Could he, the magistrates wanted to know, give any instances when his wife's behavior might be considered as that of a witch? The man's furrowed brow wrinkled even more, and he scratched his thick hair, almost white, with gnarled fingers. 'Twas hard to say, he muttered. He knew little of witches, he was a churchgoing man. But there had been that day. . . .

"Sometime last week, I fetched an ox out of the woods about noon. He lay down in the yard and I went to raise him, to yoke him to the plow, but he could not rise. He dragged his hinder parts, as if he had been hip-shot. Then Martha came out to see what was the trouble, and then the ox did rise." He gazed about him as if to see whether he had said the right thing.

"And has there been aught else?" Hathorne asked.

Again Cory scratched his head, struggling to find some answer. "I had a cat, strangely taken on the sudden, and it did make me think she would have died presently. My wife bid me knock her in the head, but I did not, and since, she is well."

"Ah," said Hathorne.

Old Cory's face lighted as if with sudden inspiration. "My wife hath been wont to sit up after I went to bed, and I have perceived her to kneel down by the hearth, as if she were at prayer, but heard nothing." He smiled about him, obviously, in his poor, blundering way, hoping he had said something to please the awesome authorities.

"And did you think she was praying to Satan?" Hathorne asked.

Giles Cory looked puzzled. "And why would Martha do that? Martha is a gospel woman."

And again, on the instant, came our chant, "Gospel witch! Gospel witch!"

And so Martha Cory, too, was taken off to the jail that already housed Sarah Good, Sarah Osburne, and Tituba. A few days later, without the benefit of a hearing, since it was felt 'twould not do for someone so young, little Dorcas Good, four years of age, was taken to join them. Her shape, Abigail had said, ran about the village like a small mad dog, biting us, the possessed, because of our accusations against her mother. Perhaps Dorcas did not mind so much. She would certainly have been better fed in prison than by the scant bits of food given her by the frugal people of Salem Village.

TEN

Those were such frightening weeks! I seemed to have lost my own will. I could not think for myself, nor speak for myself. Whatever the others did, I did also. Our brains, our bodies had become almost as one person, and I could do no more than follow. The nine of us were together most of the time, for the magistrates and the ministers did persist in their questioning of us, and at each questioning new names were mentioned.

John Proctor made it plain that he did not wish me to attend the hearings, but it was demanded that I be there. He stood staring at our little group one day as we waited to enter the meetinghouse, his face grim. Not taking his eyes from us, he spoke to Reverend Lawson, who stood next him.

"They should be at the whipping post," he said. "If they are let to continue their mischief we shall all be devils and witches!"

On the few days that I could stay at home he had barely a word for me. I longed to say to him, "This is not of my doing! I do not know what power has taken me from myself—'tis something too strong for me to pull away. Do not scorn me so. I mean no harm! Speak to me as you used, be gentle with me!" But none of this I ever said. Elizabeth Proctor in her quiet way tried to give me the understanding that John did not, and I turned it away. It was not her comfort I longed for.

Rebecca Nurse might have been a respected member of the little community, but the time had come when there was little respect for anyone in Salem Village—unless it was for us, the possessed children, and the names we threw like bones to hungry dogs. Deodat Lawson, that brave man, insisted that he be one of those to go to Goody Nurse's home and tell her there must be a hearing. I do not know what the poor old woman said when she was told. I know only that she was brought before the magistrates.

Goody Nurse was hard of hearing and so frail with age that Magistrate Hathorne was more kindly toward her than he had been to any of the other accused. Earnestly did he try to make certain she heard each word so that she might answer properly.

"I can say before my eternal Father that I am innocent," Mistress Nurse said, her voice shaking with emotion, "and God will clear my innocence."

"There is never a one in this assembly but desires it," Hathorne replied. And then, his face solemn, he added, "But if you be guilty, I pray God discover you!"

Anne's uncle, Edward Putnum, reported that he had seen his young niece in the throes of physical anguish and that she had screamed, "Rebecca Nurse is torturing me!"

"I am innocent and clear and have not been able to get out of doors these eight-nine days," Goody Nurse retorted. "I never afflicted no child, no, never in my life."

The doubt on Hathorne's face was evident. "Are you then," he asked, "an innocent person relating to this witchcraft?"

Anne Putnum called out, "Did you not bring the tall man from Boston with you? Did you not bid me tempt God and die? How often have you eaten and drunk the bloody sacrament to your own damnation?"

Anne then fell to the floor in a convulsion. The rest of us too were tipped into that same black state, writhing, moaning, and weeping.

John Hathorne turned back to Rebecca Nurse. "What do you say to them?" he demanded.

The old woman stood small in the big chair, her blue-veined hands holding tightly to the back of it, her wide eyes staring at us. "Oh, Lord help me!" she cried.

"It is awful for all to see these agonies," Hathorne said. "To see you stand there with dry eyes when there are so many wet."

"You do not know my heart."

"You would do well if you are guilty to confess."

"Would you have me belie myself?"

And she did not. No matter what was said to Rebecca Nurse, she continued to deny all knowledge and guilt. At last the magistrates ordered her removed. There were tears in Reverend Lawson's eyes as she was led away.

Outside the meetinghouse John Proctor watched the frail old creature being taken to jail, and turned his cold blue eyes on us as we emerged into late afternoon sunlight.

"Hang them! Hang *them*!" he cried, and ignored the shocked disbelief on the faces that turned toward him. He should not have spoken so. We were the poor possessed children. We were the pitied darlings of Salem Village. It was not wise to speak against us.

Oh, John! How could you have done it?

With Tituba in jail her husband, John Indian, worked doubly hard. In the Parris home he did much of the cleaning and some of the cooking that had been Tituba's work, and he continued his work at Ingersoll's tavern. In either place he could watch the behavior of the nine of us, and listen to the gossip and theories of our elders, and certainly it was plain to him that we were the protected pets of the village. Perhaps wise Tituba warned him that to stay aloof could be dangerous when the feelings of others were so aroused. Perhaps the heightened emotions that surrounded him touched some hidden well of island mysteries and superstitions on which he had been raised. Who is there now who can say? In any case, John Indian suddenly shocked us all by testifying against Sarah Cloyce.

Goody Cloyce was the sister of Rebecca Nurse. Wretched and angry after Mistress Nurse's imprisonment, she came to church on April 3, Sacrament Sunday, in the hope, I suppose, that taking the sacrament might comfort her. Her eyes were straight on Reverend Parris when he gave his text. It came from the book of St. John, and the words rang out over the congregation.

"Have not I chosen you twelve, and one of you is a devil?"

No sooner were the words uttered than Sarah Cloyce rose to her feet, glared at the preacher, stalked down the aisle, and left the church with a great bang of the door. Over the murmur of surprise and disapproval, the Reverend's next words sparked like lightning.

"Christ knows how many devils there are in His church and who they are!"

At the end of the service, as the church emptied, Elizabeth Booth came out into the sunshine. Suddenly she pointed to a spot on the fresh spring grass.

"See," she cried. "There they gather for their sacrament! The bread is red!"

"And the wine is bloody!" shrieked Susanna Sheldon.

Around us people looked where we pointed. "Who?" they asked. "What do you see? We see naught!"

"'Tis the witches! All of them! There is Goody Cloyce!"

"Oh, Goody Cloyce, I did not think to see you here," moaned Elizabeth. "Is this a time to receive the sacrament? You scorned to receive it in the meetinghouse. Is *this* a time to receive it?" And covering her eyes as though against the unholy sight, Elizabeth fell to her knees on the church steps. She was immediately joined by the rest of us.

On Monday, April ɪɪ, Goody Cloyce stood in the minister's chair, and John Indian, at his own request, was brought in to testify.

By now the problems of little Salem Village were known over a great area. No doubt they had grown apace through the telling and retelling—though they were horrible enough without any exaggeration—and the gravity of Salem's plight had enlisted the efforts of leaders of Massachusetts Bay Colony. At the hearing for Sarah Cloyce it was the deputy governor, Thomas Danforth, who did the questioning.

John Indian stood beside the heavy table, shoulders slouched. There was something furtive in his manner, yet his eyes were bright with an inner excitement as they glanced toward where the nine of us sat. 'Twas as if he knew it would be safer to become an accuser than a possible accused.

Master Danforth opened the hearing calmly, his voice low and sympathetic. "John, who has hurt you?"

When the answer came I was close to swooning. "Goody Proctor first, and then Goody Cloyce."

My heart raced, my ears hummed, I trembled in every limb. Goody Proctor! My Mistress Proctor!

"What did Goody Proctor do to you?"

"She choked me and brought the book."

"How often did she come to torment you?"

"A good many times, she and Goody Cloyce."

"Do you *know* Goody Cloyce and Goody Proctor?"

"Yes. Here is Goody Cloyce."

At this Sarah Cloyce broke in angrily. "When did I hurt thee?"

"A great many times," John Indian said, his eyes avoiding hers.

"Oh, you are a grievous liar!" the woman cried, where-upon she was hushed by Thomas Danforth, who resumed the questioning.

I sat there, disbelieving and distraught, barely able to breathe. The voices seemed to come from some great distance so I barely heard them. Elizabeth Proctor! What would John say? Would he think it was one of us who had accused his wife? Would he think—oh, dear heaven!—would he think 'twas *me*? Could I have fallen into a swoon at that moment as—God help me—I had so often before, I would have done so. My mind seemed to have been wiped clean, and I could only pray that this hearing would soon be over that I might get away to think. To try to think.

A different voice broke through into my consciousness. Mary Walcott was being questioned.

"Mary Walcott, who hurts you?"

My nails dug deep into my palms as I waited for her reply.

"Goody Cloyce," said Mary.

"Did she bring the book?"

"Yes."

Thank God! In the questions and answers that followed there was no mention of Elizabeth Proctor. When Abigail Williams was called I clutched the solid wooden seat beneath me to keep from screaming, for if there was mischief amongst us it centered in Abby. But the names she spoke were those that had been said before—Goody Nurse, Goody Cory, and Goody Cloyce. Not a syllable of Goody Proctor.

I know not what else was said. When the hearing was closed Sarah Cloyce was taken off to prison and I, unable to face either John or Elizabeth Proctor, followed dumbly when the girls repaired to Ingersoll's tavern. I found a small corner settle and huddled there, trying to straighten my thoughts. I was hardly aware when Anne Putnum squeezed in beside me.

"So Goody Proctor has been named," she said.

I could barely speak. "Yes," I whispered.

"That should teach Master Proctor a lesson!"

I stared at her. "What mean you?"

"Surely you must recall, Mary, when Goody Nurse was accused. Your great John Proctor looked upon us and said, 'Hang them. Hang *them*!' You must have heard."

"But—"

"He has called us devils. He has told any who would listen that we are mad, demented!"

"He may be right," I said. "Surely this is not sanity, this that we are doing!"

Anne's pale eyes drilled into mine with a feverish brilliance: "Take care, Mary," she said quietly. "You are one of us. One of the possessed. You dare not falter now. 'Twould go hard with you, I swear it."

"But to name the innocent—"

"Who can say who is innocent? We would have named no one had the ministers and magistrates not insisted that we must. If there is blame, surely it is theirs, not ours."

"But 'twas with us that it all started."

"Aye, as sport, and might have been done with quickly, had not our elders pressed us for the names of our tormentors."

"Tormentors! None but ourselves torment us!"

"I swear I have seen the shapes of witches! I have seen Goody Good and Goody Osburne and the others. They have come to me, to hurt me—"

"'Tis only in our twisted minds, Anne!" I grasped her arm, shaking it. "We have—have—befogged ourselves in some way that I do not understand! Best it were finished before more harm is done!"

Her thin hand removed my hand from her arm. "It is too late, Mary. And I warn you again. You cannot take yourself from us now. We must dispose of all those who would cry us down, who think us naught but foolish, misguided children. We must have the respect of all the village—respect, and our proper place. Take great care, Mary. Do not undo us. If you should—but I need not say more. You know, now, what we can do!"

With prim little steps she left me and joined Abigail and the others by the great fire. I felt desperate and sick. I was just summoning the courage to leave Ingersoll's when I was drawn out of myself by Anne's voice. She was kneeling by the fire, one arm extended, her finger pointing to one of the smoke-darkened rafters.

"There's Goody Proctor!" she shrieked. "Old witch! I'll have her hang!"

ELEVEN

Was it God or the Devil who placed John Proctor alone in his keeping room when I returned? He was sitting at the table, working on a bit of harness that had broken, his head outlined against the late afternoon sun that fell in long slanted shafts through a diamond-paned window. He looked up as I stumbled through the door. I closed it behind me and leaned back against it, too weak to stand alone.

"They have named Mistress Elizabeth," I whispered.

There was utter silence in the room. Even the fire seemed to cease its crackle. His eyes, so blue, locked with mine. After a moment he spoke.

"They?" he said. "*They*? And who, Mary, are 'they'?"

"John Indian first, at the hearing for Goody Cloyce. And later—later—Anne Putnum, at Ingersoll's. Oh, Master Proctor, it was not I! Nor did I join them!"

Suddenly I was weeping as though all the tears of a lifetime came at once. Blindly I ran to him, wanting to touch him, wanting his protection. He pushed his chair back roughly across the wooden floor and rose, catching my wrist and holding me away from him.

"I will try to believe that," he said. "But 'twill not be easy. I have seen the work of the 'possessed.' Stay away from me, Mary. I must speak to my wife."

He left the room and I could hear his step, heavy on the stairs.

When Elizabeth Proctor arrived for her hearing John stood at her side. I write this as if I had seen it, but I did not. I was not there. Instead I stayed at the farmhouse, watching the children, weeping, shaking with fright, praying. But I knew the scene so well! I could see in my mind how Mistress Proctor would look, standing above the assemblage, her figure starting to swell with the new babe. I could see John beside her, his hand most likely close to hers. Though I did not hear what was asked of her, I was later told. And it was all so familiar!

It was Thomas Danforth who questioned her. "Elizabeth Proctor," he said, "you understand whereof you are charged, to be guilty of sundry acts of witchcraft. What say you to it? Speak the truth as you will answer it before God another day."

Silently Elizabeth shook her head.

Turning to Mary Walcott, Danforth asked, "Mary Walcott, doth this woman hurt you?"

And Mary murmured, "I never saw her, so as to be hurt by her."

Danforth faced another one of us. "Mercy Lewis, does she hurt you?"

And Mercy opened her mouth, but was unable to speak.

"Anne Putnum, does she hurt you?"

And Anne stood mute and still.

"Abigail Williams, does she hurt you?"

And Abby thrust her hand into her mouth and bit hard on her own flesh.

Not one of them said a word. The girls were as silent as if dumb. And then Master Danforth turned to John Indian. "John," he said, "does she hurt you?"

And John Indian stood there and replied, "This is the woman that came in her shift and choked me."

John Proctor looked at him with angry scorn in his eyes, but made no move.

"Did she ever bring the book?" asked Danforth.

"Yes, sir."

"What? This woman?"

"Yes, sir."

"Are you sure of it?"

"Yes, sir."

The deputy governor looked soberly at Mistress Proctor. "What do you say to these things?"

I know Elizabeth Proctor's voice would have been clear and soft, but I doubt not there was a quaver in it.

"I take God in heaven to be my witness, that I know nothing of it, no more than the child unborn," she answered.

Had it not been for John Indian, Mistress Proctor might well have walked from that crowded room into the fresh air and made her way home with her husband. But with his accusations, the girls found their tongues and fell into their fits, and all was lost.

"Anne Putnum," asked Danforth again. "Doth this woman hurt you?"

"Yes, sir. A great many times."

"She does not bring the book to you, does she?"

"Yes, sir, often, and saith she hath made her bound girl set her hand to it." Thus Anne punished me!

"Abigail Williams, does this woman hurt you?"

"Yes, sir. Often."

"Does she bring the book to you?"

"Yes."

"What would she have you do with it?"

"She bade me write in it."

From where she stood Mistress Proctor gazed sadly at Abby, shaking her head slightly. Facing her directly, Abby cried out, "Did not you tell me that your bound girl had written?"

And Elizabeth Proctor answered, "Dear child, it is not so. There *is* another judgment, dear child."

And on the instant Abigail and Anne fell into the spasms that I knew so well, and Anne, pulling herself to her knees, shouted, "Look you! There is Goody Proctor upon the beam!"

John Proctor's voice cut across the room. "You look for devils, sirs, there are your devils!" And his strong hand pointed at the row of girls and John Indian.

Abigail clapped her fingers to her arm, holding it tightly. Raising her head, she glared at Master Proctor, and I know how her eyes would have narrowed and glittered.

"Why, he can pinch as well as she!" Abby said. "He is a wizard!"

And from all the girls the cry went up. "A wizard! Goodman Proctor is a wizard!"

Jumping to her feet, Abigail doubled her hand into a fist and drew it back as she moved swiftly toward John. Then, as if to strike him, the fist was thrust forward. But as it neared him the fingers opened loosely, the hand lost its force, and Abby touched his shoulder slowly and lightly, instantly shrinking back.

"Oh, my fingers! My fingers burn! The wizard hath burned my fingers!" And she threw herself to the floor and rocked back and forth, weeping.

At last word came to me that Sarah Cloyce and Elizabeth and John Proctor had been sent to the jail in Boston. At that moment I wished that my life would end.

TWELVE

The five children of Elizabeth and John Proctor could not be left alone—the youngest was but three years old—and there was no choice but that I stay with them. And so it was that I was in the house when the sheriff came.

It was stated by law that the goods of a witch were to be taken from her, just as her life could be. But it was also stated by law that this could not be done until the witch had been tried and convicted, and in the case of the Proctors, neither had taken place. They had been heard, and were being held until an actual trial took place, but they had not been convicted. But with this particular sheriff, the full extent of the law, which he was pledged to uphold, carried little weight. He arrived one morning early in April with a wagon drawn by two strong horses, and an assistant to help him lift and carry. I stopped him at the door and asked his mission.

"Why, to take the cattle and the household goods and whatever else there may be, to be sure."

"But you cannot!" I said. "The children are here—their parents have been convicted of nothing! You cannot do this!"

He spat into the new grass beside the doorsill and looked at me. "I figure 'twill take more than one lass, possessed by witches or devils or who knows what, to stop me from doing my duty. Out of the way, girl."

I tried to push the door closed against him, but he was much stronger than I. As the children and I clustered together by the hearth, he rolled the barrel of beer to the door, emptied it on the ground, and threw the barrel into the wagon. Chairs and tables, stools and settles, beds and bedding, nightstands and candlesticks, whatever the two men could lift and move, they took. When he tipped the pot of broth I had set simmering over the fire, dousing most of the small flames, and then took the very pot itself, I screamed.

"But what am I to feed us with?"

"Toad's feet and lizards, for aught I care," was his answer.

As many cattle as he could handle were roped together to the back of the wagon, and at last we watched as they drove away. I put my head in my arms and wept.

There was no scrap of news that did not reach Ingersoll's sooner or later, and generally sooner. When Mistress Sarah Ingersoll heard that the sheriff had taken from the Proctors' house all he could carry, she arrived at the door, laden with foodstuffs and comfort. We fed the children, and then sat together in the doorway, feeling the spring sun on our faces. My tears flowed uncontrollably, and whatever I said came through gulps and sobs, yet I needed to tell it to someone.

"It all started as a sort of sport," I said. "A bit of fortune-telling, the reading of our hands—Tituba did that—and sometimes Betty Parris would trance herself, and then Abby Williams saw the Devil—at least she said she did—and it all grew somehow, and when the others said they saw things, then I thought I did, too, and we all went into takings and screamed. I know not why I could not keep myself from joining them. And then Reverend Parris and the other men said we must put names to the shapes we saw. . . ."

On and on I went, spilling it all out to patient Goody Ingersoll, the while she listened and soothed me, sometimes asking questions.

"Then the girls have not told the truth?"

"'Tis more that they have dissembled than lied, I think. What they say is not true, but they have come to believe it is. Like hearing the words of Tommy Richards, who has not been right in the head since the day he was born, and who makes as much sense as a gabbling babe! But to him, I believe 'tis true."

"But you yourself, Mary. I have heard you speak when you were at the tavern. You claimed you saw all manner of things."

"And so I did, ma'am. My head was so distempered by all that went on that I must have seen the apparitions of a hundred persons. But now I think there was naught save my imagination, and the workings on me of the others, seeing the same things."

"Abigail Williams says that Goody Proctor brought you the book, and that you signed it."

"I swear 'tis not true!"

"They are saying now that Satan has made you one of his own to punish the other girls for having named so many of his witches."

"They will say anything, Goody Ingersoll, lest their game be stopped!"

"You think it all a game, then, Mary?"

"I know not what to think. There were times when one of us would call out that she was being pinched by one shape or another, and I could feel the pinches, too. When they claimed they could feel hands at their throats, then I fancied hands were tight on mine. What they did, I did—and my heavenly God, look where it has put us now!"

"'Tis no longer a game, Mary. No longer sport."

"No, ma'am. No longer."

When word reached the girls that I spoke against them and no longer considered myself as one of them, they did what I should have known they would do. They named me a witch. I warrant it was Anne Putnum who first saw my "shape" or felt my fingers at her throat, though it might have been Abby.

In any case, on April 19 I found myself standing on that chair, looking down, as others had, at a sea of faces, and I was sore afraid. As for the girls, there was naught in their eyes but satisfaction. I felt that they would have my blood!

My examination was conducted by John Hathorne and Jonathan Corwin, whom I had watched so many times before. Master Hathorne spoke first.

"Mary Warren," he said, "you stand here charged with sundry acts of witchcraft. What do you say for yourself? Are you guilty or no?"

I, who had raised my voice to cry out against other poor souls who stood where I stood now, could scarce find the voice to speak with. "I am innocent," I whispered.

Hathorne turned to the girls. "Hath she hurt you?" he asked.

I looked at their faces. Each of them stared back at me, but only Elizabeth Hubbard spoke. "Yes," she said. "Mary Warren has hurt me many times." And when I gazed at her in astonishment, she fell into a violent fit.

Now Jonathan Corwin turned to me. "You were, but a short time ago, an afflicted person. Now you are an afflicter. How comes this to pass?"

"I look up to God," I said, "and take it to be a great mercy of God."

"What! Do you take it to be a great mercy to afflict others?"

Before I could open my dry lips to answer, all eight girls I had called friends fell into hysteria. How horrible it was to see! They screeched and whimpered, they bared their teeth, they seemed to be trying to pull hands from their throats. I could feel the spirit of it stealing over me! I began to shake and could feel the old blackness rising round me like a thick cloud, but still I knew the truth and thought that I must tell it, for there was naught to help me now except the truth and I, myself. From somewhere I heard my own voice screaming, "I will speak! Oh, I am sorry for it! Oh, Lord help me! Oh, good Lord, save me! I will tell! I will tell!"

And then the blackness covered me and I felt the hard wood of the chair as I fell, and then strong arms carried me out into the air.

As I gradually came back to myself I could barely remember what I had said. I was only grateful to be away from those faces, beyond hearing of the girls' ravings. At least, I thought in my stupidity, I had told the magistrates I was innocent of their charges. I had said I would tell them all they wanted to know about our "possession." But while I sat there in the soft April air, unable to speak for myself, Anne Putnum had taken my case in her small hands.

"Mary was *trying* to confess to witchcraft, sir. You heard her promising to tell you of how it all came about. But then the shapes of Goody Cory and Goody Proctor fell upon her and choked her until she could not speak. You must have seen them yourself, sir."

"We saw nothing but an afflicted girl."

"But not as we are afflicted, sir. Mary was being set upon by the other two witches so that she might not tell of her own witchcraft. Satan must protect his own just as we must seek them out."

I knew nothing of this. I only wanted to recover from my

weakness and explain to the magistrates that I was sorry I had ever allowed myself to be guided and misled by the other girls. They will believe me, I thought. They will believe me because it is true.

I was not summoned back into the meetinghouse. Instead I was taken across the road to Ingersoll's ordinary, where the two magistrates joined me in a little room that Goody Ingersoll opened for us. That dear woman's eyes seemed to offer me sympathy and strength as she left the three of us alone.

Just being closed in with the two men brought on my trembling again. I sat crouched in my chair, my hands clenched together, trying to keep my poor brain on what was being said to me, so that I might answer correctly.

"Tell us how it is that you are now a tormentor," they said, "for surely those poor children there in the meeting-house were made to suffer by you."

"They brought me to it," I said, my teeth chattering. "I will tell, I will! They did it. They did!"

"They have done naught since you left the room. 'Twas only when you were there before them that they had their fits, as they do whenever they are faced with a witch. As you yourself once did."

"No, no," I moaned. "'Tis not that way! I will tell!"

"Have you signed the Devil's book?" Jonathan Corwin asked.

"No!"

"Have you not touched it?"

"No!"

If ever I had a nightmare, that was it. Each word I spoke they twisted until they would have it that I was a witch confessing, instead of a weak and foolish girl who had helped send innocent folk to prison. Surely Satan was punishing me then, nor could I find the hand of God. The people of Salem Village would believe what they wanted to believe, and they wanted to believe that the children were naming the witches, and that I was one. I lost all reason. I could but jibber when I wanted to speak. I fell to the floor in tears when I tried to find words to make those men understand my plight. The girls had done their work well.

I was taken to the jail in Salem Village.

THIRTEEN

At the same time that I was taken to Salem Prison so were others, named, as I was, witch. There was Giles Cory, that bewildered old man; there was Bridget Bishop, and there was Abigail Hobbs. All had been heard on the same day as I, all had been accused, and all had been taken to the village's small jail to await a formal trial.

Goody Bishop's preference for highly colorful dress may have made her unpopular with other Salem females who wore none but muted shades, and the two taverns she ran were so noisy they had brought frowns to many faces. As reasons for naming her a witch they did not seem sufficient.

As for Abigail Hobbs, she did not even live in the village, but in nearby Topsfield, where she alarmed the homeowners by wandering through the woods at night, peering through windows at what her neighbors might be doing, and uttering strange little cries in the moonlight. Even Abigail's mother, Deliverance, spoke of her daughter as a "dafter." But Abigail had relished her hearing in the meetinghouse, and had lost not a moment in admitting that she was, indeed, a witch. She had described unholy meetings held in Samuel Parris's pasture, where she had been one of ten, she claimed, who gathered there regularly. She also lightheartedly insisted that she had committed more than one murder of boys and girls who had angered her, though she could not recall who nor why. In the face of such testimony the magistrates had no choice but to deposit her in Salem Prison, where she was to bide until her trial, though they may well have doubted her story because of its all too fluent eagerness.

So there we were, and in the quiet of the small building we talked together. Except for Abigail, who made little sense at best, we knew we were not witches. It was a comfort to share our feelings, to realize that a trial would prove we were innocent of witchcraft, and that we would be released. When one *knows* one is not guilty, one cannot conceive of anyone else thinking it. After a day or so I felt myself becoming calmer. I chafed at being held prisoner, but without the questions and the accusations, without the misunderstandings and the insistence on guilt, my mind began to move smoothly and I was filled with hope and confidence. It was short-lived.

Although the magistrates and the ministers had been busy with—God help them!—nigh a dozen more accused persons, they would not let me be. They visited me and posed their questions until I trembled and shook from listening to them. So many of them! Samuel Parris and Deodat Lawson, Reverend Noyes and Reverend Hale, Magistrate Hathorne and Magistrate Corwin. Their voices struck against my wits like mallets. They stood around me, their eyes searching me as if to uncover some foul thing.

"Have you signed the Devil's book?" they asked, and I answered, "No." "Have you touched it?" they asked, and I answered, "No." "Has it not been brought before you by Goody Proctor?" they asked, and I answered, "No." And I thought of

Anne Putnum and her threats should I try to break away
from the group, and I cried out, "She saith she owes me a
spite! Avoid her! Avoid Satan, for the name of God, avoid!"
And they took it that I spoke of Mistress Elizabeth Proctor,
and they beat upon me with their questions until my lips
could speak no sense and my body shook, and I was again
pitched into the black clouds of madness.

After some hours they would leave me, and just as I
would begin to feel my poor brain settling itself into sanity,
back they would come with their drumming questions, their
accusations, their relentless voices, and their eyes. I tried to
answer them sensibly—God Himself knows I tried—but I
was so afeared of those men with their long, doubting faces,
their urging voices, their power! I sat and wept before them,
my face deep in my hands, my heart filled with shame at the
harm done to Elizabeth Proctor and John. To save them and
to save myself I must speak nothing but clear truth, I told
myself, over and over again. Naught but truth!

And thus, when John Hathorne asked me, "When you
lived in the Proctors' house, did you ever see such things as
poppets? Or great books with strange words within them?
Or ointments whose uses you did not know? Or any other
such?"

"Poppets?" I asked, confused. "You mean like doll
babies?"

"Yes. Like doll babies. Did you see such?"

"Yes. But they were for the children."

"You are sure? You never saw such a thing with, let us say,
pins stuck in it, perchance?"

"Sometimes, if Goody Proctor could find no proper cush-
ion in which to keep her pins, for the children would use the
little cushions to play with, you know, then she might place
her pins in a poppet, to keep them safe. . . ."

"And ointments?" they asked.

And speaking the truth still, I told them, "Aye, many

ointments. Goody Proctor knows a score of excellent cures."

"And books? Books with strange words?"

"There were books," I said, "but I had little time to look within them."

And in every case I spoke the truth, and still they pressed at me with their words and askings until, beside myself with confusion and fear and shame, I cried out, "Oh, Mistress Proctor! Hast thou undone me body and soul?"

And they took it as accusation against her, and with satisfaction writ large upon their faces, they left me for that day, and I sank back into the blackness which now I welcomed. But the next day, and the next, and yet the next they came, and whatever I told them was turned and twisted until there seemed no truth in all the world.

And then, the most frightful day of all, they came again.

Again they battered me with their unending questions, repeated over and over, until I felt bruised by their voices. They brought their faces close to mine and their hard eyes pinioned me. "Confess," they said. "Confess to thy witchcraft!" And when I spoke the truth and said I was no witch, they would not accept it, and urged me further, until I cowered there on my stool, my hands clasping my arms, rocking back and forth in anguish, the tears drenching my face, and when they said again, "Confess! Confess thy witchcraft and be free," I could bear no more and screamed at them, "Yes!" Whatever they asked me then, I cried out, "Yes! 'Tis true! Yes!" And they sighed at last, and smiled at their achievement, and patted me, and then they said there was but one thing more and the word *yes* was almost at my lips.

"Tell us that you know John Proctor to be a wizard," they said.

And all I wanted was to be left alone, and in my aching, tormented brain I heard John's voice saying, "Hang them." "They should be whipped," I heard his voice say. "They are devils," I heard his voice say. And last of all, "Stay away from me, Mary!" And his eyes had been as cold as ice and he had given me no comfort.

And the men around me said again, "Confess John Proctor is a wizard, so that your soul will be clean again."

And I heard my own voice rise above theirs as I fell to my knees on the stone floor of the prison. "Yes," I screamed. "Yes! I have felt a shape above me, and when I reached up and pulled it down to me I saw 'twas John Proctor!"

And then I think I must have swooned, for I knew nothing more until the day that followed when they came again, that body of men, and said I had been freed from my sin and could join my friends, those possessed children, Salem's darlings.

And gently, tenderly, they led me from the jail, and I could not speak.

FOURTEEN

here was no place for me to go. John Proctor's house had been closed. His neighbors had taken the children and were caring for them. In any case, after the harm I had done him I had no right to stay there. The Reverend Parris offered to house me, but I did not wish to be in such close company with Abigail Williams. And so it was that I went to Ingersoll's ordinary, and Sarah Ingersoll bade me stay, helping her in exchange for my bed and meals.

During the days in which I had been half out of my mind in Salem Prison the other girls had not been idle. They had thrown name after name to those stern protectors of the village, the magistrates and the ministers, and each name had been caught and repeated until its owner was brought forth and questioned. It was May by then, a soft, beautiful May, with air made heavy by the scent of lilacs, and early green shoots showing through the rich dark earth of farmlands. Some were heard to mumble that listening to witches would put no food on the table, and they proceeded to get to their planting. But in spite of the clear air, the bird song, the warm sun, and fragrant evenings, the girls continued to spend their hours at Ingersoll's, spying their witches sitting on beams or rafters and throwing themselves into their fits.

As much as I tried to keep apart from them by scouring dishes in the kitchen, or drawing pints of ale or cider in the taproom, or whatever else there was for me to do, it was impossible not to be aware of all that went on. I heard them name the parents of "daftie" Abigail Hobbs, her mother, Deliverance, and her father, William. I heard them name a woman called Sarah Wild, and another called Mary Black. I heard them name Mary Esty, the sister of Sarah Cloyce and Rebecca Nurse. And I heard them name old George Jacobs, to whom Sarah Churchill was bound.

Poor Sarah! It may have been fright at the naming of her master, for old Goodman Jacobs was a hard man who had contemptuously referred to us as "bitch witches." It may have been loyalty, or gratitude for his having given her a home. Whatever the reason, at first Sarah Churchill staunchly announced at George Jacobs's hearing that she had no cause to suspect him of being a wizard. Immediately the girls fell into such frenzies as had not been seen in some time. When Sarah rolled her eyes to heaven for strength, the eyes of every girl rolled heavenward also. When she turned her head away, ducking it toward her shoulder to shut their faces from her, every head was twisted sideways. When at last she screamed at them to "stop it!" her words were thrown back at her in a shrieking echo. And thus, because of her seeming influence over the "possessed" girls, Sarah Churchill was herself accused of being a witch.

I knew well how she felt! Weeping, half-swooning, Sarah finally shouted, "Yes!" to whatever was asked her, confessing to anything in order to be released from the torment of questioning. And with that "confession" Sarah, like me, was forgiven and allowed to return to that powerful group of girls.

I was there when Sarah came to Goody Ingersoll that evening and was brought into the kitchen, away from the group who were at their usual antics in the main room of the tavern.

"I must talk to someone, ma'am," Sarah sobbed, "but no one will hear me!"

"I will hear you, child. What is it?"

"There is no truth in what I said of George Jacobs. He is no wizard!"

"Then why said you those things?" Sarah Ingersoll's voice was soft, but firm. "Why belie yourself, thus causing great harm to an innocent man?"

"They kept asking about the book—the Devil's book, ma'am, the same they mention always—and what was there for me to say? For believe me, Goody Ingersoll, if I told Reverend Noyes but once that I had set hand to the book he would believe me, but if I told him one hundred times that I had *not* he would say I lied!" Tears drenched the girl's face, and in sympathy I took her hand.

"She speaks the truth, Goody Ingersoll," I said. "I know. Things now are such that to proclaim oneself innocent is to declare oneself guilty. Only by lies can we be believed. If we say we are witches, 'tis accepted as truth and we are forgiven. If we speak the fact, and deny all devilish doings, we are said to lie and are condemned as witches. All Salem Village has gone mad, I think, Goody Ingersoll! There is no one left to sift the lies from the truth." And I wondered suddenly within myself when I had come to know this. Experience is a hard, but efficient, teacher.

During those dark days my whole life seemed to be a lie. I was viewed by virtually everyone as a confessed witch who had been cleansed of her black powers by that confession, and I was once more regarded as one of the poor possessed children. The same was true of Sarah Churchill. Neither of us wanted more to do with the other girls, not because we lacked all fondness for them, but because we feared them—feared the enormous power in which they exulted. Again it was Anne Putnum who came to me.

At twelve years old Anne looked now like a woman of forty. By nature small and slight, she had become bone-thin. Her face had sharpened and paled; her little hands with their sticklike fingers were nigh transparent. But it was her eyes that frighted me most of all. They had always been wide and pale, but now they seemed glossed over as though the child were half-blind. They held no expression, they simply stared. To have her gaze at me—*through* me—made me want to run and hide, yet there was no escaping her.

"Mary," she said reproachfully one afternoon, stopping me as I tried to whisk past her with a tray of empty tankards. "What hath come over thee? We see little of thee now, and we miss thee. All thy true friends miss thee."

True friends! And yet, save for Goody Ingersoll, what other friends had I, true or not?

"I keep busy here," I said. "I cannot accept Goody Ingersoll's bed and board without working for it."

"But we need you, Mary. Now, when we are doing God's work as best we can, we need the wisdom of those who are older, such as you and Sarah Churchill."

"God's work?" I repeated. "You call this *God's* work?"

"But of course. To see and name those who work against Him—surely that is God's work, which He has set us to do."

My temper flared. "I do not call it God's work to imprison innocent people, old people, such as Rebecca Nurse and Giles Cory. If that be God's work I want no part of it!"

"Have a care, Mary. You admitted to witchcraft and were

forgiven. If you are no longer on the Devil's side, then you must be on God's. There is no other choice."

"There must be, or all Salem has gone mad! Think of Goody Esty, Anne! Imprisoned because you—*you*!—accused her! Mary Esty? A gentle woman who never in her life hath hurt a soul, I swear! To accuse her is *God's* work?"

"Oh, mayhap you have not heard," said Anne in her cool, precise little voice. "Goody Esty has been freed."

"What? When?"

"Just yesterday. When many who knew her insisted I might have erred in naming her, I feared lest they be right. Goody Esty was brought before us again, and none of us was sure of her guilt, and so she was set free. You see, Mary, we try to do our best, and never to harm an innocent person."

With the smallest smile she left me, and I stood like a gawk with my tray of tankards. Had Anne spoken the truth? Had the girls, in fact, allowed one poor soul her freedom? Did I misjudge them? Was it possible that if I were to join with them again I might persuade them to free others? To free John Proctor? Yes, and Elizabeth Proctor, too! If the girls had let Mary Esty go, perchance they were coming to their senses!

And it was true enough. I heard it in the tavern all that day. The woman had gone home to Topsfield and been warmly welcomed by her family and friends, and now there was great hope that her sisters, Sarah Cloyce and Rebecca Nurse, would soon walk freely from prison. And the Proctors, I prayed. Please God, the Proctors!

'Twas but two days later, and the girls were gathered in Ingersoll's ordinary. The wide door stood propped open to let in the sweet May scents, and the fresh spring air seemed to wash the room clean and fill it with hope. I found myself humming as I mopped the tables, swept the floors, and filled the tankards. I could almost believe we had reached the end of the blackness that had shrouded Salem Village all winter. It was then that Mercy Lewis suddenly screamed aloud and fell to the floor, her body twisting oddly.

For a second I stood, waiting for one or another of the girls to join Mercy in what I felt sure was but one of her usual takings, but no girl moved. Kneeling beside her, I took her hand, so burning hot to my touch it seemed to scorch me.

"Mercy!" I said. "What is it?"

"The pain, Mary! Oh, help me! I cannot stand the pain!"

"What pain? Where? Where does it hurt you?"

"My body is on fire! Oh, help me, Mary, help me!"

I turned to look at the girls who stood a little back of us. Their faces wore expressions of such bewilderment that I knew they were as puzzled as I.

"Anne," I said. "We must get Mercy home where your mother can care for her." Dumbly, Anne Putnum nodded. "Mercy, can you stand?" I asked. "Can you walk?"

"I cannot move. Oh, help me! Dear God, someone help me!"

Quickly I rose, snatched a clean napkin, and wrung it out in cool water. "Here," I said, handing it to Anne, "hold this to her face and head. I will find some way to carry her."

Goody Ingersoll took a sturdy blanket from a chest and went in search of some men to carry the girl. Laying the blanket on the floor, the girls and I lifted Mercy enough to slide her onto it, and so stiff was she in every joint she seemed made of wood. I watched from the door as Anne ran on ahead to prepare her mother, and the men, patrons of the tavern, followed with the corners of the blanket in their strong hands.

"Best send your uncle to the Putnums'," I said to Elizabeth Hubbard, Dr. Griggs's niece, "and let me know how Mercy does."

She nodded and hurried away, while I went back to my chores. As I worked I saw many of the tavern patrons wander off to stand outside the Putnums' house, waiting, most like, for another witch to be named. They, and sometimes the girls, kept bringing word back to me.

"She lies sometimes unconscious! At other times she is racked with such agony as we have never seen!"

"She prays the Lord to have mercy on her soul!"

"Dr. Griggs's medications do her no good."

"'Tis not like other times, she speaks hardly at all. Nor screams."

The afternoon turned to evening and the evening darkened into night. My tasks were done, but still I could not go to bed. At last I threw a shawl about my shoulders and walked quickly to the Putnums' house.

The room in which Mercy lay was crowded. In the dim light from the one candle that stood on a table by the bed I could see the shadowed faces of the girls who stood against the walls. Anne Putnum's parents were there, eyes fastened on their young bound girl, and Anne's uncle, Edward Putnum. Dr. Griggs leaned across the bed from time to time, hopelessly spooning drops of medicine into Mercy's mouth. The dusky room seemed filled with waiting.

Suddenly Mercy moved. Her eyes tight closed, she arched her back, her hands rushing to her throat, her head turning heavily from one side to the other on the crumpled pillow. From her dry cracked lips her voice came in a soft moan. "Oh, Lord, let them not kill me quite!"

I saw Anne reach out and take Abby Williams's hand, and together they moved to the bed, kneeling beside it. Their eyes wide, they stared at Mercy, and then around the room. It was Anne who spoke first.

"'Tis Mary Esty! The shape of Mary Esty!"

Her father, Thomas Putnum, looked up quickly. "Yet you said she was no witch," he said. "She was freed."

"Still, she is here," Abby murmured. "We can see her. Not clearly ... "

Mary Walcott rose quickly at the back of the room. "She has chains," she whispered. "She is putting chains on Mercy's neck, to choke her!"

"Who, Mary? Who is it?"

"Why, Goody Esty, of course! Oh, Goody Esty, we freed you! Free Mercy now!" And then she stood as if listening, and then spoke again. "But Mercy spoke naught against you."

Thomas Putnum spoke quietly. "What does she say?"

"Oh sir, Goody Esty says that Mercy spoke not against her, but neither did she speak for her. She says Mercy knows she is a witch. She says she cannot let Mercy live to condemn her."

"All this she tells you, Mary?"

"Aye, sir! Oh, Goody Esty, stop! Stop!" Tears streaming down her face, Mary Walcott huddled on a chair, hiding her face in her arms, swaying back and forth in distress.

It was close to midnight, and with every hour Mercy had become weaker. Now Dr. Griggs's hand on her wrist could barely find the throbbing of life. She lay stiff and straight; her jaws seemed locked together. A hushed consultation took place among the adults in the room, and presently Thomas Putnum and his brother Edward left the house to dispatch the constables for Goody Esty.

It seemed hours that we stood there, watching Mercy as sometimes she struggled weakly, and at other times lay as if dead. Somewhere a cock crew, and I saw that the morning sky was beginning to lighten so that from the window trees and rooftops were becoming visible. At that moment Mercy opened her eyes, stared blankly about the room, sighed deeply and, turning upon her side, fell into a comfortable and natural sleep.

Not long after, I heard it was at that same hour of dawn

that Mistress Esty was lifted to ride pillion behind one of the constables, and the horses' heads were turned to Salem Prison.

My heart wept with hopelessness. No matter what had happened, nor how it had happened, no witch the girls had named would ever go free.

FIFTEEN

*L*ife was a nightmare to which waking brought no end. The girls gathered constantly at Ingersoll's, where I could not avoid them, much as I tried. But they could not make me join them! My body might be there, but from somewhere I had gained the strength to stand apart from all their displays. From *somewhere*? From thinking of John and Elizabeth Proctor in that stinking jail. Elizabeth must by now be large with child. Was she kept in irons? Many of the women were, I knew. Did she weep? No, Mistress Proctor would not shed useless tears. Her thoughts would be for her husband; her efforts would go toward upholding him. And how they both must hate me! If they were freed, could they ever forgive me? And what matter if they did, since I could never forgive myself.

I went through the motions of each day's living—scrubbing and cleaning, cooking and tending the bar, getting up and going to bed—and nothing touched me. Once I thought, almost with a smile, it was as if I were but the "shape" of Mary Warren, and not the living girl. An empty shape, filled with quiet horror. For still, day after day, new witches were named.

One was Constable John Willard. How often he had been sent to bring in some poor soul whose name had rushed from the lips of the young accusers, how often he had heard the pleas of innocence from frightened prisoners! At last he stood, strong and angry, in the doorway of the ordinary, his eyes going from face to face of the girls. And, as John Proctor had done, he spoke unheedingly.

"Hang them," he cried. "They're all witches!"

A few days later a young cousin of Constable Willard's became suddenly ill. When Dr. Griggs was unable to help him, Mercy Lewis and Mary Walcott generously offered to see the boy. It took only a short while, of course, for them to cry out against Willard. His shape was plain, crushing the lad to death. When in truth the boy did die, there was no possible hope for John Willard.

There were Martha Carrier and Mistress Cary. There were Mary and Philip English. There were Elizabeth How and Dorcas Hoar. And there was the Reverend George Burroughs.

Abigail Hobbs had been the first to disclose that a pasture belonging to Samuel Parris, though at some distance from his house, was the gathering place for witches. Tituba had claimed not to know where she flew upon her stick, but now it was clear, and the girls made much of it. There was a horn, they said, that could be heard at midnight on the witches' Sabbath. No, they had not heard it themselves, for were they not clean and pure, God's children? The horn could only be heard by those who worshiped Satan. Its call would bring the witches together in the pasture, and there, in whatever evil light the moon shone down, they conducted their own hideous rites, taking their sacrament of blood, and bread as red as what they drank. Anne Putnum had seen them one mild spring night and cried out to her father.

"Oh, dreadful, dreadful!" she moaned. "Here is a minister come! What, are ministers witches too?"

Shocked, Thomas Putnum questioned his young daughter closely. "A minister, Anne? How can you be sure?"

"His clothes! His black clothes! He is small, and there is much black hair upon his head and face, and upon the backs of his hands. Now he takes his stand in front of the others. He preaches to them! To the witches!" Clapping her hands over her ears, she turned away. "I cannot listen!"

"His name, child! What is his name?"

"I know not. I have never seen him before!"

"But we must have his name!"

And Anne, insisting that she spoke to the shape standing there in the pasture, was answered and repeated it to her father.

"He tells me his name is George Burroughs."

'Twas not strange that Anne claimed never to have seen the man before. She had been but a babe of one year when Reverend Burroughs, minister to Salem Village, had left the small town and moved to Maine. But while still in Salem he and his wife had lived for some time with another branch of Anne's family, the John Putnums, and Anne's mother had taken an immediate and strong dislike to George Burroughs. Mrs. Putnum's dislikes were frequent, strong, and irrational. Had I been more perceptive then I would have realized what I now see clearly—many of the witches named by Anne were people for whom her mother did not have a good word. It was George Burroughs who had first taken a young, orphaned Mercy Lewis into his home, and it was with Anne's parents that he left Mercy when he departed for Maine. But all of that had been ten years ago. Why now did Anne fasten on his name?

It was but a day or so later, before any official action had been taken—for a charge of witchcraft against a minister must be carefully considered lest an error be made—that Abby Williams stopped just outside Ingersoll's, pointing in front of her.

"There he stands," she screamed. "The Reverend Burroughs! He is the little black man! There he stands!"

A patron of the tavern, one Benjamin Hutchinson, was just about to enter for a thirst-quenching pint of cider after working in his fields. He still held his pitchfork, and now in excitement he struck it where Abigail pointed.

"No, no, you have not touched him! He still stands there! Now he has moved—he is there—no, there—" Her finger shifted from one spot to another, and Hutchinson stabbed viciously with his pitchfork, though he could see no target.

"Ah! You have ripped his coat! I heard it tear! But now—oh! Now he follows me!"

Turning in fright, Abby ran into the ordinary, followed by Goodman Hutchinson. I heard the girl's voice ring out. "Do you see him? 'Tis the Reverend Burroughs! Do you see him?"

There was a time when I would have "seen" him just as clearly as the girls now said they did. But the guilt I felt for my own misdoings had sealed my eyes against all such visions and I was as unseeing now as Benjamin Hutchinson and the other patrons who were gathered in the room. Brave, foolish man, Hutchinson grimly wielded his weapon where Abigail pointed. "There! No, there!" At last the girl cried out, "Ah! There! You have hit him! Now he turns himself into a great gray cat! He backs toward the fire. You see him?"

"I see him! I see him!" It was Mary Walcott. "And here comes the shape of Goody Good."

Anne Putnum, her blank eyes wide, stared into the room. "Goody Good has taken the cat into her arms—she wants to hide it before it is injured again. See? There she goes away with it!" And Anne's raised hand pointed a moving path across the room and out the door, while every eye in the room followed intently. Every eye save mine. Thank God, I could no longer "see"!

*   *   *

Months ago during Tituba's hearing, when she had spoken
of the "little black man," she had spoken too of a "tall man
from Boston." In their thorough way the magistrates must
have pondered on who might fit that description, but surely
they had been kept busy with the endless stream of unfor-
tunates who were constantly being named by the afflicted
girls. But now a new name had been mentioned, though it is
odd to note that the accuser was never identified. The tall
man from Boston, it seemed, might well be that doughty sea
captain and soldier, he who had fought in wars against the
Indians and who had become an admired authority on
Indian lore and life, that son of two of Massachusetts's ear-
liest settlers, Captain John Alden, Jr.

Summoned to report to Salem Village, Captain Alden
strode into the crowded courtroom one mild May morning,
broad hat jauntily on his head, sword at his side. With him
was a friend, one Captain Hill. The girls were in their usual
place, and already whimpering and moaning over the mischief that Captain Alden, whom they had never actually
seen, was doing them.

Magistrates Hathorne and Corwin had been joined today
by a good friend of Captain Alden's, Bartholomew Gedney.
Now, before any move was made toward the tall, handsome,
middle-aged man who had just entered, Hathorne told the
girls to identify him. Turning from their seats in the front
row they scanned the room, some of them rising in their
seats to see better. As their eyes went quickly from one face
to another they seemed confused. At last Elizabeth Booth
raised an uncertain finger, pointing at Captain Hill.

"There he stands," she said.

A man close to her leaned forward quickly and whispered, and Elizabeth's finger changed its aim.

"Alden! Alden!" she said.

"How do you know it is Alden?" Hathorne asked.

The unguarded surprise was clear on her face. "The man told me so," she said.

Now Susanna Sheldon spoke, her voice shrill. "There stands Alden! A bold fellow who wears his hat before the judges! He sells powder and shot to the Indians and the French, and lies with Indian squaws and has Indian papooses!" Looking rather pleased with herself, Susanna sank back into her seat as John Alden faced her.

"There is not a word of truth in it," he snapped.

Nevertheless, his hat and sword were taken from him—the girls cringing from the sharp pricks they said his sword had been giving them—and John Alden's hearing was begun.

In their usual way the girls twisted and cowered and whimpered, saying the Captain was pinching them, pulling their hair, tweaking at their clothes. He had been instructed not to look upon his accusers, and now, his eyes firmly upon the magistrates, he spoke.

"Just why do your honors suppose I have no better things to do than to come to Salem to afflict these persons that I never knew or saw before?"

"It is not up to you to ask the questions," he was told calmly. "Turn now, and face the children."

It was all so familiar to me! The moment Captain Alden looked at the girls they fell to the floor, writhing and shrieking.

"Set his hand to theirs," Corwin ordered.

An officer of the court held Alden's hand and touched it to each girl in turn. Immediately they were quiet as the "wizard" drew back into himself the evil he had put upon them. Gazing at them with scorn, Alden shook his head slowly and faced Magistrate Gedney.

"What's the reason *you* don't fall down when I look at you? Can you give me one?"

"Confess and give glory to God," Gedney replied.

"I hope to give glory to God, but not to gratify the Devil. I wonder at God in suffering these creatures to accuse innocent people."

"These creatures, as you call them, are filled with God's spirit."

Captain Alden's icy blue eyes ranged slowly along the row of girls. "Spirit they may be filled with," he said, "but it is a lying spirit!"

John Alden was a strong man, so much like my John Proctor! His strength did him little good now, for he was held to await trial on charges of being a wizard. However, unlike John Proctor, Captain Alden was an important man throughout Massachusetts. Instead of being jailed he was placed under guard in his own home in Boston.

SIXTEEN

'Twas the end of May then, that beautiful month of promise, but not mayhap so beautiful nor so promising to the thirty or more accused witches who lay in various jails awaiting trial. The stories that came from those jails terrified me! Filthy, most of them were, and now overcrowded, since no prison built by God-fearing, dutiful Puritans had ever been expected to hold more than a handful of lawbreakers.

The prisoners for the most part were heavily chained, though that seemed a useless precaution since their shapes were so often still seen by the girls. Their food was of the poorest, and ill-prepared. They were constantly forced to submit to physical examinations of the most debasing kind, the search for any small growth that might answer the description of a "witch's teat." Cruelty had grown among the authorities, whose cool sanity seemed to have deserted them, and two of Martha Carrier's young sons were tied head to heels in an effort to make them accuse their mother. Bravely they resisted until the blood came from their mouths and then they said whatever their torturers wanted

to hear. And oh, God help us all, John Proctor's eldest son
was chained in the same manner when he visited his parents in prison, and being only human he finally moaned
"yes" to everything, and was allowed to take his racked and
agonized body safely away. Salem Village and the country-
side around it had gone mad, and who is to say where the
most guilt lay—with the young accusers, or with the older
believers?

No wonder then that the actual trials were longed for,
since they promised to end the suffering one way or another.
Even though it was well known that a recognized witch
would not be permitted to live, those poor souls who filled
the jails must have felt that an honest trial, conducted by
the clearest, wisest minds in Massachusetts, would prove
their innocence. And so all of Salem awaited the opening of
the witchcraft trials.

I do believe that the seven men who were selected as
judges were chosen as wisely as was possible. Certainly they
were aware of what had absorbed all of Massachusetts, but
few had been close to the affair. Samuel Sewall, John Richards, Wait Winthrop, and William Sergeant came from
Boston. The man named presiding justice, Deputy Governor
William Stoughton, was of Dorchester, and Nathaniel
Saltonstall came from Haverhill. Only one was a Salem
man, the same Bartholomew Gedney who had been present
when Captain John Alden was examined. Stephen Sewall,
whose Salem Town house still sheltered little Betty Parris,
was named clerk of the court, and Thomas Newton was
King's Attorney. The two magistrates who had conducted
the examinations for so long, Hathorne and Corwin, were at
the same task as the girls continued with their "God-given"
gift of discovering witches.

The first trial was held on June 2, and Bridget Bishop
stood as the accused. Although no longer young, she was a
well-featured woman, with brilliant black eyes and a

shapely figure. Her liking for such fripperies as scarlet bodices and fancy laces was disapproved of by Salem women, but more serious was the charge that the two taverns she ran were frequented by young people of Salem Town and Beverly, who roused peaceful villagers from sleep with their lusty singing and riotous games of shovel-board. In themselves these complaints might not have been sufficient to condemn her as a witch, but now her trial brought forth more damning stories. Bridget was accused of having a "smooth and flattering manner" toward men, and there were male witnesses aplenty to swear to this. They told of being visited at night by her shape, of spending sleepless hours as she hovered much too close above their beds. They told of how, when they refused to look at or speak to her in their daily lives, pursuing their virtuous ways, she had caused the deaths of children of three of them.

The mother of wild-tongued Abigail Hobbs, Deliverance, who had unwittingly confessed to being a witch and was therefore released, was brought to describe how Goody Bishop had helped to serve the witches' Sabbath in Reverend Parris's pasture. In short, there was none to speak for her, and many willing to speak against her. The jury took scarcely any time to pronounce Bridget Bishop guilty of witchcraft, and on June 10 she was taken to the top of Gallows Hill, where High Sheriff George Corwin hanged her from the sturdy branch of a giant oak tree.

She was the first.

I could tell myself that I had had no part in Bridget Bishop's death, but I knew it was not true. Her hearing had taken place on the same day as mine, and had followed mine so that I was not present to make any display against her. But there was no denying that I was a part of the band of girls who had named her and, though I could not remember distinctly, might well have added my voice to theirs. I had come to know her well in Salem Prison, her and Giles Cory and Abigail Hobbs. Bridget Bishop and I had talked much together, and I had developed a liking for her spirited and friendly ways. To think that I, however unknowingly, had been one of those who sent Bridget to her death brought a shock that nigh undid me.

The girls still made Ingersoll's their meeting place, and though I was believed to be one of them again, within myself I knew that I was with them in body, but not of them in spirit. They knew it too, and it showed in their cold faces. If they felt any touch of guilt for Bridget Bishop's death I could not detect it. If anything, it had made them stronger. They held Salem Village in their hands, and though they were doubted and avoided by a few, they were pampered by the many who watched them in fearsome delight as they went about their godly search for witches and wizards and devils.

It was June 28 before the next trials were opened, and it was frail Rebecca Nurse who was the first. She said little for herself. Her deafness was such that only shouted questions could reach her, and even those were most likely not clear. She stood quietly, her rheumy eyes fixed on space, unheeding of what went on about her. There were many to speak for her, those who knew of her deep love for her family and her constant readiness to help those in need, but she did not hear these voices. And it may have been as well, for neither, then, did she hear those who spoke against her.

She did not hear Anne Putnum's parents testify that she had killed six children. She did not hear a woman named Sarah Holton blame her for the death of her husband after he had let his hogs get into the Nurses' garden. But most sadly, she did not hear her loyal daughter swear she had seen one Goody Bibber take pins from her own clothing and clasp them in her hands, then cry out that Goody Nurse had pricked her.

The jury, new and inexperienced in such matters as witchcraft, tended to take the accusations of murder as unprovable. They knew that saying so did not make it so, and they were more ready to add their knowledge of her as a reputable person to the testimony that was given in her defense. Accordingly, after but a brief discussion among themselves, the jury returned with the verdict of "not guilty."

My heart sang! There *was* justice in Salem! I would have shouted for joy, knowing that most of those gathered there would join me, but I had no chance. There was a shrill scream from Anne, and then, like a pack of young wolves, the girls opened their throats. Never before had they fallen into howls and shrieks such as these. Never had they twisted their bodies in such terrifying convulsions. The sound beat upon my ears, the dreadful sound of young voices raised in animal-like baying, the sound of young bodies thrashing upon the wooden floor. Dear God! And I had once been part of that!

Chief Justice Stoughton, a cold, solemn man, summoned the spokesman of the jury, Thomas Fisk. Lifting his voice until it could be partially heard above the raging of the girls, he said, "I will not impose upon the jury, but I must ask you if you considered one statement made by the prisoner."

Those words were enough to reach the girls, and gradually their howling ceased. Stoughton paused for complete quiet, and then went on, his words plain now to everyone in the courtroom.

"When Deliverance Hobbs was brought into court to testify, the prisoner turned her head toward her and said, 'What, do you bring her? She is one of us.' Has the jury weighed the implications of this statement?"

Master Fisk, his face bewildered, turned to look upon the jury. Silently, with small shakes of their heads and shrugs of their shoulders, they indicated they had heard no such statement.

"We have no recollection of those words, sir," Fisk murmured.

"Nevertheless, they were spoken by the prisoner," the Chief Justice stated. "And does it not come to you that Rebecca Nurse recognized Goody Hobbs as another witch? One with whom she had shared indecent revels on past occasions? Plainly, that Rebecca Nurse was admitting openly that she herself was a witch?"

"If your honor will permit, the jury will meet again."

"I think that would be wise, Master Fisk."

There was no doubt then. The girls had won, would always win. Sarah Churchill, sitting next me, laid her hand on mine. Neither of us had words.

Rebecca Nurse was found guilty of witchcraft. I do not think she knew what was being said. Mutely she walked to the door between two burly officers, looking smaller and frailer than ever. They took her back to jail.

The rest of those who were tried that day and during the few following days were also found guilty: Elizabeth How, Goody Good, Sarah Wild, and Susanna Martin. All five were hanged on Gallows Hill on the nineteenth day of July, that black year of 1692.

They were buried on the slope of the hill, but somehow— somehow—Goody Nurse's body was moved. 'Twas said her children had quietly taken her home, to lie in her own acres beneath her lilac trees. Somehow no one saw it happen.

SEVENTEEN

I had heard that old Goody Osburne had died in jail, quietly, peacefully, just fading away, and I rejoiced. A far better way! And now I heard that Mistress Cary, who had been accused by John Indian with the support of the girls, had been spirited away by her husband, Nathaniel Cary. No one knew how, no one knew where. When his wife had been led away from him after her hearing, Cary had shouted violently, "God will take vengeance! God will deliver us out of the hands of unmerciful men!"

Whether 'twas God who helped Mistress Cary to escape, or her husband with the aid of friends, no one could say. They had gone and could not be found.

And after them, heartened by their success, went Bridget Bishop's stepson, Edward, and his wife, Sarah. Off—away— and who could say where? And then Mary and Philip English. And finally Captain John Alden, Jr. He had been kept under guard in his home, but at last his short patience was exhausted. In some manner he departed one night, arriving in Duxbury to beat upon the door of friends, crying, "The Devil is after me!" He was never seen again in Salem.

Whispers had it that most of these were given protection
and sanctuary in New York. Little effort was made to find
them, and in truth there was little surprise that escape had
been possible. By now there were many in whom doubt
about the trials had been raised, many who had had enough
of accusations and executions. The guards and jailers themselves may well have felt so. It is of small wonder that they
chanced to be absorbed in other duties at convenient times.

It gave me new heart. If Mistress Cary, the younger Bish-
ops, the Englishes, and Captain Alden could gain their freedom, why not the Proctors? They were respected throughout
the community, they had friends, they had courage. I prayed.
Dear God, how I prayed! Tituba had once said that I held
John's life in my hands. I tried desperately now to think
how I might save that life. It was hinted that jailers might
have been bribed for those earlier escapes, but I had no
money for bribery. I considered going to see them, for all
prisoners were permitted visitors, and perhaps I could have
put the thought of escape in their minds. Yet I could not.
Shame and horror at what I had done consumed me, as they
do today, and I knew I could not face them. The memory of
John's eyes when he had held me off from him, when he had
said, "Stay away from me, Mary," was still too clear. And so,
with naught else to do, I continued to pray.

Prayer! Prayer can avail you nothing!

On August 5 trials began for Constable John Willard, for
Sarah Churchill's aged master, George Jacobs, for Martha
Carrier, for the minister—the "little black man"—George
Burroughs, and for John and Elizabeth Proctor. Sarah
Churchill and I were ushered to seats with the favored band
of accusers, and we sat at the far end of the row, our hands
clasped tightly together. I think not once during the days of
the trial did either of us speak. What was there to say? It
had been our own words that had brought three of those
people there.

I know I sat there. I know the trials went on around me. I know that from time to time the girls were called upon to give evidence of things they had seen or agonies they had suffered at the hands of these followers of Satan. I seemed to hear nothing, to feel nothing, except at one moment when John Proctor's eyes met mine. Unthinking, I leaned forward in my chair, my hand lifted toward him, and my lips, Sarah told me, breathed his name. There was no expression in John's eyes at all. None. After a moment he turned his head away, and never did he look back.

I know not how many days it lasted. Elizabeth Proctor was given a stay of execution until her child should be born. All the rest were condemned to die by hanging.

The road from the jail to Gallows Hill led past Ingersoll's. It was the nineteenth day of August, hot, people said, though I felt nothing. I stood scouring the counter in the taproom, my hand moving round and round as if it had a life of its own. It must have had. There was no other life in me. The sound of the heavy prison wagons was unmistakable, their wheels rumbling on the hard-packed dirt of the road, the horses' hooves clopping slowly. If ever I knew Hell it was at that moment. I laid the scouring cloth neatly below the counter, walked through the taproom, the main room, and the kitchen, and went out the back door of the tavern. Sarah Ingersoll saw me go and said nothing.

In the fields that led away from Salem Village the uncut grass grew tall, brushing thickly against my skirt as I walked. I could feel the sun on my head, but there was no warmth in it. I recall being in a small wood where a stream rilled through. I think I sat beside it for a while, dropping leaves and small twigs into the water and watching them drift away. I remember climbing a hill somewhere and looking down on a small cove of Massachusetts Bay, smelling the fresh scent of the water, watching the sun sparkle on it.

I must have walked for most of the day, for there came a moment when I saw the sun was flinging its brilliant orange streamers from low in the west. I turned back toward Ingersoll's.

I walked in as quietly as I had walked out. The taproom was filled, but strangely quiet. A few faces turned toward me and then turned away. There was no sign of the girls. Goody Ingersoll looked at me, made a movement as though to come to me, and then paused.

"Are you all right, Mary?" she asked softly.

"Yes, ma'am," I said.

She hesitated, then took the few steps that brought her to me. She laid a hand on my shoulder, and her face was filled with compassion.

"'Tis said he looked strong, Mary, and was very calm," she said.

I bowed my head. "Thank you," I whispered.

"Go to your room now, Mary. I can manage tonight without you."

"Thank you," I said again.

I closed the door of my room quietly behind me, undressed, brushed my hair, and lay down on the bed. Stretched out on my back, stiff and still, I watched as night moved into every corner of my room. I remembered each word John had ever said to me, the rare sound of his laughter, the touch of his hand. In the darkness I could see his thick, rough hair that I had so often yearned to lay my hand on. I could see the deep blue of his eyes, and the strong width of his shoulders. And then against the darkness my mind saw the outline of Gallows Hill, and a body swinging, swinging, swinging—

Suddenly I was choking with sobs. I pulled the pillow across my face to stifle the crying. I turned and thrust my face hard against the mattress. I drowned in tears that brought no relief, I ached with sobs, I beat my clenched fists against the bed. Then there were arms around me and Sarah Ingersoll pulled me close, rocking back and forth, pressing my head against her shoulder.

"There, child, there," she murmured, and her voice was choked with sorrow too. I reached my hand up to touch her cheek; it was as wet with tears as my own. For a long time we stayed so, she whispering soothing words such as one might use to a babe, rocking me slightly, wiping my face and her own with a corner of the bedclothes. The storm of weeping slowed until there were but a few last shuddering sobs. Goody Ingersoll laid my head gently back on the pillow, smoothing the wet hair away from my face. Leaning forward, she kissed my forehead.

"Sleep now, Mary. Sleep, child. God will help you."

EIGHTEEN

1t was not the end, of course. There were further trials in September. I went to none of them; in fact, rarely did I leave the tavern and the strength that Goody Ingersoll gave me, but I heard. I could not help but hear. The girls continued to gather there, and the change in them sickened me. No longer did they see shapes, nor scream, nor cry out names. Instead they sat quietly and modestly, acknowledging their position in the village with grave nods or a few words. For there were many now who felt it only wise to be as friendly as the girls would permit. Their power had been seen, and only fools would choose to doubt it. But their faces! Pale, they were, and hard and cold. Even their skin seemed to have thickened. Their eyes were blank and empty, their hands shook over needlework. The beautiful knitting that Mary Walcott had once done so skillfully was now botched, stitches dropped and hanging. They spoke to me. I answered. We said nothing.

Abigail Hobbs, she who had so eagerly professed herself to be not only a witch but a murderer, was among the first to be tried in September, and with her five others, Rebecca

Eames, Dorcas Hoar, Mary Bradbury, and two women from Andover whom Anne Putnum and Mary Walcott had named, Mary Lacy and Ann Foster. Perhaps they learned from Abigail Hobbs while they awaited trial in jail. In any case, each confessed herself a witch. As witches they were condemned, and as confessed, and therefore supposedly reformed, witches they were reprieved and allowed to go in freedom. Such was justice.

But a little later in the month others did not fare so well. Their names were Alice Parker and Ann Pudeator, Samuel Wardwell and Wilmot Redd, Mary Parker and Margaret Scott. I knew little of any of them. But there were also Martha Cory and Mary Esty—Goody Esty, who had once known that brief taste of freedom before Mercy Lewis's illness pulled her back. All eight of them were hanged on Gallows Hill on the twenty-second of September, and may God have mercy on their souls!

They were the last, or rather let us say they were the last to meet death in that particular way. For there was also Giles Cory, that slow, stubborn, honorable old man, who throughout his trial refused to say a word. He stood as tall in court as his bent back would permit, and remained utterly mute, although he was told what the punishment would be for refusing to answer the questions put to him. Mayhap he no longer cared. He had not been able to help his wife, Martha. Why try to help himself?

He was taken into an open field beside the jail and stretched upon the ground while heavy stones were placed upon his chest in an effort to make him speak. Finally he did.

"More weight," he said. "More weight."

At last the crushed chest stopped that tired, valiant heart.

The sun rises and the sun sets, and nothing changes this. The days go on, becoming weeks and months and years, fifteen years now since it all happened. Gradually Salem's wounds began to heal, though there are many who will suffer always. Elizabeth Proctor left the jail after her baby was born, and no one chose to recall that her execution had been but stayed, not dismissed. Still, as someone who was considered legally dead, she had no rights to her home nor to the possessions that had been taken from it. Friends took her in, for the Proctors had friends in plenty.

The Reverend Parris found that he had not. For months he had protected the girls from the slow shift of opinion against them. As shock invaded Salem Village at the deaths of friends and neighbors and family members, so hatred grew toward the undeniable cause of those deaths, the possessed girls. The villagers remembered too that it was in Samuel Parris's house that all the trouble had started, that his slaves, Tituba and John Indian, had figured largely, that his niece, Abigail Williams, had seemed to lead the girls, that his daughter, Betty, had been sent away to safety. The large family of Rebecca Nurse refused to attend Parris's church services, and as the weeks passed others supported them, until each Sabbath saw more seats empty than filled.

From his pulpit Samuel Parris read a document in which he offered sympathy to those who had suffered "through Satan's wiles," and he prayed that "all may be covered with the mantle of love and may forgive each other heartily." It was not enough.

The Reverend was relieved of his church and departed Salem Village, taking his wife, his daughter, Betty, and Abigail Williams. As they drove away in Samuel Parris's buggy, their household goods piled in a wagon that followed, Abby sat straight on the seat, her narrow eyes downcast, her face expressionless. Beside her Betty looked even smaller, staring blankly ahead with huge unseeing eyes.

Abby and Betty—and Tituba. That was where it all began.

Long before the Parris family left the village, Tituba was released from jail into the care of a new master, a weaver with a mind so practical as to have put little faith in Salem's turmoil. The fact that he might be giving a home to a confessed witch seemed to weigh far less with him than Tituba's ability to cook delicious meals and sew an almost invisible seam.

She stopped one day at Ingersoll's soon after she had left the jail, to meet John Indian, who still did much of the heavy work about the ordinary. I watched her as she entered, her back still straight, her white-kerchiefed head high, her eyes calm.

"Good day, Tituba," I said.

She turned and saw me and smiled. "You speak to me, Mary Warren?"

"Of course. Why should I not?"

"There be those who never will. They say that Tituba—"

I interrupted her gently. "There has been too much 'they say,'" I told her. "I no longer listen to what 'they say.'"

Her dark eyes filled with sympathy. "You be a growed woman now, Mary, and a wise one. But the wisdom, it come hard, I think."

"Very hard."

She took one of my hands, her cool slim fingers turning it palm upward. Looking down at it, she said, "Tituba tried to warn you, child. 'Twas all there, right here in your hand. Tituba knowed it was bad, but only God knowed how bad." She closed my hand again, her eyes lifting to mine. "Be you at peace now?"

Suddenly I felt the sting of tears. "At peace?" I asked. "No, Tituba, never at peace again. But I can live."

"That be all any of us can do, Mary," she said, and with a little pat on my hand she went her way.

And the others? After that last hanging on September 22

there were still several unfortunate souls left in prison. Their trials were never held. Instead, Governor Phips, a merciful man with a conscience, and the superior of the cold Chief Justice Stoughton, issued a general release to all who remained in jails. For many it came too late, but because of it a few were spared to live.

And the girls themselves. Or must I say *ourselves*? For surely I cannot escape the blame that I will always feel. In the time that has passed since that nightmare year, Mary Walcott and Elizabeth Booth have married and moved away from Salem. Elizabeth Hubbard lives on in old Dr. Griggs's house, caring for him since the death of his wife, for he is feeble now. Sarah Churchill left the village quietly one day, and I know not where she went. I have never heard of her since. Mercy Lewis and Susanna Sheldon come often to the ordinary. They drink far too much and their voices rise and coarsen, and their eyes blur and stare into space. Who knows what they may be seeing?

Anne Putnum, after the death of her mother, began to suffer what must truly be called "the tortures of the damned." At last she stood before her church and begged for forgiveness and acceptance.

"I desire to be humbled before God," she said. "It was a great delusion of Satan that deceived me in that sad time. I did it not out of any anger, malice, or ill will. And particularly as I was a chief instrument of accusing Goodwife Nurse and her two sisters, I desire to lie in the dust and be humbled for it, in that I was a cause with others of so sad a calamity to them and to their families. I desire to lie in the dust and earnestly beg forgiveness of all those unto whom I have given just cause of sorrow and offense, whose relations were taken away and accused."

Fourteen years had passed before Anne made her plea,

and the passage of time dims even great sorrows. She was taken back into her church.

And I. I remain still at Ingersoll's, doing all that I can to assist dear Sarah in her work. I smile, I chat with customers, I see myself slowly aging and care not.

I met Elizabeth Proctor upon the road today. As she always does, she gave me a small, sad smile.

BIBLIOGRAPHY

Boyer, Paul, and Stephen Nissenbaum. *Salem Possessed: The Social Origins of Witchcraft*. Cambridge, Mass.: Harvard University Press, 1974.

Boyer, Paul, and Stephen Nissenbaum. *The Salem Witchcraft Papers: Verbatim Transcripts*. New York: Da Capo Press, 1977.

Miller, Arthur. *The Crucible: A Play in Four Acts*. New York: Viking Press, 1953.

Petry, Ann. *Tituba of Salem Village*. New York: Thomas Y. Crowell Co., 1964.

Smith, Page. *Daughters of the Promised Land: Women in American History*. Boston: Little, Brown and Co., 1970.

Starkey, Marion L. *Devil in Massachusetts: A Modern Enquiry into the Salem Witch Trials*. New York: Doubleday/Anchor Press, 1969.

Upham, Charles W. *Salem Witchcraft*. New York: Frederick Ungar Publishing Co., 1959.

READ ON FOR MORE
ABOUT PATRICIA CLAPP. . . .

ABOUT PATRICIA CLAPP

by her children

Patricia Clapp was born in Boston, Massachusetts. She moved to Montclair, New Jersey, when she was six years old but continued to spend her summers in Cape Cod. Her Boston childhood shaped her life, and though she spent her adult years in New Jersey, she always considered herself a New Englander. Her New England roots appear in both *Jane-Emily* and *Witches' Children*.

From the time Clapp was little, words were her music. Whether it was the written word or the spoken word, she delighted in the use of words and the magic they could convey. She began writing when she was a teenager, at first short stories and poems. A few of her teenage writings were published, and the writing bug had bitten. After she graduated from high school, she attended Columbia University to study writing.

As the mother of three children, Clapp expanded her writing to include plays, hastily written for a backyard production or a school or Girl Scout assembly. Writing plays for children came easily to her, and she soon had the first of many plays published. She continued writing plays, raising children, and performing in virtually every production at a local theater in Montclair, the Studio Players.

As her children grew and the daily demands of motherhood lessened, she did some research on her family's genealogy and discovered a *Mayflower* ancestor, Constance Hopkins. Her writer's gift realized there was a story behind the brief cold facts of a teenage girl's experience on the *Mayflower*. After much research, she wrote her first book,

Constance: A Story of Early Plymouth. Unlike many beginning writers, she sold her book to the first publisher she queried, and a wonderful writing career was born.

Clapp's publisher recognized that there was an emerging market for fiction aimed at teenage girls, books with a strong female protagonist. *Constance* was followed by two works of fiction, *Jane-Emily* and *King of the Dollhouse,* and four more historical fiction books: *Doctor Elizabeth, The Tamarack Tree, I'm Deborah Sampson,* and *Witches' Children.* Her books won numerous awards and have been translated into many languages, including Danish, Dutch, and Japanese.

Clapp loved being with children, reading to them, writing for them, directing them in plays, giving book talks to local schools, and answering many times the all-important schoolroom question, "What do you have to do to become a writer?" Her standard one-word answer was, "Write." As the mother of three, grandmother of eleven, and great-grandmother of thirty-five, she has passed her love of writing down to her descendants.

One of her favorite family stories originated in a grandson's fifth-grade classroom. One of Clapp's books was being discussed in class, and her grandson volunteered that his grandmother had written the book. A classmate sarcastically replied, "Right, and my grandmother is Santa Claus." Well, for the world of children's books, perhaps Ms. Clapp was a Santa Claus, or at least a Mrs. Claus, giving the gift of books and reading to children around the world.

Clapp passed away in December 2003.

IN HER OWN WORDS

Patricia Clapp on the writing and origins of
Jane-Emily and *Witches' Children*

I remember virtually nothing about my first four years. The records show that I was born on June 9, 1912, in Boston, and that my father, Howard Clapp, died when I was nine months old. He was hospitalized for much of that time, and Mother hired a Negro woman named Edna to take care of me so that she would still be free to visit my father. The name "Edna" still gives me a warm, safe feeling whenever I hear it. It was also the name of my first book editor.

My father had been a dentist, and with his father, Dwight M. Clapp, dean of the Harvard School of Dentistry, he had expanded into the manufacture and importation of toothbrushes. This was long before the use of plastics, and the toothbrushes came from England equipped with "genuine bone handles" and "pure boar bristles," marks of quality that appealed to the affluent. Since Mother could not become a dentist overnight to support us, she became a businesswoman, importing toothbrushes. She did amazingly well! She was an attractive young woman with a great deal of natural charm, and her pre-liberated woman's efforts proved successful. With Edna to care for me, she worked very hard and very long hours.

Like most people, I had two grandmothers. They were both New Englanders, but by and large any similarity stops there. My father's mother I knew as Grandmère (Mother always addressed her as Mère), and I was called Patricia. There were no pet names, no diminutives. I was in awe of Grandmère, a petite woman, small-boned, brunette, and always formal. She was deaf and used an ear trumpet — to a child a frightening black snake with an earpiece at one end and a mouthpiece at the other. Mother could manage it, but for me conversation was impossible. All words died in my throat.

Grandmère's silvering hair was dressed high, she sat with her small feet close together, and there were little grainy marks in the creases of her skin. As I recall, she dressed in gray or black or lavender, all mourning colors, in memory of her two children and her husband. Her dresses made a soft noise when she moved. They had high-boned lace collars and sometimes jabots. Except for a wide, heavy gold wedding band I don't remember her wearing jewelry, though I eventually inherited several pieces, including a handsome black locket on a long jet chain. It had a picture of her daughter, Ethel, and what I always thought was a diamond set in the front. Not long ago, my brother told me it was a yellow sapphire. There was also an onyx cross and a flat oval gold locket, which opened to display space for two tiny photographs. It was empty when I got it.

I know Grandmère had a house in Lynn, Massachusetts, where I was taken to visit when I was small. I have a picture in my mind of a tall house surrounded by a beautiful garden. I know there were pansies in the garden. I know (because I now own it) that Grandmère had a purple leather notebook in which she wrote in her meticulous hand anecdotes and sayings of her children, Ethel and Howard. Ethel died of pneumonia at the age of twelve. Put these things together, and you have the seeds from which my second novel, *Jane-Emily*, sprang years later.

After we moved from Boston to New Jersey, Mother took me back from time to time to visit Grandmère. By then she lived in the second-floor apartment of a narrow brownstone building with a companion named Miss Eaton and an unpleasant Boston bulldog that snuffled. I dreaded those visits, though I liked staying with Mother at the Copley-Plaza Hotel.

Now that I am a grandmother—even a great-grandmother—myself, I could weep for Grandmère and myself. I was her only grandchild, and I am sure she wanted to love me. I could not have made it easy for her. Her formality, her dry, withered kisses on my young cheek, her eagerness to have me tell her of my life and my inability to communicate through that hateful learning aid—all these created a chasm between us. Only in letters did we come a little closer. She wrote me frequently, the letter consisting mostly of questions. Since I have always liked writing letters, I was much more at ease on paper. I hope now that perhaps she understood. I hope that my letters to her helped to lessen the gap between us.

Grandmère died when I was twelve, and Mother and I went to Boston for the funeral. I remember seeing my grandmother lying on her heavy, carved mahogany bed, beautifully dressed, her hair coiffed just so, her narrow hands, with the heavy wedding band, folded on her breast. I can't remember what my thoughts were. Mother and I stayed at the Copley-Plaza for three or four days. At dinner the first night I ordered a napoleon from the French pastry tray for dessert. However, as so often happens with me, my eyes were bigger than my stomach, so I wrapped it in a napkin and put it in a drawer in our bedroom. I forgot about it until we packed to leave. It had blue fuzz on it.

Mother's mother was Granny. I adored her. She, too, was short in stature, but pleasantly rounded. Sometimes she called me "Child" since she had a flock of grandchildren, and it was probably easier than trying to remember that I was "Patty," her alternative name for me. She lived on a small farm on Cape Cod with her second husband, and they—and the farm—figure largely in my life.

The story goes that when Granny was seventeen, she was sitting on the back stoop, wearing a scarlet flannel dress, drying her hair after washing it. It was still, when I knew her, beautiful hair: very long, thick, shining, dark, and if given a chance, it whisked into tiny ringlets around her face. Along came Benjamin Franklin Blachford, probably fifteen or twenty years older than she. He was a pilot, hired to take ships in and out of tricky harbors. He was then on his way to China. And—so the story goes—they met and talked, and he told the young Estella Treffrey that he would return in a year to marry her. He did. Off to China they sailed, where they had four daughters, my mother, Elizabeth, being the youngest. When Mother was twelve (so many things in this record happen to girls when they are twelve!), her father died. He had made good money, which he chose to spend on his family and his style of living. There was very little left upon his death. Granny packed up her daughters and her belongings and came home to Cape Cod. I now own a yellow tin trunk that made the voyage. Granny's name is stenciled on the lid. The transition must not have been easy. In due course she became housekeeper to a widower and expeditiously married him. He was the only "Grandpa" I ever knew. I loved him.

I had, in recent years [1955–1965], written nothing but plays and poetry, so my first reaction [to discovering the girl Constance Hopkins in my husband's genealogical records] was to make a full-length play about her. It never got off the ground. Too large a cast, too much time to cover, too many sets required to give it a sense of space and movement—it wouldn't work. So then I just started writing, and it came out as Constance's journal. I didn't plan it that way. It just took off by itself and happened.

So I wrote and wrote and wrote—no children in the house, none of their happy distractions—only Mother's apologetic bell when she needed to turn over in bed and couldn't, or required a bedpan, or wanted a cigarette. I am a confirmed smoker, too, but Mother's hands shook so that if she had a cigarette when she was alone, visions of fire alarms danced in my head. So I'd stop typing and answer Mother's bell and visit with her for a while, and we'd have a cigarette. She'd ask what I was doing, and I'd say I was writing something but I didn't know how it would turn out. Or even if. Perhaps my deepest regret is that Mother never knew it was published as a book. She would have been so proud! But she had died by then.

Not only was *Constance* published, it was a runner-up for the National Book Award in the Young Adult Literature division. I didn't even know what the National Book Award was! That was in 1968. It is now 1987, and she is still selling. I think it was my best book. Not the most popular — *Jane-Emily* holds that title — but the one I am proudest of.

And time marched on, [my daughter] Patsy had some more babies, and [my daughter] Pam had some, and [my son] Kit came home from Africa and got married, and then he and his new wife returned to the [Episcopal] mission [in Liberia] for another round. I didn't want to be a one-book author, so I wrote *Jane-Emily*, and that, too, was published and is still selling well.

Even now, when there are seven books in print, I am always astonished to see reviews of the books or ads for them or to receive letters from readers. At that time, when *Constance* and *Jane-Emily* were new, I was overwhelmed. I felt like the woman in the nursery rhyme who cried, "Lawkamercy on us, this is none of I!" I found it both hysterically funny and terribly impressive that anyone would be addressing me as an author. I didn't (and don't) feel like one. I dislike authors' gatherings and autograph parties and all those adjuncts to the profession. Sometimes, under duress, I do them, but I much prefer not to. What I do enjoy is talking to youngsters in schools or libraries. Actually I talk *with* them, not *to* them. They ask innumerable questions — generally the same ones — and I answer as well as I can. One of those questions is invariably, "How long does it take to write a book?" When I say, "From six months to a year, and maybe more," that idea floats almost visibly out the window. There is always some child who asks, "When did you decide to become a writer?" And, of course, I never did. It was just one of those things that happened to me, like getting married and having children and working in a theatre.

Because I write under my maiden name, at least two-thirds of my friends and neighbors have no idea that I do anything as unconventional as write books. I like it that way.

With one exception, each of my books takes place in the past and grew from a particular interest. *Jane-Emily* came from Grandmère's house in Lynn (though it was no more to me than a fragile memory) and from the early death of her daughter, Ethel, and from such tangible objects as the black locket and the purple leather notebook. Somehow, all stirred up together, they made that short story when I was at Columbia [University], and later, greatly expanded, became a book. *Constance* was . . . because there came a point when I had to put her on paper. Had to make her live. The New England landscape and scents and weather and nature sounds came naturally to me after summers and summers spent with Granny. *Dr. Elizabeth*, the story of Elizabeth Blackwell, who became the first woman doctor, happened because a house in which she frequently visited is around a couple of corners from where I now live. Another house, owned by her sister-in-law, Lucy Stone Blackwell, still stands here in Montclair, with the old well in the front yard. It was in that yard that the two women sometimes sat and talked, enjoying the country atmosphere and quiet surroundings. They must have had a lot to discuss together. Both Lucy and Elizabeth had flouted the current ideas and ideals of female behavior, and proved that they were quite able to work and to think as intelligent men did.

As for *Witches' Children*, I went back to New England again to see what I could make of that dreadful time of witch-calling. It seems to me to have been largely a case of mass hysteria, and heaven knows we meet that frequently nowadays. Rock concerts, for example, where young girls weep and scream and gyrate. The modern accusations of sexual abuse, many of which have ended when the alleged victims admitted that they lied. The youthful female is volatile. If, as in Puritan communities in the early days, she must keep her emotions bottled up, something will eventually loosen the cork, and the release can be sheer disaster. I have seen it happen more than once in my lifetime.

There is one aspect of writing historical fiction that I particularly enjoy: the research. I have access to two excellent libraries, and I come home weighed down with assorted volumes and submerge myself for weeks. Architecture, clothing, food, pastimes, politics, education, language—all of these must be as familiar to me as the events I am writing about. Every period has its own flavor, and unless that is clearly conveyed, the reader will lose half the story. I prefer to release this background in small snatches rather than long paragraphs of description. In studying female fashions of the Civil War period, I was fascinated by the number of garments young women wore, even in the hot climate of Mississippi, but to say "she had on this and that and thus and so—" would have made any reader's eye flick to the next paragraph. I chose, in *The Tamarack Tree*, to describe Mary Byrd's attire, after she had removed her dress, in more "visible" terms:

She sat cross-legged on her pink-canopied bed as we talked. Dressed only in her corset, laced to make her small waist even smaller, her long drawers trimmed with delicate lace, her chemise, her underpetticoat, her

white petticoat with three starched flounces, a final
thin muslin petticoat, her lacy knitted stockings, and
thin white slippers on her feet, she looked like a drift
of white cloud that had settled.

I can see her. I hope my reader can.

In historical fiction, language is a problem. We cannot *hear* how people spoke a hundred or more years ago; we must rely on what they wrote. But by and large people don't speak as they write. Speaking is usually less formal, apt to be interrupted, not as carefully thought out as the written word. Still, in the written word one can find the flavor, a suggestion of how people of many years ago actually spoke. Reading the things they wrote helps give the rhythm of their speech and the words that were in usage. That reading can also become addictive. I came out of a haze of colonial reading one day when [my husband] Edward called me, and answered innocently, "Yes, dear? What dost thou want?" It took a long time to live that one down.

For me there is only one big problem with historical research. I become so carried away by it that I want to read on and on. It is difficult to say sternly to myself, "All right, Patricia, that's enough! Get to work."

One more thought about the "work" of writing. ("Work!" It is exciting, joyous, stimulating, fulfilling, exhausting, and I am never happier than when I can sit and type and type and *type*! It's just hard getting started.) As I was saying, those people who *do* know that I write are relentless! As soon as a book is published they start the "What is the next one going to be about?" routine. It's like getting up from an overly abundant lunch and having someone say, "What's for dinner?" As I write this, I am recovering from a fractured knee. It has been a little more than three months, and I can't count the number of loyal friends who have said, "What a wonderful time to start another book!" Well, one doesn't just sit down at the typewriter, roll in the paper, and start another book. At least I don't. Not until the seed has sprouted and grown, until it fills my mind. Not until the research has been done and the outline made. Not until I know my characters as well as I know myself. My typewriter may turn on with a switch, but my writing doesn't.